THE
BEST
STORIES
of
ANTON
CHEKHOV

THE
BEST
STORIES
—of—
ANTON
CHEKHOV

EDITED BY JOHN KULKA

BARNES
&NOBLE
BOOKS
NEW YORK

2000 Barnes & Noble Books

ISBN 0-7607-1981-0

Printed and bound in the United States of America

00 01 02 03 MP 9 8 7 6 5 4 3 2 1

FG

CONTENTS

INTRODUCTION

Anton Pavlovich Chekhov was born on January 17, 1860, in the southern Russian seaport town of Taganrog. He was the third child in a family of five boys and a girl. If not for 3,500 rubles scraped together by a shrewd and ambitious grandfather, with which he purchased his own and his family's freedom, the future writer would have been born a serf. The writer's father, Pavel, rose further into lower-middle-class respectability as the proprietor of a small grocery in Taganrog. He was a religious, church-going man and a strict disciplinarian who took it as his parental duty to beat his children. Chekhov thought him a tyrant. "It is sickening and dreadful to recall," he wrote to his brother Alexander, "the extent to which despotism and lying mutilated our childhood."

Chekhov's mother, on the other hand, was kind but unable to alter the course of the situation at home. When the grocery business failed in 1876, Pavel fled to Moscow to escape an angry creditor. The rest of the family soon followed—all but the sixteen-year-old Anton, who remained behind to appease the creditor by tutoring his son for a pittance. Left to fend for himself, Chekhov finished

Introduction

high school in Taganrog, then rejoined the family and enrolled in Moscow University to study medicine.

Chekhov's beginnings as a writer were humble. While attending the university, he began to write humorous sketches for periodicals to ease the family's poverty. He would later recall these earliest efforts as "trash." The first of his stories was published in 1880, and in the next half-dozen years he finished perhaps as many as six hundred. In 1884, he took up the practice of medicine in a provincial district—by no means a lucrative career move, but one that appealed to Chekhov's civic-mindedness. He continued to earn his living chiefly through his pen, however. As a provincial doctor, Chekhov came into close contact with the peasants, army officers, petty officials, and innumerable provincial types that became the subjects of his stories. It was only his poor health that dictated his decision to give up the practice of medicine. (Before graduating from the university, he had already contracted the tuberculosis that would kill him.) Chekhov had always seen medicine and writing as allied in his quest for spiritual fulfillment.

Speckled Tales, Chekhov's first collection of short stories, appeared in 1886 to public and critical acclaim. In the same year, Dimitry Grigorovich, a venerable old man of letters, wrote encouragingly to Chekhov after reading "The Huntsman" in the *Petersburg Gazette* and hailed

Introduction

him as a writer possessed of talents that "set you far above other writers of the younger generation." This bit of recognition was nearly as important to the future of Russian literature as Emerson's congratulatory letter to Walt Whitman was to the future of our own. From this time on, Chekhov was considered among Russia's leading writers, and he published his stories in the most important periodicals of the day. He enjoyed an enormous popular following. Recognition as a playwright came somewhat later. Not until 1898, when Stanislavski's Moscow Art Theatre presented *The Seagull*—a miserable failure in its first production in 1896—did Chekhov finally find an appreciative audience for his plays.

In 1901, Chekhov married Olga Knipper, a gifted actress in the Moscow Art Theatre. Husband and wife spent little of their married life together. For health reasons, Chekhov relocated to Yalta, while Olga pursued her theatrical career in Moscow. Much of their relationship was carried on by correspondence that reveals genuine feeling on both sides. Olga was with Chekhov at a health resort in Badenweiler, Germany, when he died of a severe pulmonary hemorrhage on July 2, 1904. His body was transported to Moscow in a refrigeration car bearing the legend "Fresh Oysters."

Chekhov inspires almost universal praise and adoration among readers. His stories are especially

Introduction

admired by other writers. His champions comprise a wide and surprisingly diverse group of talents: Leo Tolstoy, William Faulkner, Virginia Woolf, James T. Farrell, V. S. Pritchett, Vladimir Nabokov, John Cheever, John Barth, and Flannery O'Connor. For Tolstoy, Chekhov was the most astute and gifted photographer of the Russian countryside; James T. Farrell proclaimed him the most influential practitioner of the short story form; and Nabokov—not one to mince words—insisted that to prefer Dostoyevsky or Gorky to Chekhov is to be unable to grasp "the essentials of universal literary art." What other writer commands such high praise from fellow writers? Ovid. Dante. Shakespeare. James Joyce, perhaps, in our own age.

Chekhov is a simple writer, one who easily exceeds the sum of his parts. He is neither a stylistic innovator nor a writer of pretty prose. He rarely engages in metaphor or simile, and his working vocabulary is small. He is the antithesis of a clever writer. Instead, his modest prose, always in the service of his art, is notable for swiftness, compression, understatement, gray and twilight tonalities, freedom from all temporizing, and, above all else, emotional truth. His stories give the impression of being very close to direct experience, yet few stories have been written that equal the heartbreaking beauty of "The Lady with the Dog," or "Ward Six."

Introduction

Chekhov is arguably the first writer to employ understatement and suggestion to convey stabbing pathos. In "The Lady with the Dog," he rarely discusses Gurov's moods or feelings, and he never touches on the difficult moral dilemma of marital infidelity. Instead, he captures these elements through the details of his character's life. When Gurov breaks off his affair with Anna (the lady with the dog), and returns to Moscow, he settles into the routine of winter life with the rest of the city. It is the tedium of life that contrasts so sharply with the affair. Unable to contain himself any longer, he speaks warmly but abstractly on the subject of love to his wife, who, with raised eyebrow, merely responds, "The part of a lady-killer does not suit you at all, Dmitri." The narrator reports nothing further about this exchange, but we feel Gurov's silently mounting frustration, and we understand exactly how the comment cuts him. In the hands of a lesser artist, this scene would have been protracted and explained, with questions raised about the wife's suspicions.

Part of Chekhov's genius lay in knowing exactly when to summarize thought, when to reveal it in dialogue, and when to merely suggest it through detail. In "The Lady with the Dog," when Chekhov describes the day in which the relationship between Gurov and Anna moves from flirtation to physical intimacy, he first care-

Introduction

fully distances us from Gurov and then brings us close to him to startling effect. It is a hot day, and Gurov entreats Anna to share an ice. Then they walk together to the harbor to watch a steamer dock as daylight gradually dwindles. Whatever passes through Gurov's mind is not mentioned, and any exchanges between the couple are reported indirectly and at a great distance: "She talked a great deal and asked disconnected questions, forgetting next moment what she had asked; then she dropped her lorgnette in the crush." When Gurov's proposition finally comes, it is all the more jarring for what has passed so hazily before, more profound and vivid in the way that certain details seem in recollection: "'Let us go to your hotel,' he said softly." Chekhov reports Gurov's thoughts only afterward, in a moment of postcoital melancholy as Gurov attempts to place "the lady with the dog" in his apparently considerable catalog of sexual exploits. We plunge directly into his mind with: "'What different people one meets in the world!'" It is a chilling moment, as if we were suddenly granted access to the thoughts of our own inscrutable lover.

Chekhov's most characteristic stories lack plot in the normal sense of rising action, climax, and denouement. They have, as John Galsworthy once noted, "apparently neither head nor tail, they seem all middle like a tortoise." But, as

Introduction

Galsworthy goes on to point out, Chekhov's many imitators fail "to realize the heads and tails are merely tucked in." For example, "Gusev" seems particularly shapeless. It allows retelling no more than does a poem by Thomas Hardy. A consumptive military orderly on sick leave travels home by steamer; he engages in conversation with some of the other men in the infirmary; he goes briefly above deck; and then he dies. The story continues for a page or two beyond Gusev's brusquely noted death. We follow his body into the water, where it slowly sinks, drifts, and then is cautiously approached by a shark that eventually attacks it, ripping open the body bag. In a sense, the story is all anticlimax because Gusev is already dying when the story opens. The most dynamic event in the story is the shark attack on the body, and even that is implied rather than seen. The interior passages in which Gusev reflects on home provide no narrative tissue— only broken glimpses of Gusev's former life, seen through the gauze of fever. "Gusev," for all its lack of plot, is always compelling. When we read the story, we give ourselves up to a twilight mood that washes through us like the ebb and flow of dark waters.

Chekhov's stories frequently end abruptly and inconclusively, or they simply fade out. In his letters, Chekhov insisted on the necessity of the incompleteness of his art. "You are right in

Introduction

demanding that an artist approach his work consciously," he wrote to his friend Aleksey Suvorin in 1888, "but you are confusing two concepts: the solution of a problem and the correct formulation of a problem. Only the second is required of the artist." "The Lady with the Dog" breaks every rule of conventional storytelling, ending at the very place any other writer would begin a story about marital infidelity. The story comes full circle with the realization that "it was clear to both of them that the end was still far off, and that what was to be most complicated and difficult for them was just beginning." Even in the stories that end with death, there is often no real closure or resolution, only cessation of suffering and disappointed hopes. And not always in those stories is there an end to suffering because so long as some character remains alive, suffering continues. By calculated design, Chekhov ends his stories—as things tend to end in real life—on broken musical notes.

—*John Kulka*
March 2000

Note on this collection and translation: Few would argue that the stories included here are not among Chekhov's best, but some will undoubtedly complain about those stories that are missing: some overlooked favorite or ignored classic. The

THE
BEST
STORIES
of
ANTON
CHEKHOV

THE BEST STORIES
OF ANTON CHEKHOV

THE LADY WITH THE DOG

I

IT was said that a new person had appeared on the sea-front: a lady with a little dog. Dmitri Dmitritch Gurov, who had by then been a fort-night at Yalta, and so was fairly at home there, had begun to take an interest in new arrivals. Sitting in Verney's pavilion, he saw, walking on the sea-front, a fair-haired young lady of medium height, wearing a *béret*; a white Pomeranian dog was running behind her.

And afterwards he met her in the public gardens and in the square several times a day. She was walking alone, always wearing the same *béret,* and always with the same white dog; no one knew who she was, and every one called her simply " the lady with the dog."

" If she is here alone without a husband or friends, it wouldn't be amiss to make her ac-quaintance," Gurov reflected.

He was under forty, but he had a daughter already twelve years old, and two sons at school. He had been married young, when he was a student in his second year, and by now his wife seemed half as old again as he. She was a tall, erect woman with dark eyebrows, staid and dignified, and, as she said of herself, intellectual. She read a great deal, used phonetic spelling, called her husband, not Dmitri, but Dimitri, and he secretly considered her unintelligent, narrow, inelegant, was afraid of her, and did not like to be at home. He had begun being unfaithful to her long ago — had been unfaithful to her often, and, probably on that account, almost always spoke ill of women, and when they were talked about in his presence, used to call them " the lower race."

It seemed to him that he had been so schooled by bitter experience that he might call them what he liked, and yet he could not get on for two days together without " the lower race." In the society of men he was bored and not himself, with them he was cold and uncommunicative; but when he was in the company of women he felt free, and knew what to say to them and how to behave; and he was at ease with them even when he was silent. In his appearance, in his character, in his whole nature, there was something attractive and elusive which allured women and disposed them in his favour; he knew that, and some force seemed to draw him, too, to them.

Experience often repeated, truly bitter experience, had taught him long ago that with decent people, especially Moscow people — always slow to move and irresolute — every intimacy, which at first so agreeably diversifies life and appears a light and charming adventure, inevitably grows into a regular problem of extreme intricacy, and in the long run the situation becomes unbearable. But at every fresh meeting with an interesting woman this experience seemed to slip out of his memory, and he was eager for life, and everything seemed simple and amusing.

One evening he was dining in the gardens, and the lady in the *béret* came up slowly to take the next table. Her expression, her gait, her dress, and the way she did her hair told him that she was a lady, that she was married, that she was in Yalta for the first time and alone, and that she was dull there. . . . The stories told of the immorality in such places as Yalta are to a great extent untrue; he despised them, and knew that such stories were for the most part made up by persons who would themselves have been glad to sin if they had been able; but when the lady sat down at the next table three paces from him, he remembered these tales of easy conquests, of trips to the mountains, and the tempting thought of a swift, fleeting love affair, a romance with an unknown woman, whose name he did not know, suddenly took possession of him.

He beckoned coaxingly to the Pomeranian, and when the dog came up to him he shook his finger at it. The Pomeranian growled: Gurov shook his finger at it again.

The lady looked at him and at once dropped her eyes.

" He doesn't bite," she said, and blushed.

" May I give him a bone? " he asked; and when

she nodded he asked courteously, " Have you been long in Yalta ? "

" Five days."

" And I have already dragged out a fortnight here."

There was a brief silence.

" Time goes fast, and yet it is so dull here! " she said, not looking at him.

" That's only the fashion to say it is dull here. A provincial will live in Belyov or Zhidra and not be dull, and when he comes here it's ' Oh, the dulness! Oh, the dust! ' One would think he came from Grenada."

She laughed. Then both continued eating in silence, like strangers, but after dinner they walked side by side; and there sprang up between them the light jesting conversation of people who are free and satisfied, to whom it does not matter where they go or what they talk about. They walked and talked of the strange light on the sea : the water was of a soft warm lilac hue, and there was a golden streak from the moon upon it. They talked of how sultry it was after a hot day. Gurov told her that he came from Moscow, that he had taken his degree in Arts, but had a post in a bank; that he had trained as an opera-singer, but had given it up, that he owned two houses in Moscow. . . . And from her he learnt that she had grown up in Petersburg, but had lived in S—— since her marriage two years before, that she was staying another month in Yalta, and that her husband, who needed a holiday too, might perhaps come and fetch her. She was not sure whether her husband had a post in a Crown Department or under the Provincial Council — and was amused by her own ignorance. And Gurov learnt, too, that she was called Anna Sergeyevna.

Afterwards he thought about her in his room at the hotel — thought she would certainly meet him next day; it would be sure to happen. As he got into bed he thought how lately she had been a girl at school, doing lessons like his own daughter; he recalled the diffidence, the angularity, that was still manifest in her laugh and her manner of talking with a stranger. This must have been the first time in her life she had been alone in surroundings in which she was followed, looked at, and spoken to merely from a secret motive which she could hardly fail to guess. He recalled her slender, delicate neck, her lovely grey eyes.

" There's something pathetic about her, anyway," he thought, and fell asleep.

II

A week had passed since they had made acquaintance. It was a holiday. It was sultry indoors, while in the street the wind whirled the dust round and round, and blew people's hats off. It was a thirsty day, and Gurov often went into the pavilion, and pressed Anna Sergeyevna to have syrup and water or an ice. One did not know what to do with oneself.

In the evening when the wind had dropped a little, they went out on the groyne to see the steamer come in. There were a great many people walking about the harbour; they had gathered to welcome some one, bringing bouquets. And two peculiarities of a well-dressed Yalta crowd were very conspicuous: the elderly ladies were dressed like young ones, and there were great numbers of generals.

Owing to the roughness of the sea, the steamer arrived late, after the sun had set, and it was a long time turning about before it reached the groyne. Anna Sergeyevna looked through her lorgnette at the steamer and the passengers as though looking for acquaintances, and when she turned to Gurov her eyes were shining. She talked a great deal and asked disconnected questions, forgetting next moment what she had asked; then she dropped her lorgnette in the crush.

The festive crowd began to disperse; it was too dark to see people's faces. The wind had completely dropped, but Gurov and Anna Sergeyevna still stood as though waiting to see some one else come from the steamer. Anna Sergeyevna was silent now, and sniffed the flowers without looking at Gurov.

"The weather is better this evening," he said. "Where shall we go now? Shall we drive somewhere?"

She made no answer.

Then he looked at her intently, and all at once put his arm round her and kissed her on the lips, and breathed in the moisture and the fragrance of the flowers; and he immediately looked round him, anxiously wondering whether any one had seen them.

The Lady with the Dog

" Let us go to your hotel," he said softly. And both walked quickly.

The room was close and smelt of the scent she had bought at the Japanese shop. Gurov looked at her and thought: " What different people one meets in the world ! " From the past he preserved memories of careless, good-natured women, who loved cheerfully and were grateful to him for the happiness he gave them, however brief it might be ; and of women like his wife who loved without any genuine feeling, with superfluous phrases, affectedly, hysterically, with an expression that suggested that it was not love nor passion, but something more significant ; and of two or three others, very beautiful, cold women, on whose faces he had caught a glimpse of a rapacious expression — an obstinate desire to snatch from life more than it could give, and these were capricious, unreflecting, domineering, unintelligent women not in their first youth, and when Gurov grew cold to them their beauty excited his hatred, and the lace on their linen seemed to him like scales.

But in this case there was still the diffidence, the angularity of inexperienced youth, an awkward feeling ; and there was a sense of consternation as though some one had suddenly knocked at the door. The attitude of Anna Sergeyevna — " the lady with the dog " — to what had happened was somehow peculiar, very grave, as though it were her fall — so it seemed, and it was strange and inappropriate. Her face dropped and faded, and on both sides of it her long hair hung down mournfully ; she mused in a dejected attitude like " the woman who was a sinner " in an old-fashioned picture.

" It's wrong," she said. " You will be the first to despise me now."

There was a water-melon on the table. Gurov cut himself a slice and began eating it without haste. There followed at least half an hour of silence.

Anna Sergeyevna was touching; there was about her the purity of a good, simple woman who had seen little of life. The solitary candle burning on the table threw a faint light on her face, yet it was clear that she was very unhappy.

" How could I despise you? " asked Gurov. " You don't know what you are saying."

" God forgive me," she said, and her eyes filled with tears. " It's awful."

" You seem to feel you need to be forgiven."

" Forgiven? No. I am a bad, low woman; I despise myself and don't attempt to justify myself. It's not my husband but myself I have deceived. And not only just now; I have been deceiving myself for a long time. My husband may be a good, honest man, but he is a flunkey! I don't know what he does there, what his work is, but I know he is a flunkey! I was twenty when I was married to him. I have been tormented by curiosity; I wanted something better. ' There must be a different sort of life,' I said to myself. I wanted to live! To live, to live! . . . I was fired by curiosity . . . you don't understand it, but, I swear to God, I could not control myself; something happened to me: I could not be restrained. I told my husband I was ill, and came here. . . . And here I have been walking about as though I were dazed, like a mad creature; . . . and now I have become a vulgar, contemptible woman whom any one may despise."

Gurov felt bored already, listening to her. He was irritated by the naïve tone, by this remorse, so unexpected and inopportune; but for the tears in her eyes, he might have thought she was jesting or playing a part.

" I don't understand," he said softly. " What is it you want? "

She hid her face on his breast and pressed close to him.

" Believe me, believe me, I beseech you . . ." she said. " I love a pure, honest life, and sin is loathsome to me. I don't know what I am doing. Simple people say: ' The Evil One has beguiled me.' And I may say of myself now that the Evil One has beguiled me."

" Hush, hush! . . ." he muttered.

He looked at her fixed, scared eyes, kissed her, talked softly and affectionately, and by degrees she was comforted, and her gaiety returned; they both began laughing.

Afterwards when they went out there was not a soul on the sea-front. The town with its cypresses had quite a deathlike air, but the sea still broke noisily on the shore; a single barge was rocking on the waves, and a lantern was blinking sleepily on it.

They found a cab and drove to Oreanda.

" I found out your surname in the hall just now:
it was written on the board — Von Diderits," said
Gurov. " Is your husband a German? "

" No; I believe his grandfather was a German,
but he is an Orthodox Russian himself."

At Oreanda they sat on a seat not far from the
church, looked down at the sea, and were silent.
Yalta was hardly visible through the morning mist;
white clouds stood motionless on the mountain-tops.
The leaves did not stir on the trees, grasshoppers
chirruped, and the monotonous hollow sound of
the sea rising up from below, spoke of the peace, of
the eternal sleep awaiting us. So it must have
sounded when there was no Yalta, no Oreanda here;
so it sounds now, and it will sound as indifferently
and monotonously when we are all no more. And
in this constancy, in this complete indifference to
the life and death of each of us, there lies hid, perhaps, a pledge of our eternal salvation, of the unceasing movement of life upon earth, of unceasing
progress towards perfection. Sitting beside a
young woman who in the dawn seemed so lovely,
soothed and spellbound in these magical surroundings — the sea, mountains, clouds, the open sky —
Gurov thought how in reality everything is beautiful
in this world when one reflects: everything except
what we think or do ourselves when we forget our
human dignity and the higher aims of our existence.

A man walked up to them — probably a keeper —
looked at them and walked away. And this detail
seemed mysterious and beautiful, too. They saw

a steamer come from Theodosia, with its lights out in the glow of dawn.

"There is dew on the grass," said Anna Sergeyevna, after a silence.

"Yes. It's time to go home."

They went back to the town.

Then they met every day at twelve o'clock on the sea-front, lunched and dined together, went for walks, admired the sea. She complained that she slept badly, that her heart throbbed violently; asked the same questions, troubled now by jealousy and now by the fear that he did not respect her sufficiently. And often in the square or gardens, when there was no one near them, he suddenly drew her to him and kissed her passionately. Complete idleness, these kisses in broad daylight while he looked round in dread of some one's seeing them, the heat, the smell of the sea, and the continual passing to and fro before him of idle, well-dressed, well-fed people, made a new man of him; he told Anna Sergeyevna how beautiful she was, how fascinating. He was impatiently passionate, he would not move a step away from her, while she was often pensive and continually urged him to confess that he did not respect her, did not love her in the least, and thought of her as nothing but a common woman. Rather late almost every evening they drove somewhere out of town, to Oreanda or to the waterfall; and the expedition was always a success, the scenery invariably impressed them as grand and beautiful.

They were expecting her husband to come, but a letter came from him, saying that there was something wrong with his eyes, and he entreated his wife to come home as quickly as possible. Anna Sergeyevna made haste to go.

" It's a good thing I am going away," she said to Gurov. " It's the finger of destiny ! "

She went by coach and he went with her. They were driving the whole day. When she had got into a compartment of the express, and when the second bell had rung, she said:

" Let me look at you once more . . . look at you once again. That's right."

She did not shed tears, but was so sad that she seemed ill, and her face was quivering.

" I shall remember you . . . think of you," she said. " God be with you; be happy. Don't remember evil against me. We are parting forever — it must be so, for we ought never to have met. Well, God be with you."

The train moved off rapidly, its lights soon vanished from sight, and a minute later there was no sound of it, as though everything had conspired together to end as quickly as possible that sweet delirium, that madness. Left alone on the platform, and gazing into the dark distance, Gurov listened to the chirrup of the grasshoppers and the hum of the telegraph wires, feeling as though he had only just waked up. And he thought, musing, that there had been another episode or adventure in his life, and it, too, was at an end, and nothing was left of it but a memory. . . . He was moved, sad, and conscious of a slight remorse. This young woman whom he would never meet again had not been happy with him; he was genuinely warm and affectionate with her, but yet in his manner, his tone, and his caresses there had been a shade of light irony, the coarse condescension of a happy man who was, besides, almost twice her age. All the time she had called him kind, exceptional, lofty; obviously he had seemed to her different from what he really was, so he had unintentionally deceived her. . . .

Here at the station was already a scent of autumn; it was a cold evening.

" It's time for me to go north," thought Gurov as he left the platform. " High time! "

III

At home in Moscow everything was in its winter routine; the stoves were heated, and in the morning it was still dark when the children were having breakfast and getting ready for school, and the nurse would light the lamp for a short time. The frosts had begun already. When the first snow has fallen, on the first day of sledge-driving it is pleasant to see the white earth, the white roofs, to draw soft, delicious breath, and the season brings back the days of one's youth. The old limes and birches, white with hoar-frost, have a good-natured expression; they are nearer to one's heart than cypresses and palms, and near them one doesn't want to be thinking of the sea and the mountains.

Gurov was Moscow born; he arrived in Moscow on a fine frosty day, and when he put on his fur coat and warm gloves, and walked along Petrovka, and when on Saturday evening he heard the ringing of the bells, his recent trip and the places he had seen lost all charm for him. Little by little he became absorbed in Moscow life, greedily read three newspapers a day, and declared he did not read the Moscow papers on principle! He already felt a longing to go to restaurants, clubs, dinner-parties, anniversary celebrations, and he felt flattered at entertaining distinguished lawyers and artists, and at playing cards with a professor at the doctors' club. He could already eat a whole plateful of salt fish and cabbage. . . .

In another month, he fancied, the image of Anna Sergeyevna would be shrouded in a mist in his memory, and only from time to time would visit him in his dreams with a touching smile as others did. But more than a month passed, real winter had come, and everything was still clear in his memory as though he had parted with Anna Sergeyevna only the day before. And his memories glowed more and more vividly. When in the evening stillness he heard from his study the voices of his children, preparing their lessons, or when he listened to a song or the organ at the restaurant, or the storm howled in the chimney, suddenly everything would rise up in his memory: what had happened on the groyne, and the early morning with the mist on the mountains, and the steamer coming from Theodosia, and the kisses. He would pace a long time about his room, remembering it all and smiling; then his memories passed into dreams, and in his fancy the past was mingled with what was to come. Anna Sergey-

evna did not visit him in dreams, but followed him
about everywhere like a shadow and haunted him.
When he shut his eyes he saw her as though she were
living before him, and she seemed to him lovelier,
younger, tenderer than she was; and he imagined
himself finer than he had been in Yalta. In the
evenings she peeped out at him from the bookcase,
from the fireplace, from the corner — he heard her
breathing, the caressing rustle of her dress. In the
street he watched the women, looking for some one
like her.

He was tormented by an intense desire to confide
his memories to some one. But in his home it was
impossible to talk of his love, and he had no one outside; he could not talk to his tenants nor to any one
at the bank. And what had he to talk of? Had he
been in love, then? Had there been anything beautiful, poetical, or edifying or simply interesting in his
relations with Anna Sergeyevna? And there was
nothing for him but to talk vaguely of love, of
woman, and no one guessed what it meant; only
his wife twitched her black eyebrows, and said:
"The part of a lady-killer does not suit you at all,
Dimitri."

One evening, coming out of the doctors' club with
an official with whom he had been playing cards, he
could not resist saying:

"If only you knew what a fascinating woman I
made the acquaintance of in Yalta!"

The official got into his sledge and was driving
away, but turned suddenly and shouted:

"Dmitri Dmitritch!"

" What? "

" You were right this evening: the sturgeon was a bit too strong! "

These words, so ordinary, for some reason moved Gurov to indignation, and struck him as degrading and unclean. What savage manners, what people! What senseless nights, what uninteresting, uneventful days! The rage for card-playing, the gluttony, the drunkenness, the continual talk always about the same thing. Useless pursuits and conversations always about the same things absorb the better part of one's time, the better part of one's strength, and in the end there is left a life grovelling and curtailed, worthless and trivial, and there is no escaping or getting away from it — just as though one were in a madhouse or a prison.

Gurov did not sleep all night, and was filled with indignation. And he had a headache all next day. And the next night he slept badly; he sat up in bed, thinking, or paced up and down his room. He was sick of his children, sick of the bank; he had no desire to go anywhere or to talk of anything.

In the holidays in December he prepared for a journey, and told his wife he was going to Petersburg to do something in the interests of a young friend — and he set off for S———. What for? He did not very well know himself. He wanted to see Anna Sergeyevna and to talk with her — to arrange a meeting, if possible.

He reached S——— in the morning, and took the best room at the hotel, in which the floor was covered with grey army cloth, and on the table was an

The Lady with the Dog

inkstand, grey with dust and adorned with a figure on horseback, with its hat in its hand and its head broken off. The hotel porter gave him the necessary information; Von Diderits lived in a house of his own in Old Gontcharny Street — it was not far from the hotel: he was rich and lived in good style, and had his own horses; every one in the town knew him. The porter pronounced the name " Dridirits."

Gurov went without haste to Old Gontcharny Street and found the house. Just opposite the house stretched a long grey fence adorned with nails.

" One would run away from a fence like that," thought Gurov, looking from the fence to the windows of the house and back again.

He considered: to-day was a holiday, and the husband would probably be at home. And in any case it would be tactless to go into the house and upset her. If he were to send her a note it might fall into her husband's hands, and then it might ruin everything. The best thing was to trust to chance. And he kept walking up and down the street by the fence, waiting for the chance. He saw a beggar go in at the gate and dogs fly at him; then an hour later he heard a piano, and the sounds were faint and indistinct. Probably it was Anna Sergeyevna playing. The front door suddenly opened, and an old woman came out, followed by the familiar white Pomeranian. Gurov was on the point of calling to the dog, but his heart began beating violently, and in his excitement he could not remember the dog's name.

He walked up and down, and loathed the grey fence more and more, and by now he thought irritably that Anna Sergeyevna had forgotten him, and was perhaps already amusing herself with some one else, and that that was very natural in a young woman who had nothing to look at from morning till night but that confounded fence. He went back to his hotel room and sat for a long while on the sofa, not knowing what to do, then he had dinner and a long nap.

" How stupid and worrying it is ! " he thought when he woke and looked at the dark windows : it was already evening. " Here I've had a good sleep for some reason. What shall I do in the night ? "

He sat on the bed, which was covered by a cheap grey blanket, such as one sees in hospitals, and he taunted himself in his vexation :

" So much for the lady with the dog . . . so much for the adventure. . . . You're in a nice fix. . . ."

That morning at the station a poster in large letters had caught his eye. " The Geisha " was to be performed for the first time. He thought of this and went to the theatre.

" It's quite possible she may go to the first performance," he thought.

The theatre was full. As in all provincial theatres, there was a fog above the chandelier, the gallery was noisy and restless ; in the front row the local dandies were standing up before the beginning of the performance, with their hands behind them ; in the Governor's box the Governor's daughter, wearing a boa, was sitting in the front seat, while the Governor himself lurked modestly behind the curtain with only his hands visible ; the orchestra was a long time tuning up; the stage curtain swayed. All the time the audience were coming in and taking their seats Gurov looked at them eagerly.

Anna Sergeyevna, too, came in. She sat down in the third row, and when Gurov looked at her his heart contracted, and he understood clearly that for him there was in the whole world no creature so near, so precious, and so important to him; she, this little woman, in no way remarkable, lost in a provincial crowd, with a vulgar lorgnette in her hand, filled his whole life now, was his sorrow and his joy, the one happiness that he now desired for himself, and to the sounds of the inferior orchestra, of the wretched provincial violins, he thought how lovely she was. He thought and dreamed.

A young man with small side-whiskers, tall and stooping, came in with Anna Sergeyevna and sat down beside her; he bent his head at every step and seemed to be continually bowing. Most likely this was the husband whom at Yalta, in a rush of bitter feeling, she had called a flunkey. And there really was in his long figure, his side-whiskers, and the small bald patch on his head, something of the flunkey's obsequiousness; his smile was sugary, and in his buttonhole there was some badge of distinction like the number on a waiter.

During the first interval the husband went away to smoke; she remained alone in her stall. Gurov, who was sitting in the stalls, too, went up to her and said in a trembling voice, with a forced smile:

" Good-evening."

She glanced at him and turned pale, then glanced

again with horror, unable to believe her eyes, and tightly gripped the fan and the lorgnette in her hands, evidently struggling with herself not to faint. Both were silent. She was sitting, he was standing, frightened by her confusion and not venturing to sit down beside her. The violins and the flute began tuning up. He felt suddenly frightened; it seemed as though all the people in the boxes were looking at them. She got up and went quickly to the door; he followed her, and both walked senselessly along passages, and up and down stairs, and figures in legal, scholastic, and civil service uniforms, all wearing badges, flitted before their eyes. They caught glimpses of ladies, of fur coats hanging on pegs; the draughts blew on them, bringing a smell of stale tobacco. And Gurov, whose heart was beating violently, thought:

" Oh, heavens! Why are these people here and this orchestra! . . ."

And at that instant he recalled how when he had seen Anna Sergeyevna off at the station he had thought that everything was over and they would never meet again. But how far they were still from the end!

On the narrow, gloomy staircase over which was written " To the Amphitheatre," she stopped.

" How you have frightened me! " she said, breathing hard, still pale and overwhelmed. " Oh, how you have frightened me! I am half dead. Why have you come? Why? "

" But do understand, Anna, do understand . . ."

he said hastily in a low voice. "I entreat you to understand. . . ."

She looked at him with dread, with entreaty, with love; she looked at him intently, to keep his features more distinctly in her memory.

"I am so unhappy," she went on, not heeding him. "I have thought of nothing but you all the time; I live only in the thought of you. And I wanted to forget, to forget you; but why, oh, why, have you come?"

On the landing above them two schoolboys were smoking and looking down, but that was nothing to Gurov; he drew Anna Sergeyevna to him, and began kissing her face, her cheeks, and her hands.

"What are you doing, what are you doing!" she cried in horror, pushing him away. "We are mad. Go away to-day; go away at once. . . . I beseech you by all that is sacred, I implore you. . . . There are people coming this way!"

Some one was coming up the stairs.

"You must go away," Anna Sergeyevna went on in a whisper. "Do you hear, Dmitri Dmitritch? I will come and see you in Moscow. I have never been happy; I am miserable now, and I never, never shall be happy, never! Don't make me suffer still more! I swear I'll come to Moscow. But now let us part. My precious, good, dear one, we must part!"

She pressed his hand and began rapidly going downstairs, looking round at him, and from her eyes he could see that she really was unhappy. Gurov stood for a little while, listened, then, when all sound had died away, he found his coat and left the theatre.

IV

And Anna Sergeyevna began coming to see him in Moscow. Once in two or three months she left S——, telling her husband that she was going to consult a doctor about an internal complaint — and her husband believed her, and did not believe her. In Moscow she stayed at the Slaviansky Bazaar hotel, and at once sent a man in a red cap to Gurov. Gurov went to see her, and no one in Moscow knew of it.

Once he was going to see her in this way on a winter morning (the messenger had come the evening before when he was out). With him walked his daughter, whom he wanted to take to school: it was on the way. Snow was falling in big wet flakes.

" It's three degrees above freezing-point, and yet it is snowing," said Gurov to his daughter. " The thaw is only on the surface of the earth; there is quite a different temperature at a greater height in the atmosphere."

" And why are there no thunderstorms in the winter, father? "

He explained that, too. He talked, thinking all the while that he was going to see *her,* and no living soul knew of it, and probably never would know. He had two lives: one, open, seen and known by all who cared to know, full of relative truth and of relative falsehood, exactly like the lives of his friends and acquaintances; and another life running its course in secret. And through some strange, perhaps accidental, conjunction of circumstances, everything that was essential, of interest and of value to him, everything in which he was sincere and did not deceive himself, everything that made the kernel of his life, was hidden from other people; and all that was false in him, the sheath in which he hid himself to conceal the truth — such, for instance, as his work in the bank, his discussions at the club, his " lower race," his presence with his wife at anniversary festivities — all that was open. And he judged of others by himself, not believing in what he saw, and always believing that every man had his real, most interesting life under the cover of secrecy and under the cover of night. All personal life rested on secrecy, and possibly it was partly on that account that civilised man was so nervously anxious that personal privacy should be respected.

After leaving his daughter at school, Gurov went on to the Slaviansky Bazaar. He took off his fur coat below, went upstairs, and softly knocked at the door. Anna Sergeyevna, wearing his favourite grey dress, exhausted by the journey and the suspense, had been expecting him since the evening before. She was pale; she looked at him, and did not smile, and he had hardly come in when she fell on his breast. Their kiss was slow and prolonged, as though they had not met for two years.

" Well, how are you getting on there? " he asked. " What news? "

" Wait; I'll tell you directly. . . . I can't talk."

She could not speak; she was crying. She turned away from him, and pressed her handkerchief to her eyes.

"Let her have her cry out. I'll sit down and wait," he thought, and he sat down in an arm-chair.

Then he rang and asked for tea to be brought him, and while he drank his tea she remained standing at the window with her back to him. She was crying from emotion, from the miserable consciousness that their life was so hard for them; they could only meet in secret, hiding themselves from people, like thieves! Was not their life shattered?

"Come, do stop!" he said.

It was evident to him that this love of theirs would not soon be over, that he could not see the end of it. Anna Sergeyevna grew more and more attached to him. She adored him, and it was unthinkable to say to her that it was bound to have an end some day; besides, she would not have believed it!

He went up to her and took her by the shoulders to say something affectionate and cheering, and at that moment he saw himself in the looking-glass.

His hair was already beginning to turn grey. And it seemed strange to him that he had grown so much older, so much plainer during the last few years. The shoulders on which his hands rested were warm and quivering. He felt compassion for this life, still so warm and lovely, but probably already not far from beginning to fade and wither like his own. Why did she love him so much? He always seemed to women different from what he was, and they loved in him not himself, but the man created by their imagination, whom they had been eagerly seeking all their lives; and afterwards, when they noticed their mistake, they loved him all the same. And not one of them had been happy with him. Time passed, he had made their acquaintance, got on with them, parted, but he had never once loved; it was anything you like, but not love.

And only now when his head was grey he had fallen properly, really in love — for the first time in his life.

Anna Sergeyevna and he loved each other like people very close and akin, like husband and wife, like tender friends; it seemed to them that fate itself had meant them for one another, and they could not understand why he had a wife and she a husband; and it was as though they were a pair of birds of passage, caught and forced to live in different cages. They forgave each other for what they were ashamed of in their past, they forgave everything in the present, and felt that this love of theirs had changed them both.

In moments of depression in the past he had comforted himself with any arguments that came into his mind, but now he no longer cared for arguments; he felt profound compassion, he wanted to be sincere and tender. . . .

"Don't cry, my darling," he said. "You've had your cry; that's enough. . . . Let us talk now, let us think of some plan."

Then they spent a long while taking counsel together, talked of how to avoid the necessity for secrecy, for deception, for living in different towns and not seeing each other for long at a time. How could they be free from this intolerable bondage?

"How? How?" he asked, clutching his head. "How?"

And it seemed as though in a little while the solution would be found, and then a new and splendid life would begin; and it was clear to both of them that they had still a long, long road before them, and that the most complicated and difficult part of it was only just beginning.

1899

GUSEV

I

It was getting dark; it would soon be night.

Gusev, a discharged soldier, sat up in his hammock and said in an undertone:

"I say, Pavel Ivanitch. A soldier at Sutchan told me: while they were sailing a big fish came into collision with their ship and stove a hole in it."

The nondescript individual whom he was addressing, and whom everyone in the ship's hospital called Pavel Ivanitch, was silent, as though he had not heard.

And again a stillness followed. . . . The wind frolicked with the rigging, the screw throbbed, the waves lashed, the hammocks creaked, but the ear had long ago become accustomed to these sounds, and it seemed that everything around was asleep and silent. It was dreary. The three invalids — two soldiers and a sailor — who had been playing cards all the day were asleep and talking in their dreams.

It seemed as though the ship were beginning to rock. The hammock slowly rose and fell under Gusev, as though it were heaving a sigh, and this was repeated once, twice, three times. . . . Something crashed on to the floor with a clang: it must have been a jug falling down.

" The wind has broken loose from its chain . . ." said Gusev, listening.

This time Pavel Ivanitch cleared his throat and answered irritably:

" One minute a vessel's running into a fish, the next, the wind's breaking loose from its chain. . . . Is the wind a beast that it can break loose from its chain? "

" That's how christened folk talk."

" They are as ignorant as you are then. . . . They say all sorts of things. One must keep a head on one's shoulders and use one's reason. You are a senseless creature."

Pavel Ivanitch was subject to sea-sickness. When the sea was rough he was usually ill-humoured, and the merest trifle would make him irritable. And in Gusev's opinion there was absolutely nothing to be vexed about. What was there strange or wonderful, for instance, in the fish or in the wind's breaking loose from its chain? Suppose the fish were as big as a mountain and its back were as hard as a sturgeon: and in the same way, supposing that away yonder at the end of the world there stood great stone walls and the fierce winds were chained up to the walls . . . if they had not broken loose, why did they tear about all over the sea like maniacs, and struggle to escape like dogs? If they were not chained up, what did become of them when it was calm?

Gusev pondered for a long time about fishes as big as a mountain and stout, rusty chains, then he began to feel dull and thought of his native place to which he was returning after five years' service in the East. He pictured an immense pond covered with snow. . . . On one side of the pond the red-brick building of the potteries with a tall chimney and clouds of black smoke; on the other side — a village. . . . His brother Alexey comes out in a sledge from the fifth yard from the end; behind him sits his little son Vanka in big felt over-boots, and his little girl Akulka, also in big felt boots. Alexey has been drinking, Vanka is laughing, Akulka's face he could not see, she had muffled herself up.

"You never know, he'll get the children frozen . . ." thought Gusev. "Lord send them sense and judgment that they may honour their father and mother and not be wiser than their parents."

"They want re-soling," a delirious sailor says in a bass voice. "Yes, yes!"

Gusev's thoughts break off, and instead of a pond there suddenly appears apropos of nothing a huge bull's head without eyes, and the horse and sledge are not driving along, but are whirling round and round in a cloud of smoke. But still he was glad he had seen his own folks. He held his breath from delight, shudders ran all over him, and his fingers twitched.

"The Lord let us meet again," he muttered feverishly, but he at once opened his eyes and sought in the darkness for water.

He drank and lay back, and again the sledge was moving, then again the bull's head without eyes, smoke, clouds. . . . And so on till daybreak.

II

The first outline visible in the darkness was a blue circle — the little round window; then little by little Gusev could distinguish his neighbour in the next hammock, Pavel Ivanitch. The man slept sitting up, as he could not breathe lying down. His face was grey, his nose was long and sharp, his eyes looked huge from the terrible thinness of his face, his temples were sunken, his beard was skimpy, his hair was long. . . . Looking at him you could not make out of what class he was, whether he were a gentleman, a merchant, or a peasant. Judging from his expression and his long hair he might have been a hermit or a lay brother in a monastery — but if one listened to what he said it seemed that he could not be a monk. He was worn out by his cough and his illness and by the stifling heat, and breathed with difficulty, moving his parched lips. Noticing that Gusev was looking at him he turned his face towards him and said:

" I begin to guess. . . . Yes. . . . I understand it all perfectly now."

" What do you understand, Pavel Ivanitch? "

" I'll tell you. . . . It has always seemed to me strange that terribly ill as you are you should be here in a steamer where it is so hot and stifling and we are always being tossed up and down, where, in fact, everything threatens you with death; now it is all clear to me. . . . Yes. . . . Your doctors put you on the steamer to get rid of you. They

get sick of looking after poor brutes like you. . . .
You don't pay them anything, they have a bother
with you, and you damage their records with your
deaths — so, of course, you are brutes! It's not
difficult to get rid of you. . . . All that is necessary
is, in the first place, to have no conscience or humanity, and, secondly, to deceive the steamer authorities. The first condition need hardly be considered,
in that respect we are artists; and one can always
succeed in the second with a little practice. In a
crowd of four hundred healthy soldiers and sailors
half a dozen sick ones are not conspicuous; well,
they drove you all on to the steamer, mixed you with
the healthy ones, hurriedly counted you over, and in
the confusion nothing amiss was noticed, and when
the steamer had started they saw that there were
paralytics and consumptives in the last stage lying
about on the deck. . . ."

Gusev did not understand Pavel Ivanitch; but supposing he was being blamed, he said in self-defence:

" I lay on the deck because I had not the strength
to stand; when we were unloaded from the barge
on to the ship I caught a fearful chill."

" It's revolting," Pavel Ivanitch went on. " The
worst of it is they know perfectly well that you can't
last out the long journey, and yet they put you here.
Supposing you get as far as the Indian Ocean, what
then? It's horrible to think of it. . . . And that's
their gratitude for your faithful, irreproachable
service! "

Pavel Ivanitch's eyes looked angry; he frowned
contemptuously and said, gasping:

" Those are the people who ought to be plucked in the newspapers till the feathers fly in all directions."

The two sick soldiers and the sailor were awake and already playing cards. The sailor was half reclining in his hammock, the soldiers were sitting near him on the floor in the most uncomfortable attitudes. One of the soldiers had his right arm in a sling, and the hand was swathed up in a regular bundle so that he held his cards under his right arm or in the crook of his elbow while he played with the left. The ship was rolling heavily. They could not stand up, nor drink tea, nor take their medicines.

" Were you an officer's servant? " Pavel Ivanitch asked Gusev.

" Yes, an officer's servant."

" My God, my God! " said Pavel Ivanitch, and he shook his head mournfully. " To tear a man out of his home, drag him twelve thousand miles away, then to drive him into consumption and . . . and what is it all for, one wonders? To turn him into a servant for some Captain Kopeikin or midshipman Dirka! How logical! "

" It's not hard work, Pavel Ivanitch. You get up in the morning and clean the boots, get the samovar, sweep the rooms, and then you have nothing more to do. The lieutenant is all the day drawing plans, and if you like you can say your prayers, if you like you can read a book or go out into the street. God grant everyone such a life."

" Yes, very nice, the lieutenant draws plans all

the day and you sit in the kitchen and pine for home. . . . Plans indeed! . . . It is not plans that matter, but a human life. Life is not given twice, it must be treated mercifully."

"Of course, Pavel Ivanitch, a bad man gets no mercy anywhere, neither at home nor in the army, but if you live as you ought and obey orders, who has any need to insult you? The officers are educated gentlemen, they understand. . . . In five years I was never once in prison, and I was never struck a blow, so help me God, but once."

"What for?"

"For fighting. I have a heavy hand, Pavel Ivanitch. Four Chinamen came into our yard; they were bringing firewood or something, I don't remember. Well, I was bored and I knocked them about a bit, one's nose began bleeding, damn the fellow. . . . The lieutenant saw it through the little window, he was angry and gave me a box on the ear."

"Foolish, pitiful man . . ." whispered Pavel Ivanitch. "You don't understand anything."

He was utterly exhausted by the tossing of the ship and closed his eyes; his head alternately fell back and dropped forward on his breast. Several times he tried to lie down but nothing came of it; his difficulty in breathing prevented it.

"And what did you hit the four Chinamen for?" he asked a little while afterwards.

"Oh, nothing. They came into the yard and I hit them."

And a stillness followed. . . . The card-players

had been playing for two hours with enthusiasm and loud abuse of one another, but the motion of the ship overcame them, too; they threw aside the cards and lay down. Again Gusev saw the big pond, the brick building, the village. . . . Again the sledge was coming along, again Vanka was laughing and Akulka, silly little thing, threw open her fur coat and stuck her feet out, as much as to say: "Look, good people, my snowboots are not like Vanka's, they are new ones."

"Five years old, and she has no sense yet," Gusev muttered in delirium. "Instead of kicking your legs you had better come and get your soldier uncle a drink. I will give you something nice."

Then Andron with a flintlock gun on his shoulder was carrying a hare he had killed, and he was followed by the decrepit old Jew Isaitchik, who offers to barter the hare for a piece of soap; then the black calf in the shed, then Domna sewing at a shirt and crying about something, and then again the bull's head without eyes, black smoke. . . .

Overhead someone gave a loud shout, several sailors ran by, they seemed to be dragging something bulky over the deck, something fell with a crash. Again they ran by. . . . Had something gone wrong? Gusev raised his head, listened, and saw that the two soldiers and the sailor were playing cards again; Pavel Ivanitch was sitting up moving his lips. It was stifling, one hadn't strength to breathe, one was thirsty, the water was warm, disgusting. The ship heaved as much as ever.

Suddenly something strange happened to one of

34

the soldiers playing cards. . . . He called hearts diamonds, got muddled in his score, and dropped his cards, then with a frightened, foolish smile looked round at all of them.

"I shan't be a minute, mates, I'll . . ." he said, and lay down on the floor.

Everybody was amazed. They called to him, he did not answer.

"Stephan, maybe you are feeling bad, eh?" the soldier with his arm in a sling asked him. "Perhaps we had better bring the priest, eh?"

"Have a drink of water, Stepan . . ." said the sailor. "Here, lad, drink."

"Why are you knocking the jug against his teeth?" said Gusev angrily. "Don't you see, turnip head?'

"What?"

"What?" Gusev repeated, mimicking him. "There is no breath in him, he is dead! That's what! What nonsensical people, Lord have mercy on us . . . !"

III

The ship was not rocking and Pavel Ivanitch was more cheerful. He was no longer ill-humoured. His face had a boastful, defiant, mocking expression. He looked as though he wanted to say: "Yes, in a minute I will tell you something that will make you split your sides with laughing." The little round window was open and a soft breeze was blowing on Pavel Ivanitch. There was a sound of

35

voices, of the plash of oars in the water. . . . Just under the little window someone began droning in a high, unpleasant voice: no doubt it was a Chinaman singing.

" Here we are in the harbour," said Pavel Ivanitch, smiling ironically. " Only another month and we shall be in Russia. Well, worthy gentlemen and warriors! I shall arrive at Odessa and from there go straight to Harkov. In Harkov I have a friend, a literary man. I shall go to him and say, ' Come, old man, put aside your horrid subjects, ladies' amours and the beauties of nature, and show up human depravity.' "

For a minute he pondered, then said:

" Gusev, do you know how I took them in? "

" Took in whom, Pavel Ivanitch? "

" Why, these fellows. . . . You know that on this steamer there is only a first-class and a third-class, and they only allow peasants — that is the riff-raff — to go in the third. If you have got on a reefer jacket and have the faintest resemblance to a gentleman or a bourgeois you must go first-class, if you please. You must fork out five hundred roubles if you die for it. Why, I ask, have you made such a rule? Do you want to raise the prestige of educated Russians thereby? Not a bit of it. We don't let you go third-class simply because a decent person can't go third-class; it is·very horrible and disgusting. Yes, indeed. I am very grateful for such solicitude for decent people's welfare. But in any case, whether it is nasty there or nice, five hundred roubles I haven't got. I haven't pilfered government money. I haven't exploited the natives, I haven't trafficked in contraband, I have flogged no one to death, so judge whether I have the right to travel first-class and even less to reckon myself of the educated class? But you won't catch them with logic. . . . One has to resort to deception. I put on a workman's coat and high boots, I assumed a drunken, servile mug and went to the agents: 'Give us a little ticket, your honour,' said I. . . ."

"Why, what class do you belong to?" asked a sailor.

"Clerical. My father was an honest priest, he always told the great ones of the world the truth to their faces; and he had a great deal to put up with in consequence."

Pavel Ivanitch was exhausted with talking and gasped for breath, but still went on:

"Yes, I always tell people the truth to their faces. I am not afraid of anyone or anything. There is a vast difference between me and all of you in that respect. You are in darkness, you are blind, crushed; you see nothing and what you do see you don't understand. . . . You are told the wind breaks loose from its chain, that you are beasts, Petchenyegs, and you believe it; they punch you in the neck, you kiss their hands; some animal in a sable-lined coat robs you and then tips you fifteen kopecks and you: 'Let me kiss your hand, sir.' You are pariahs, pitiful people. . . . I am a different sort. My eyes are open, I see it all as clearly as a hawk or an eagle when it floats over the earth, and I understand it all. I am a living protest. I see irresponsible tyranny — I protest. I see cant and hypocrisy — I protest. I see swine triumphant — I protest. And I cannot be suppressed, no Spanish Inquisition can make me hold my tongue. No. . . . Cut out my tongue and I would protest in dumb show; shut me up in a cellar — I will shout from it to be heard half a mile away, or I will starve myself to death that they may have another weight on their black consciences. Kill me and I will haunt them with my ghost. All my acquaintances say to me: ' You are a most insufferable person, Pavel Ivanitch.' I am proud of such a reputation. I have served three years in the far East, and I shall be remembered there for a hundred years: I had rows with everyone. My friends write to me from Russia, ' Don't come back,' but here I am going back to spite them . . . yes. . . . That is life as I understand it. That is what one can call life."

Gusev was looking at the little window and was not listening. A boat was swaying on the transparent, soft, turquoise water all bathed in hot, dazzling sunshine. In it there were naked Chinamen holding up cages with canaries and calling out:

" It sings, it sings! "

Another boat knocked against the first; the steam cutter darted by. And then there came another boat with a fat Chinaman sitting in it, eating rice with little sticks.

Languidly the water heaved, languidly the white seagulls floated over it.

Gusev

" I should like to give that fat fellow one in the neck," thought Gusev, gazing at the stout Chinaman, with a yawn.

He dozed off, and it seemed to him that all nature was dozing, too. Time flew swiftly by; imperceptibly the day passed, imperceptibly the darkness came on. . . . The steamer was no longer standing still, but moving on further.

IV

Two days passed, Pavel Ivanitch lay down instead of sitting up; his eyes were closed, his nose seemed to have grown sharper.

" Pavel Ivanitch," Gusev called to him. " Hey, Pavel Ivanitch."

Pavel Ivanitch opened his eyes and moved his lips.

" Are you feeling bad? "

" No . . . it's nothing . . ." answered Pavel Ivanitch, gasping. " Nothing; on the contrary . . . I am rather better. . . . You see I can lie down. . . . I am a little easier. . . ."

" Well, thank God for that, Pavel Ivanitch."

" When I compare myself with you I am sorry for you . . . poor fellow. My lungs are all right, it is only a stomach cough. . . . I can stand hell, let alone the Red Sea. Besides I take a critical attitude to my illness and to the medicines they give me for it. While you . . . you are in darkness. . . . It's hard for you, very, very hard! "

The ship was not rolling, it was calm, but as hot

and stifling as a bath-house; it was not only hard to speak but even hard to listen. Gusev hugged his knees, laid his head on them and thought of his home. Good heavens, what a relief it was to think of snow and cold in that stifling heat! You drive in a sledge, all at once the horses take fright at something and bolt. . . . Regardless of the road, the ditches, the ravines, they dash like mad things, right through the village, over the pond by the pottery works, out across the open fields. " Hold on," the pottery hands and the peasants shout, meeting them. " Hold on." But why? Let the keen, cold wind beat in one's face and bite one's hands; let the lumps of snow, kicked up by the horses' hoofs, fall on one's cap, on one's back, down one's collar, on one's chest; let the runners ring on the snow, and the traces and the sledge be smashed, deuce take them one and all! And how delightful when the sledge upsets and you go flying full tilt into a drift, face downwards in the snow, and then you get up white all over with icicles on your moustaches; no cap, no gloves, your belt undone. . . . People laugh, the dogs bark. . . .

Pavel Ivanitch half opened one eye, looked at Gusev with it, and asked softly:

" Gusev, did your commanding officer steal? "

" Who can tell, Pavel Ivanitch! We can't say, it didn't reach us."

And after that a long time passed in silence. Gusev brooded, muttered something in delirium, and kept drinking water; it was hard for him to talk and hard to listen, and he was afraid of being talked to.   An hour passed, a second, a third; evening came on, then night, but he did not notice it.   He still sat dreaming of the frost.

There was a sound as though someone came into the hospital, and voices were audible, but a few minutes passed and all was still again.

" The Kingdom of Heaven and eternal peace," said the soldier with his arm in a sling.   " He was an uncomfortable man."

" What ? " asked Gusev.   " Who ? "

" He is dead, they have just carried him up."

" Oh, well," muttered Gusev, yawning, " the Kingdom of Heaven be his."

" What do you think ? " the soldier with his arm in a sling asked Gusev.   " Will he be in the Kingdom of Heaven or not ? "

" Who is it you are talking about ? "

" Pavel Ivanitch."

" He will be . . . he suffered so long.   And there is another thing, he belonged to the clergy, and the priests always have a lot of relations.   Their prayers will save him."

The soldier with the sling sat down on a hammock near Gusev and said in an undertone:

" And you, Gusev, are not long for this world. You will never get to Russia."

" Did the doctor or his assistant say so ? " asked Gusev.

" It isn't that they said so, but one can see it. . . . One can see directly when a man's going to die. You don't eat, you don't drink; it's dreadful to see how thin you've got.   It's consumption, in fact.   I say it, not to upset you, but because maybe you would like to have the sacrament and extreme unction. And if you have any money you had better give it to the senior officer."

" I haven't written home . . ." Gusev sighed. " I shall die and they won't know."

" They'll hear of it," the sick sailor brought out in a bass voice. " When you die they will put it down in the *Gazette,* at Odessa they will send in a report to the commanding officer there and he will send it to the parish or somewhere. . . ."

Gusev began to be uneasy after such a conversation and to feel a vague yearning. He drank water — it was not that; he dragged himself to the window and breathed the hot, moist air — it was not that; he tried to think of home, of the frost — it was not that. . . . At last it seemed to him one minute longer in the ward and he would certainly expire.

" It's stifling, mates . . ." he said. " I'll go on deck. Help me up, for Christ's sake."

" All right," assented the soldier with the sling. " I'll carry you, you can't walk, hold on to my neck."

Gusev put his arm round the soldier's neck, the latter put his unhurt arm round him and carried him up. On the deck sailors and time-expired soldiers were lying asleep side by side; there were so many of them it was difficult to pass.

" Stand down," the soldier with the sling said softly. " Follow me quietly, hold on to my shirt. . . ."

It was dark. There was no light on deck, nor

on the masts, nor anywhere on the sea around. At
the furthest end of the ship the man on watch was
standing perfectly still like a statue, and it looked
as though he were asleep. It seemed as though the
steamer were abandoned to itself and were going
at its own will.

"Now they will throw Pavel Ivanitch into the
sea," said the soldier with the sling. "In a sack
and then into the water."

"Yes, that's the rule."

"But it's better to lie at home in the earth. Anyway, your mother comes to the grave and weeps."

"Of course."

There was a smell of hay and of dung. There
were oxen standing with drooping heads by the
ship's rail. One, two, three; eight of them! And
there was a little horse. Gusev put out his hand
to stroke it, but it shook its head, showed its teeth,
and tried to bite his sleeve.

"Damned brute . . ." said Gusev angrily.

The two of them, he and the soldier, threaded
their way to the head of the ship, then stood at
the rail and looked up and down. Overhead deep
sky, bright stars, peace and stillness, exactly as at
home in the village, below darkness and disorder.
The tall waves were resounding, no one could tell
why. Whichever wave you looked at each one was
trying to rise higher than all the rest and to chase
and crush the next one; after it a third as fierce
and hideous flew noisily, with a glint of light on its
white crest.

The sea has no sense and no pity. If the steamer

had been smaller and not made of thick iron, the waves would have crushed it to pieces without the slightest compunction, and would have devoured all the people in it with no distinction of saints or sinners. The steamer had the same cruel and meaningless expression. This monster with its huge beak was dashing onwards, cutting millions of waves in its path; it had no fear of the darkness nor the wind, nor of space, nor of solitude, caring for nothing, and if the ocean had its people, this monster would have crushed them, too, without distinction of saints or sinners.

" Where are we now? " asked Gusev.

" I don't know. We must be in the ocean."

" There is no sight of land. . . ."

" No indeed! They say we shan't see it for seven days."

The two soldiers watched the white foam with the phosphorus light on it and were silent, thinking. Gusev was the first to break the silence.

" There is nothing to be afraid of," he said, " only one is full of dread as though one were sitting in a dark forest; but if, for instance, they let a boat down on to the water this minute and an officer ordered me to go a hundred miles over the sea to catch fish, I'd go. Or, let's say, if a Christian were to fall into the water this minute, I'd go in after him. A German or a Chinaman I wouldn't save, but I'd go in after a Christian."

" And are you afraid to die? "

" Yes. I am sorry for the folks at home. My brother at home, you know, isn't steady; he drinks, he beats his wife for nothing, he does not honour his parents. Everything will go to ruin without me, and father and my old mother will be begging their bread, I shouldn't wonder. But my legs won't bear me, brother, and it's hot here. Let's go to sleep."

V

Gusev went back to the ward and got into his hammock. He was again tormented by a vague craving, and he could not make out what he wanted. There was an oppression on his chest, a throbbing in his head, his mouth was so dry that it was difficult for him to move his tongue. He dozed, and murmured in his sleep, and, worn out with nightmares, his cough, and the stifling heat, towards morning he fell into a sound sleep. He dreamed that they were just taking the bread out of the oven in the barracks and he climbed into the stove and had a steam bath in it, lashing himself with a bunch of birch twigs. He slept for two days, and at midday on the third two sailors came down and carried him out.

He was sewn up in sailcloth and to make him heavier they put with him two iron weights. Sewn up in the sailcloth he looked like a carrot or a radish: broad at the head and narrow at the feet. . . . Before sunset they brought him up to the deck and put him on a plank; one end of the plank lay on the side of the ship, the other on a box, placed on a stool. Round him stood the soldiers and the officers with their caps off.

" Blessed be the Name of the Lord . . ." the priest began. " As it was in the beginning, is now, and ever shall be."

" Amen," chanted three sailors.

The soldiers and the officers crossed themselves and looked away at the waves. It was strange that a man should be sewn up in sailcloth and should soon be flying into the sea. Was it possible that such a thing might happen to anyone?

The priest strewed earth upon Gusev and bowed down. They sang " Eternal Memory."

The man on watch duty tilted up the end of the plank, Gusev slid off and flew head foremost, turned a somersault in the air and splashed into the sea. He was covered with foam and for a moment looked as though he were wrapped in lace, but the minute passed and he disappeared in the waves.

He went rapidly towards the bottom. Did he reach it? It was said to be three miles to the bottom. After sinking sixty or seventy feet, he began moving more and more slowly, swaying rhythmically, as though he were hesitating and, carried along by the current, moved more rapidly sideways than downwards.

Then he was met by a shoal of the fish called harbour pilots. Seeing the dark body the fish stopped as though petrified, and suddenly turned round and disappeared. In less than a minute they flew back swift as an arrow to Gusev, and began zig-zagging round him in the water.

After that another dark body appeared. It was a shark. It swam under Gusev with dignity and no show of interest, as though it did not notice him, and sank down upon its back, then it turned belly upwards, basking in the warm, transparent water and languidly opened its jaws with two rows of teeth. The harbour pilots are delighted, they stop to see what will come next. After playing a little with the body the shark nonchalantly puts its jaws under it, cautiously touches it with its teeth, and the sail-cloth is rent its full length from head to foot; one of the weights falls out and frightens the harbour pilots, and striking the shark on the ribs goes rapidly to the bottom.

Overhead at this time the clouds are massed together on the side where the sun is setting; one cloud like a triumphal arch, another like a lion, a third like a pair of scissors. . . . From behind the clouds a broad, green shaft of light pierces through and stretches to the middle of the sky; a little later another, violet-coloured, lies beside it; next that, one of gold, then one rose-coloured. . . . The sky turns a soft lilac. Looking at this gorgeous, enchanted sky, at first the ocean scowls, but soon it, too, takes tender, joyous, passionate colours for which it is hard to find a name in human speech.

1890

AN UPHEAVAL

MASHENKA PAVLETSKY, a young girl who had only just finished her studies at a boarding school, returning from a walk to the house of the Kushkins, with whom she was living as a governess, found the household in a terrible turmoil. Mihailo, the porter who opened the door to her, was excited and red as a crab.

Loud voices were heard from upstairs.

"Madame Kushkin is in a fit, most likely, or else she has quarrelled with her husband," thought Mashenka.

In the hall and in the corridor she met maid-servants. One of them was crying. Then Mashenka saw, running out of her room, the master of the house himself, Nikolay Sergeitch, a little man with a flabby face and a bald head, though he was not old. He was red in the face and twitching all over. He passed the governess without noticing her, and throwing up his arms, exclaimed:

"Oh, how horrible it is! How tactless! How stupid! How barbarous! Abominable!"

Mashenka went into her room, and then, for the first time in her life, it was her lot to experience in all its acuteness the feeling that is so familiar to persons in dependent positions, who eat the bread of the rich and powerful, and cannot speak their minds. There was a search going on in her room. The lady of the house, Fedosya Vassilyevna, a stout, broad-shouldered, uncouth woman with thick black eyebrows, a faintly perceptible moustache, and red hands, who was exactly like a plain, illiterate cook in face and manners, was standing, without her cap on, at the table, putting back into Mashenka's work-bag balls of wool, scraps of materials, and bits of paper. . . . Evidently the governess's arrival took her by surprise, since, on looking round and seeing the girl's pale and astonished face, she was a little taken aback, and muttered:

"*Pardon.* I . . . I upset it accidentally. . . . My sleeve caught in it. . . ."

And saying something more, Madame Kushkin rustled her long skirts and went out. Mashenka looked round her room with wondering eyes, and, unable to understand it, not knowing what to think, shrugged her shoulders, and turned cold with dismay. What had Fedosya Vassilyevna been looking for in her work-bag? If she really had, as she said, caught her sleeve in it and upset everything, why had Nikolay Sergeitch dashed out of her room so excited and red in the face? Why was one drawer of the table pulled out a little way? The money-box, in which the governess put away ten kopeck pieces and old stamps, was open. They had opened it, but did not know how to shut it, though they had scratched the lock all over. The whatnot with her books on it, the things on the table, the bed — all bore fresh traces of a search. Her linen-basket, too. The linen had been carefully folded, but it was not in the same order as Mashenka had left it when she went out. So the search had been thorough, most thorough. But what was it for? Why? What had happened? Mashenka remembered the excited porter, the general turmoil which was still going on, the weeping servant-girl; had it not all some connection with the search that had just been made in her room? Was not she mixed up in something dreadful? Mashenka turned pale, and feeling cold all over, sank on to her linen-basket.

A maid-servant came into the room.

" Liza, you don't know why they have been rummaging in my room? " the governess asked her.

" Mistress has lost a brooch worth two thousand," said Liza.

" Yes, but why have they been rummaging in my room? "

" They've been searching every one, miss. They've searched all my things, too. They stripped us all naked and searched us. . . . God knows, miss, I never went near her toilet-table, let alone touching the brooch. I shall say the same at the police-station."

" But . . . why have they been rummaging here? " the governess still wondered.

" A brooch has been stolen, I tell you. The mistress has been rummaging in everything with her own hands. She even searched Mihailo, the porter, herself. It's a perfect disgrace! Nikolay Sergeitch simply looks on and cackles like a hen. But you've no need to tremble like that, miss. They

51

found nothing here. You've nothing to be afraid of if you didn't take the brooch."

" But, Liza, it's vile . . . it's insulting," said Mashenka, breathless with indignation. " It's so mean, so low! What right had she to suspect me and to rummage in my things?"

" You are living with strangers, miss," sighed Liza. " Though you are a young lady, still you are . . . as it were . . . a servant. . . . It's not like living with your papa and mamma."

Mashenka threw herself on the bed and sobbed bitterly. Never in her life had she been subjected to such an outrage, never had she been so deeply insulted. . . . She, well-educated, refined, the daughter of a teacher, was suspected of theft; she had been searched like a street-walker! She could not imagine a greater insult. And to this feeling of resentment was added an oppressive dread of what would come next. All sorts of absurd ideas came into her mind. If they could suspect her of theft, then they might arrest her, strip her naked, and search her, then lead her through the street with an escort of soldiers, cast her into a cold, dark cell with mice and woodlice, exactly like the dungeon in which Princess Tarakanov was imprisoned. Who would stand up for her? Her parents lived far away in the provinces; they had not the money to come to her. In the capital she was as solitary as in a desert, without friends or kindred. They could do what they liked with her.

" I will go to all the courts and all the lawyers," Mashenka thought, trembling. " I will explain to them, I will take an oath. . . . They will believe that I could not be a thief! "

Mashenka remembered that under the sheets in her basket she had some sweetmeats, which, following the habits of her schooldays, she had put in her pocket at dinner and carried off to her room. She felt hot all over, and was ashamed at the thought that her little secret was known to the lady of the house; and all this terror, shame, resentment, brought on an attack of palpitation of the heart, which set up a throbbing in her temples, in her heart, and deep down in her stomach.

" Dinner is ready," the servant summoned Mashenka.

" Shall I go, or not? "

Mashenka brushed her hair, wiped her face with a wet towel, and went into the dining-room. There they had already begun dinner. At one end of the table sat Fedosya Vassilyevna with a stupid, solemn, serious face; at the other end Nikolay Sergeitch. At the sides there were the visitors and the children. The dishes were handed by two footmen in swallow-tails and white gloves. Every one knew that there was an upset in the house, that Madame Kushkin was in trouble, and every one was silent. Nothing was heard but the sound of munching and the rattle of spoons on the plates.

The lady of the house, herself, was the first to speak.

" What is the third course? " she asked the footman in a weary, injured voice.

" *Esturgeon à la russe*," answered the footman.

"I ordered that, Fenya," Nikolay Sergeitch hastened to observe. "I wanted some fish. If you don't like it, *ma chère*, don't let them serve it. I just ordered it. . . ."

Fedosya Vassilyevna did not like dishes that she had not ordered herself, and now her eyes filled with tears.

"Come, don't let us agitate ourselves," Mamikov, her household doctor, observed in a honeyed voice, just touching her arm, with a smile as honeyed. "We are nervous enough as it is. Let us forget the brooch! Health is worth more than two thousand roubles!"

"It's not the two thousand I regret," answered the lady, and a big tear rolled down her cheek. "It's the fact itself that revolts me! I cannot put up with thieves in my house. I don't regret it— I regret nothing; but to steal from me is such ingratitude! That's how they repay me for my kindness. . . ."

They all looked into their plates, but Mashenka fancied after the lady's words that every one was looking at her. A lump rose in her throat; she began crying and put her handkerchief to her lips.

"*Pardon*," she muttered. "I can't help it. My head aches. I'll go away."

And she got up from the table, scraping her chair awkwardly, and went out quickly, still more overcome with confusion.

"It's beyond everything!" said Nikolay Sergeitch, frowning. "What need was there to search her room? How out of place it was!"

An Upheaval

" I don't say she took the brooch," said Fedosya Vassilyevna, " but can you answer for her? To tell the truth, I haven't much confidence in these learned paupers."

" It really was unsuitable, Fenya. . . . Excuse me, Fenya, but you've no kind of legal right to make a search."

" I know nothing about your laws. All I know is that I've lost my brooch. And I will find the brooch! " She brought her fork down on the plate with a clatter, and her eyes flashed angrily. " And you eat your dinner, and don't interfere in what doesn't concern you! "

Nikolay Sergeitch dropped his eyes mildly and sighed. Meanwhile Mashenka, reaching her room, flung herself on her bed. She felt now neither alarm nor shame, but she felt an intense longing to go and slap the cheeks of this hard, arrogant, dull-witted, prosperous woman.

Lying on her bed she breathed into her pillow and dreamed of how nice it would be to go and buy the most expensive brooch and fling it into the face of this bullying woman. If only it were God's will that Fedosya Vassilyevna should come to ruin and wander about begging, and should taste all the horrors of poverty and dependence, and that Mashenka, whom she had insulted, might give her alms! Oh, if only she could come in for a big fortune, could buy a carriage, and could drive noisily past the windows so as to be envied by that woman! But all these were only dreams, in reality there was only one thing left to do — to get away as

55

quickly as possible, not to stay another hour in this place. It was true it was terrible to lose her place, to go back to her parents, who had nothing; but what could she do? Mashenka could not bear the sight of the lady of the house nor of her little room; she felt stifled and wretched here. She was so disgusted with Fedosya Vassilyevna, who was so obsessed by her illnesses and her supposed aristocratic rank, that everything in the world seemed to have become coarse and unattractive because this woman was living in it. Mashenka jumped up from the bed and began packing.

"May I come in?" asked Nikolay Sergeitch at the door; he had come up noiselessly to the door, and spoke in a soft, subdued voice. "May I?"

"Come in."

He came in and stood still near the door. His eyes looked dim and his red little nose was shiny. After dinner he used to drink beer, and the fact was perceptible in his walk, in his feeble, flabby hands.

"What's this?" he asked, pointing to the basket.

"I am packing. Forgive me, Nikolay Sergeitch, but I cannot remain in your house. I feel deeply insulted by this search!"

"I understand. . . . Only you are wrong to go. . . . Why should you? They've searched your things, but you . . . what does it matter to you? You will be none the worse for it."

Mashenka was silent and went on packing. Nikolay Sergeitch pinched his moustache, as though wondering what he should say next, and went on in an ingratiating voice:

An Upheaval

"I understand, of course, but you must make allowances. You know my wife is nervous, headstrong; you mustn't judge her too harshly."

Mashenka did not speak.

"If you are so offended," Nikolay Sergeitch went on, "well, if you like, I'm ready to apologise. I ask your pardon."

Mashenka made no answer, but only bent lower over her box. This exhausted, irresolute man was of absolutely no significance in the household. He stood in the pitiful position of a dependent and hanger-on, even with the servants, and his apology meant nothing either.

"H'm! . . . You say nothing! That's not enough for you. In that case, I will apologise for my wife. In my wife's name. . . . She behaved tactlessly, I admit it as a gentleman. . . ."

Nikolay Sergeitch walked about the room, heaved a sigh, and went on:

"Then you want me to have it rankling here, under my heart. . . . You want my conscience to torment me. . . ."

"I know it's not your fault, Nikolay Sergeitch," said Mashenka, looking him full in the face with her big tear-stained eyes. "Why should you worry yourself?"

"Of course, no. . . . But still, don't you . . . go away. I entreat you."

Mashenka shook her head. Nikolay Sergeitch stopped at the window and drummed on the pane with his finger-tips.

"Such misunderstandings are simply torture to

me," he said. "Why, do you want me to go down on my knees to you, or what? Your pride is wounded, and here you've been crying and packing up to go; but I have pride, too, and you do not spare it! Or do you want me to tell you what I would not tell as Confession? Do you? Listen; you want me to tell you what I won't tell the priest on my death-bed?"

Mashenka made no answer.

"I took my wife's brooch," Nikolay Sergeitch said quickly. "Is that enough now? Are you satisfied? Yes, I . . . took it. . . . But, of course, I count on your discretion. . . . For God's sake, not a word, not half a hint to any one!"

Mashenka, amazed and frightened, went on packing; she snatched her things, crumpled them up, and thrust them anyhow into the box and the basket. Now, after this candid avowal on the part of Nikolay Sergeitch, she could not remain another minute, and could not understand how she could have gone on living in the house before.

"And it's nothing to wonder at," Nikolay Sergeitch went on after a pause. "It's an everyday story! I need money, and she . . . won't give it to me. It was my father's money that bought this house and everything, you know! It's all mine, and the brooch belonged to my mother, and . . . it's all mine! And she took it, took possession of every-thing. . . . I can't go to law with her, you'll admit. . . . I beg you most earnestly, overlook it . . . stay on. *Tout comprendre, tout pardonner.* Will you stay?"

58

An Upheaval

"No!" said Mashenka resolutely, beginning to tremble. "Let me alone, I entreat you!"

"Well, God bless you!" sighed Nikolay Sergeitch, sitting down on the stool near the box. "I must own I like people who still can feel resentment, contempt, and so on. I could sit here forever and look at your indignant face. . . . So you won't stay, then? I understand. . . . It's bound to be so. . . . Yes, of course. . . . It's all right for you, but for me — wo-o-o-o! . . . I can't stir a step out of this cellar. I'd go off to one of our estates, but in every one of them there are some of my wife's rascals . . . stewards, experts, damn them all! They mortgage and remortgage. . . . You mustn't catch fish, must keep off the grass, mustn't break the trees."

"Nikolay Sergeitch!" his wife's voice called from the drawing-room. "Agnia, call your master!"

"Then you won't stay?" asked Nikolay Sergeitch, getting up quickly and going towards the door. "You might as well stay, really. In the evenings I could come and have a talk with you. Eh? Stay! If you go, there won't be a human face left in the house. It's awful!"

Nikolay Sergeitch's pale, exhausted face besought her, but Mashenka shook her head, and with a wave of his hand he went out.

Half an hour later she was on her way.

1886

59

NEIGHBOURS

Pyotr Mihalitch Ivashin was very much out of humour: his sister, a young girl, had gone away to live with Vlassitch, a married man. To shake off the despondency and depression which pursued him at home and in the fields, he called to his aid his sense of justice, his genuine and noble ideas — he had always defended free-love! — but this was of no avail, and he always came back to the same conclusion as their foolish old nurse, that his sister had acted wrongly and that Vlassitch had abducted his sister. And that was distressing.

His mother did not leave her room all day long; the old nurse kept sighing and speaking in whispers; his aunt had been on the point of taking her departure every day, and her trunks were continually being brought down to the hall and carried up again to her room. In the house, in the yard, and in the garden it was as still as though there were some one dead in the house. His aunt, the servants, and even the peasants, so it seemed to Pyotr Mihalitch, looked at him enigmatically and with perplexity, as though they wanted to say " Your sister has been seduced; why are you doing nothing? " And he reproached himself for inactivity, though he did not know precisely what action he ought to have taken.

So passed six days. On the seventh — it was Sunday afternoon — a messenger on horseback brought a letter. The address was in a familiar feminine handwriting: "Her Excy. Anna Nikolaevna Ivashin." Pyotr Mihalitch fancied that there was something defiant, provocative, in the handwriting and in the abbreviation "Excy." And advanced ideas in women are obstinate, ruthless, cruel.

"She'd rather die than make any concession to her unhappy mother, or beg her forgiveness," thought Pyotr Mihalitch, as he went to his mother with the letter.

His mother was lying on her bed, dressed. Seeing her son, she rose impulsively, and straightening her grey hair, which had fallen from under her cap, asked quickly:

"What is it? What is it?"

"This has come . . ." said her son, giving her the letter.

Zina's name, and even the pronoun "she" was not uttered in the house. Zina was spoken of impersonally: "this has come," "Gone away," and so on. . . . The mother recognised her daughter's handwriting, and her face grew ugly and unpleasant, and her grey hair escaped again from her cap.

"No!" she said, with a motion of her hands, as though the letter scorched her fingers. "No, no, never! Nothing would induce me!"

The mother broke into hysterical sobs of grief

and shame; she evidently longed to read the letter, but her pride prevented her. Pyotr Mihalitch realised that he ought to open the letter himself and read it aloud, but he was overcome by anger such as he had never felt before; he ran out into the yard and shouted to the messenger:

" Say there will be no answer! There will be no answer! Tell them that, you beast! "

And he tore up the letter; then tears came into his eyes, and feeling that he was cruel, miserable, and to blame, he went out into the fields.

He was only twenty-seven, but he was already stout. He dressed like an old man in loose, roomy clothes, and suffered from asthma. He already seemed to be developing the characteristics of an elderly country bachelor. He never fell in love, never thought of marriage, and loved no one but his mother, his sister, his old nurse, and the gardener, Vassilitch. He was fond of good fare, of his nap after dinner, and of talking about politics and exalted subjects. He had in his day taken his degree at the university, but he now looked upon his studies as though in them he had discharged a duty incumbent upon young men between the ages of eighteen and twenty-five; at any rate, the ideas which now strayed every day through his mind had nothing in common with the university or the subjects he had studied there.

In the fields it was hot and still, as though rain were coming. It was steaming in the wood, and there was a heavy fragrant scent from the pines and rotting leaves. Pyotr Mihalitch stopped several times and wiped his wet brow. He looked at his winter corn and his spring oats, walked round the clover-field, and twice drove away a partridge with its chicks which had strayed in from the wood. And all the while he was thinking that this insufferable state of things could not go on for ever, and that he must end it one way or another. End it stupidly, madly, but he must end it.

" But how? What can I do? " he asked himself, and looked imploringly at the sky and at the trees, as though begging for their help.

But the sky and the trees were mute. His noble ideas were no help, and his common sense whispered that the agonising question could have no solution but a stupid one, and that to-day's scene with the messenger was not the last one of its kind. It was terrible to think what was in store for him!

As he returned home the sun was setting. By now it seemed to him that the problem was incapable of solution. He could not accept the accomplished fact, and he could not refuse to accept it, and there was no intermediate course. When, taking off his hat and fanning himself with his handkerchief, he was walking along the road, and had only another mile and a half to go before he would reach home, he heard bells behind him. It was a very choice and successful combination of bells, which gave a clear crystal note. No one had such bells on his horses but the police captain, Medovsky, formerly an officer in the hussars, a man in broken-down health, who had been a great rake and spend-thrift, and was a distant relation of Pyotr Mihalitch. He was like one of the family at the Ivashins' and had a tender, fatherly affection for Zina, as well as a great admiration for her.

" I was coming to see you," he said, overtaking Pyotr Mihalitch. " Get in; I'll give you a lift."

He was smiling and looked cheerful. Evidently he did not yet know that Zina had gone to live with Vlassitch; perhaps he had been told of it already, but did not believe it. Pyotr Mihalitch felt in a difficult position.

" You are very welcome," he muttered, blushing till the tears came into his eyes, and not knowing how to lie or what to say. " I am delighted," he went on, trying to smile, " but . . . Zina is away and mother is ill."

" How annoying! " said the police captain, look-ing pensively at Pyotr Mihalitch. " And I was meaning to spend the evening with you. Where has Zinaida Mihalovna gone? "

" To the Sinitskys', and I believe she meant to go from there to the monastery. I don't quite know."

The police captain talked a little longer and then turned back. Pyotr Mihalitch walked home, and thought with horror what the police captain's feel-ings would be when he learned the truth. And Pyotr Mihalitch imagined his feelings, and actually experiencing them himself, went into the house. "Lord help us," he thought, "Lord help us!"

At evening tea the only one at the table was his aunt. As usual, her face wore the expression that seemed to say that though she was a weak, defenceless woman, she would allow no one to insult her. Pyotr Mihalitch sat down at the other end of the table (he did not like his aunt) and began drinking tea in silence.

"Your mother has had no dinner again to-day," said his aunt. "You ought to do something about it, Petrusha. Starving oneself is no help in sorrow."

It struck Pyotr Mihalitch as absurd that his aunt should meddle in other people's business and should make her departure depend on Zina's having gone away. He was tempted to say something rude to her, but restrained himself. And as he restrained himself he felt the time had come for action, and that he could not bear it any longer. Either he must act at once or fall on the ground, and scream and bang his head upon the floor. He pictured Vlassitch and Zina, both of them progressive and self-satisfied, kissing each other somewhere under a maple tree, and all the anger and bitterness that had been accumulating in him for the last seven days fastened upon Vlassitch.

"One has seduced and abducted my sister," he thought, "another will come and murder my mother, a third will set fire to the house and sack the place.

Neighbours

. . . And all this under the mask of friendship, lofty ideas, unhappiness!"

"No, it shall not be!" Pyotr Mihalitch cried suddenly, and he brought his fist down on the table.

He jumped up and ran out of the dining-room. In the stable the steward's horse was standing ready saddled. He got on it and galloped off to Vlassitch. There was a perfect tempest within him. He felt a longing to do something extraordinary, startling, even if he had to repent of it all his life afterwards. Should he call Vlassitch a blackguard, slap him in the face, and then challenge him to a duel? But Vlassitch was not one of those men who do fight duels; being called a blackguard and slapped in the face would only make him more unhappy, and would make him shrink into himself more than ever. These unhappy, defenceless people are the most insufferable, the most tiresome creatures in the world. They can do anything with impunity. When the luckless man responds to well-deserved reproach by looking at you with eyes full of deep and guilty feeling, and with a sickly smile bends his head submissively, even justice itself could not lift its hand against him.

"No matter. I'll horsewhip him before her eyes and tell him what I think of him," Pyotr Mihalitch decided.

He was riding through his wood and waste land, and he imagined Zina would try to justify her conduct by talking about the rights of women and individual freedom, and about there being no difference between legal marriage and free union. Like a woman, she would argue about what she did not understand. And very likely at the end she would ask, " How do you come in? What right have you to interfere? "

" No, I have no right," muttered Pyotr Mihalitch. " But so much the better. . . . The harsher I am, the less right I have to interfere, the better."

It was sultry. Clouds of gnats hung over the ground and in the waste places the peewits called plaintively. Everything betokened rain, but he could not see a cloud in the sky. Pyotr Mihalitch crossed the boundary of his estate and galloped over a smooth, level field. He often went along this road and knew every bush, every hollow in it. What now in the far distance looked in the dusk like a dark cliff was a red church; he could picture it all down to the smallest detail, even the plaster on the gate and the calves that were always grazing in the church enclosure. Three-quarters of a mile to the right of the church there was a copse like a dark blur — it was Count Koltonovitch's. And beyond the church Vlassitch's estate began.

From behind the church and the count's copse a huge black storm-cloud was rising, and there were ashes of white lightning.

" Here it is! " thought Pyotr Mihalitch. " Lord help us, Lord help us! "

The horse was soon tired after its quick gallop,

and Pyotr Mihalitch was tired too. The storm-cloud looked at him angrily and seemed to advise him to go home. He felt a little scared.

" I will prove to them they are wrong," he tried to reassure himself. " They will say that it is free-love, individual freedom; but freedom means self-control and not subjection to passion. It's not liberty but license ! "

He reached the count's big pond; it looked dark blue and frowning under the cloud, and a smell of damp and slime rose from it. Near the dam, two willows, one old and one young, drooped tenderly towards one another. Pyotr Mihalitch and Vlassitch had been walking near this very spot only a fortnight before, humming a students' song:

" ' Youth is wasted, life is nought, when the heart is cold and love-
    less.' "

A wretched song !

It was thundering as Pyotr Mihalitch rode through the copse, and the trees were bending and rustling in the wind. He had to make haste. It was only three-quarters of a mile through a meadow from the copse to Vlassitch's house. Here there were old birch-trees on each side of the road. They had the same melancholy and unhappy air as their owner Vlassitch, and looked as tall and lanky as he. Big drops of rain pattered on the birches and on the grass; the wind had suddenly dropped, and there was a smell of wet earth and poplars. Be-

69

fore him he saw Vlassitch's fence with a row of yellow acacias, which were tall and lanky too; where the fence was broken he could see the neglected orchard.

Pyotr Mihalitch was not thinking now of the horsewhip or of a slap in the face, and did not know what he would do at Vlassitch's. He felt nervous. He felt frightened on his own account and on his sister's, and was terrified at the thought of seeing her. How would she behave with her brother? What would they both talk about? And had he not better go back before it was too late? As he made these reflections, he galloped up the avenue of lime-trees to the house, rode round the big clumps of lilacs, and suddenly saw Vlassitch.

Vlassitch, wearing a cotton shirt, and top-boots, bending forward, with no hat on in the rain, was coming from the corner of the house to the front door. He was followed by a workman with a hammer and a box of nails. They must have been mending a shutter which had been banging in the wind. Seeing Pyotr Mihalitch, Vlassitch stopped.

"It's you!" he said, smiling. "That's nice."

"Yes, I've come, as you see," said Pyotr Mihalitch, brushing the rain off himself with both hands.

"Well, that's capital! I'm very glad," said Vlassitch, but he did not hold out his hand: evidently he did not venture, but waited for Pyotr Mihalitch to hold out his. "It will do the oats good," he said, looking at the sky.

Neighbours

" Yes."

They went into the house in silence. To the right of the hall was a door leading to another hall and then to the drawing-room, and on the left was a little room which in winter was used by the steward. Pyotr Mihalitch and Vlassitch went into this little room.

" Where were you caught in the rain? "

" Not far off, quite close to the house."

Pyotr Mihalitch sat down on the bed. He was glad of the noise of the rain and the darkness of the room. It was better: it made it less dreadful, and there was no need to see his companion's face. There was no anger in his heart now, nothing but fear and vexation with himself. He felt he had made a bad beginning, and that nothing would come of this visit.

Both were silent for some time and affected to be listening to the rain.

" Thank you, Petrusha," Vlassitch began, clearing his throat. " I am very grateful to you for coming. It's generous and noble of you. I understand it, and, believe me, I appreciate it. Believe me."

He looked out of the window and went on, standing in the middle of the room:

" Everything happened so secretly, as though we were concealing it all from you. The feeling that you might be wounded and angry has been a blot on our happiness all these days. But let me justify myself. We kept it secret not because we did not trust you. To begin with, it all happened suddenly, by a kind of inspiration; there was no time to discuss it. Besides, it's such a private, delicate matter, and it was awkward to bring a third person in, even some one as intimate as you. Above all, in all this we reckoned on your generosity. You are a very noble and generous person. I am infinitely grateful to you. If you ever need my life, come and take it."

Vlassitch talked in a quiet, hollow bass, always on the same droning note; he was evidently agitated. Pyotr Mihalitch felt it was his turn to speak, and that to listen and keep silent would really mean playing the part of a generous and noble simpleton, and that had not been his idea in coming. He got up quickly and said, breathlessly in an undertone:

"Listen, Grigory. You know I liked you and could have desired no better husband for my sister; but what has happened is awful! It's terrible to think of it!"

"Why is it terrible?" asked Vlassitch, with a quiver in his voice. "It would be terrible if we had done wrong, but that isn't so."

"Listen, Grigory. You know I have no prejudices; but, excuse my frankness, to my mind you have both acted selfishly. Of course, I shan't say so to my sister — it will distress her; but you ought to know: mother is miserable beyond all description."

"Yes, that's sad," sighed Vlassitch. "We foresaw that, Petrusha, but what could we have done? Because one's actions hurt other people, it doesn't prove that they are wrong. What's to be done! Every important step one takes is bound to distress somebody. If you went to fight for freedom, that would distress your mother, too. What's to be done! Any one who puts the peace of his family before everything has to renounce the life of ideas completely."

There was a vivid flash of lightning at the window, and the lightning seemed to change the course of Vlassitch's thoughts. He sat down beside Pyotr Mihalitch and began saying what was utterly beside the point.

"I have such a reverence for your sister, Petrusha," he said. "When I used to come and see you, I felt as though I were going to a holy shrine, and I really did worship Zina. Now my reverence for her grows every day. For me she is something higher than a wife — yes, higher!" Vlassitch waved his hands. "She is my holy of holies. Since she is living with me, I enter my house as though it were a temple. She is an extraordinary, rare, most noble woman!"

"Well, he's off now!" thought Pyotr Mihalitch; he disliked the word "woman."

"Why shouldn't you be married properly?" he asked. "How much does your wife want for a divorce?"

"Seventy-five thousand."

" It's rather a lot. But if we were to negotiate with her? "

" She won't take a farthing less. She is an awful woman, brother," sighed Vlassitch. " I've never talked to you about her before — it was unpleasant to think of her; but now that the subject has come up, I'll tell you about her. I married her on the impulse of the moment — a fine, honourable impulse. An officer in command of a battalion of our regiment — if you care to hear the details — had an affair with a girl of eighteen; that is, to put it plainly, he seduced her, lived with her for two months, and abandoned her. She was in an awful position, brother. She was ashamed to go home to her parents; besides, they wouldn't have received her. Her lover had abandoned her; there was nothing left for her but to go to the barracks and sell herself. The other officers in the regiment were indignant. They were by no means saints themselves, but the baseness of it was so striking. Besides, no one in the regiment could endure the man. And to spite him, you understand, the indignant lieutenants and ensigns began getting up a subscription for the unfortunate girl. And when we subalterns met together and began to subscribe five or ten roubles each, I had a sudden inspiration. I felt it was an opportunity to do something fine. I hastened to the girl and warmly expressed my sympathy. And while I was on my way to her, and while I was talking to her, I loved her fervently as a woman

insulted and injured. Yes. . . . Well, a week later
I made her an offer. The colonel and my comrades thought my marriage out of keeping with the
dignity of an officer. That roused me more than
ever. I wrote a long letter, do you know, in which
I proved that my action ought to be inscribed in
the annals of the regiment in letters of gold, and
so on. I sent the letter to my colonel and copies
to my comrades. Well, I was excited, and, of
course, I could not avoid being rude. I was asked
to leave the regiment. I have a rough copy of it
put away somewhere; I'll give it to you to read sometime. It was written with great feeling. You will
see what lofty and noble sentiments I was experiencing. I resigned my commission and came here with
my wife. My father had left a few debts, I had
no money, and from the first day my wife began
making acquaintances, dressing herself smartly, and
playing cards, and I was obliged to mortgage the
estate. She led a bad life, you understand, and you
are the only one of the neighbours who hasn't been
her lover. After two years I gave her all I had to
set me free and she went off to town. Yes. . . .
And now I pay her twelve hundred roubles a year.
She is an awful woman! There is a fly, brother,
which lays an egg in the back of a spider so that
the spider can't shake it off: the grub fastens upon
the spider and drinks its heart's blood. That was
how this woman fastened upon me and sucks the
blood of my heart. She hates and despises me for

being so stupid; that is, for marrying a woman like her. My chivalry seems to her despicable. 'A wise man cast me off,' she says, 'and a fool picked me up.' To her thinking no one but a pitiful idiot could have behaved as I did. And that is insufferably bitter to me, brother. Altogether, I may say in parenthesis, fate has been hard upon me, very hard."

Pyotr Mihalitch listened to Vlassitch and wondered in perplexity what it was in this man that had so charmed his sister. He was not young — he was forty-one — lean and lanky, narrow-chested, with a long nose, and grey hairs in his beard. He talked in a droning voice, had a sickly smile, and waved his hands awkwardly as he talked. He had neither health, nor pleasant, manly manners, nor *savoir-faire,* nor gaiety, and in all his exterior there was something colourless and indefinite. He dressed without taste, his surroundings were depressing, he did not care for poetry or painting because " they have no answer to give to the questions of the day "— that is, he did not understand them; music did not touch him. He was a poor farmer.

His estate was in a wretched condition and was mortgaged; he was paying twelve per cent. on the second mortgage and owed ten thousand on personal securities as well. When the time came to pay the interest on the mortgage or to send money to his wife, he asked every one to lend him money with as much agitation as though his house were on fire, and, at the same time losing his head, he would sell the whole of his winter store of fuel for five roubles and a stack of straw for three roubles, and then have his garden fence or old cucumber-frames chopped up to heat his stoves. His meadows were ruined by pigs, the peasants' cattle strayed in the undergrowth in his woods, and every year the old trees were fewer and fewer: beehives and rusty pails lay about in his garden and kitchen-garden. He had neither talents nor abilities, nor even ordinary capacity for living like other people. In practical life he was a weak, naïve man, easy to deceive and to cheat, and the peasants with good reason called him " simple."

He was a Liberal, and in the district was regarded as a " Red," but even his progressiveness was a bore. There was no originality nor moving power about his independent views: he was revolted, indignant, and delighted always on the same note; it was always spiritless and ineffective. Even in moments of strong enthusiasm he never raised his head or stood upright. But the most tiresome thing of all was that he managed to express even his best and finest ideas so that they seemed in him commonplace and out of date. It reminded one of something old one had read long ago, when slowly and with an air of profundity he would begin discoursing of his noble, lofty moments, of his best years; or when he went into raptures over the younger generation, which has always been, and still is, in advance of

society; or abused Russians for donning their dressing-gowns at thirty and forgetting the principles of
their *alma mater*. If you stayed the night with him,
he would put Pissarev or Darwin on your bedroom
table; if you said you had read it, he would go and
bring Dobrolubov.

In the district this was called free-thinking, and
many people looked upon this free-thinking as an
innocent and harmless eccentricity; it made him profoundly unhappy, however. It was for him the
maggot of which he had just been speaking; it had
fastened upon him and was sucking his life-blood.
In his past there had been the strange marriage in
the style of Dostoevsky; long letters and copies written in a bad, unintelligible hand-writing, but with
great feeling, endless misunderstandings, explana-
tions, disappointments, then debts, a second mortgage, the allowance to his wife, the monthly borrowing of money — and all this for no benefit to any
one, either himself or others. And in the present,
as in the past, he was still in a nervous flurry, on
the lookout for heroic actions, and poking his nose
into other people's affairs; as before, at every
favourable opportunity there were long letters and
copies, wearisome, stereotyped conversations about
the village community, or the revival of handicrafts
or the establishment of cheese factories — conversations as like one another as though he had prepared
them, not in his living brain, but by some mechanical

process.   And finally this scandal with Zina of which one could not see the end!

And meanwhile Zina was young — she was only twenty-two — good-looking, elegant, gay; she was fond of laughing, chatter, argument, a passionate musician; she had good taste in dress, in furniture, in books, and in her own home she would not have put up with a room like this, smelling of boots and cheap vodka.   She, too, had advanced ideas, but in her free-thinking one felt the overflow of energy, the vanity of a young, strong, spirited girl, passionately eager to be better and more original than others. . . . How had it happened that she had fallen in love with Vlassitch?

" He is a Quixote, an obstinate fanatic, a maniac," thought Pyotr Mihalitch, " and she is as soft, yielding, and weak in character as I am. . . . She and I give in easily, without resistance.   She loves him; but, then, I, too, love him in spite of everything."

Pyotr Mihalitch considered Vlassitch a good, straightforward man, but narrow and one-sided. In his perturbations and his sufferings, and in fact in his whole life, he saw no lofty aims, remote or immediate; he saw nothing but boredom and incapacity for life.   His self-sacrifice and all that Vlassitch himself called heroic actions or noble impulses seemed to him a useless waste of force, unnecessary blank shots which consumed a great deal of powder.

And Vlassitch's fanatical belief in the extraordinary loftiness and faultlessness of his own way of thinking struck him as naïve and even morbid; and the fact that Vlassitch all his life had contrived to mix the trivial with the exalted, that he had made a stupid marriage and looked upon it as an act of heroism, and then had affairs with other women and regarded that as a triumph of some idea or other was simply incomprehensible.

Nevertheless, Pyotr Mihalitch was fond of Vlassitch; he was conscious of a sort of power in him, and for some reason he had never had the heart to contradict him.

Vlassitch sat down quite close to him for a talk in the dark, to the accompaniment of the rain, and he had cleared his throat as a prelude to beginning on something lengthy, such as the history of his marriage. But it was intolerable for Pyotr Mihalitch to listen to him; he was tormented by the thought that he would see his sister directly.

" Yes, you've had bad luck," he said gently; " but, excuse me, we've been wandering from the point. That's not what we are talking about."

" Yes, yes, quite so. Well, let us come back to the point," said Vlassitch, and he stood up. " I tell you, Petrusha, our conscience is clear. We are not married, but there is no need for me to prove to you that our marriage is perfectly legitimate. You are as free in your ideas as I am, and, happily, there can be no disagreement between us

on that point. As for our future, that ought not to
alarm you. I'll work in the sweat of my brow, I'll
work day and night — in fact, I will strain every
nerve to make Zina happy. Her life will be a
splendid one! You may ask, am I able to do it. I
am, brother! When a man devotes every minute
to one thought, it's not difficult for him to attain
his object. But let us go to Zina; it will be a joy
to her to see you."

Pyotr Mihalitch's heart began to beat. He got
up and followed Vlassitch into the hall, and from
there into the drawing-room. There was nothing
in the huge gloomy room but a piano and a long
row of old chairs ornamented with bronze, on which
no one ever sat. There was a candle alight on
the piano. From the drawing-room they went in
silence into the dining-room. This room, too, was
large and comfortless; in the middle of the room
there was a round table with two leaves with six
thick legs, and only one candle. A clock in a large
mahogany case like an ikon stand pointed to half-
past two.

Vlassitch opened the door into the next room and
said:

"Zina, here is Petrusha come to see us!"

At once there was the sound of hurried footsteps
and Zina came into the dining-room. She was tall,
plump, and very pale, and, just as when he had seen
her for the last time at home, she was wearing a
black skirt and a red blouse, with a large buckle on

her belt. She flung one arm round her brother and kissed him on the temple.

"What a storm!" she said. "Grigory went off somewhere and I was left quite alone in the house."

She was not embarrassed, and looked at her brother as frankly and candidly as at home; looking at her, Pyotr Mihalitch, too, lost his embarrassment.

"But you are not afraid of storms," he said, sitting down at the table.

"No," she said, "but here the rooms are so big, the house is so old, and when there is thunder it all rattles like a cupboard full of crockery. It's a charming house altogether," she went on, sitting down opposite her brother. "There's some pleasant memory in every room. In my room, only fancy, Grigory's grandfather shot himself."

"In August we shall have the money to do up the lodge in the garden," said Vlassitch.

"For some reason when it thunders I think of that grandfather," Zina went on. "And in this dining-room somebody was flogged to death."

"That's an actual fact," said Vlassitch, and he looked with wide-open eyes at Pyotr Mihalitch. "Sometime in the forties this place was let to a Frenchman called Olivier. The portrait of his daughter is lying in an attic now — a very pretty girl. This Olivier, so my father told me, despised Russians for their ignorance and treated them with cruel derision. Thus, for instance, he insisted on the priest walking without his hat for half a mile round his house, and on the church bells being rung when the Olivier family drove through the village. The serfs and altogether the humble of this world, of course, he treated with even less ceremony. Once there came along this road one of the simple-hearted sons of wandering Russia, somewhat after the style of Gogol's divinity student, Homa Brut. He asked for a night's lodging, pleased the bailiffs, and was given a job at the office of the estate. There are many variations of the story. Some say the divinity student stirred up the peasants, others that Olivier's daughter fell in love with him. I don't know which is true, only one fine evening Olivier called him in here and cross-examined him, then ordered him to be beaten. Do you know, he sat here at this table drinking claret while the stable-boys beat the man. He must have tried to wring something out of him. Towards morning the divinity student died of the torture and his body was hidden. They say it was thrown into Koltovitch's pond. There was an inquiry, but the Frenchman paid some thousands to some one in authority and went away to Alsace. His lease was up just then, and so the matter ended."

" What scoundrels! " said Zina, shuddering.

" My father remembered Olivier and his daughter well. He used to say she was remarkably beautiful and eccentric. I imagine the divinity student had done both — stirred up the peasants and won the daughter's heart. Perhaps he wasn't a divinity student at all, but some one travelling incognito."

Zina grew thoughtful; the story of the divinity student and the beautiful French girl had evidently carried her imagination far away. It seemed to Pyotr Mihalitch that she had not changed in the least during the last week, except that she was a little paler. She looked calm and just as usual, as though she had come with her brother to visit Vlassitch. But Pyotr Mihalitch felt that some change had taken place in himself. Before, when she was living at home, he could have spoken to her about anything, and now he did not feel equal to asking her the simple question, "How do you like being here?" The question seemed awkward and unnecessary. Probably the same change had taken place in her. She was in no haste to turn the conversation to her mother, to her home, to her relations with Vlassitch; she did not defend herself, she did not say that free unions are better than marriages in the church; she was not agitated, and calmly brooded over the story of Olivier. . . . And why had they suddenly begun talking of Olivier?

"You are both of you wet with the rain," said Zina, and she smiled joyfully; she was touched by this point of resemblance between her brother and Vlassitch.

And Pyotr Mihalitch felt all the bitterness and horror of his position. He thought of his deserted home, the closed piano, and Zina's bright little room into which no one went now; he thought there were no prints of little feet on the garden-paths, and that

before tea no one went off, laughing gaily, to bathe.
What he had clung to more and more from his
childhood upwards, what he had loved thinking
about when he used to sit in the stuffy class-room or
the lecture theatre — brightness, purity, and joy,
everything that filled the house with life and light,
had gone never to return, had vanished, and was
mixed up with a coarse, clumsy story of some battalion officer, a chivalrous lieutenant, a depraved
woman and a grandfather who had shot himself.
. . . And to begin to talk about his mother or to
think that the past could ever return would mean
not understanding what was clear.

Pyotr Mihalitch's eyes filled with tears and his
hand began to tremble as it lay on the table. Zina
guessed what he was thinking about, and her eyes,
too, glistened and looked red.

" Grigory, come here," she said to Vlassitch.

They walked away to the window and began talking of something in a whisper. From the way that
Vlassitch stooped down to her and the way she
looked at him, Pyotr Mihalitch realised again that
everything was irreparably over, and that it was no
use to talk of anything. Zina went out of the
room.

" Well, brother! " Vlassitch began, after a brief
silence, rubbing his hands and smiling. " I called
our life happiness just now, but that was, so to speak,
poetical license. In reality, there has not been a
sense of happiness so far. Zina has been thinking

all the time of you, of her mother, and has been worrying; looking at her, I, too, felt worried. Hers is a bold, free nature, but, you know, it's difficult when you're not used to it, and she is young, too. The servants call her ' Miss '; it seems a trifle, but it upsets her. There it is, brother."

Zina brought in a plateful of strawberries. She was followed by a little maidservant, looking crushed and humble, who set a jug of milk on the table and made a very low bow: she had something about her that was in keeping with the old furniture, something petrified and dreary.

The sound of the rain had ceased. Pyotr Mihalitch ate strawberries while Vlassitch and Zina looked at him in silence. The moment of the inevitable but useless conversation was approaching, and all three felt the burden of it. Pyotr Mihalitch's eyes filled with tears again; he pushed away his plate and said that he must be going home, or it would be getting late, and perhaps it would rain again. The time had come when common decency required Zina to speak of those at home and of her new life.

"How are things at home?" she asked rapidly, and her pale face quivered. "How is mother?"

"You know mother . . ." said Pyotr Mihalitch, not looking at her.

"Petrusha, you've thought a great deal about what has happened," she said, taking hold of her brother's sleeve, and he knew how hard it was for her to speak. "You've thought a great deal: tell

Neighbours

me, can we reckon on mother's accepting Grigory
. . . and the whole position, one day?"

She stood close to her brother, face to face with
him, and he was astonished that she was so beautiful, and that he seemed not to have noticed it before.
And it seemed to him utterly absurd that his sister,
so like his mother, pampered, elegant, should be living with Vlassitch and in Vlassitch's house, with the
petrified servant, and the table with six legs — in the
house where a man had been flogged to death, and
that she was not going home with him, but was
staying here to sleep.

"You know mother," he said, not answering her
question. "I think you ought to have . . . to do
something, to ask her forgiveness or something. . . ."

"But to ask her forgiveness would mean pretend-
ing we had done wrong. I'm ready to tell a lie to
comfort mother, but it won't lead anywhere. I
know mother. Well, what will be, must be!" said
Zina, growing more cheerful now that the most unpleasant had been said. "We'll wait for five years,
ten years, and be patient, and then God's will be
done."

She took her brother's arm, and when she walked
through the dark hall she squeezed close to him.
They went out on the steps. Pyotr Mihalitch said
good-bye, got on his horse, and set off at a walk;
Zina and Vlassitch walked a little way with him. It
was still and warm, with a delicious smell of hay;
stars were twinkling brightly between the clouds.

Vlassitch's old garden, which had seen so many gloomy stories in its time, lay slumbering in the darkness, and for some reason it was mournful riding through it.

"Zina and I to-day after dinner spent some really exalted moments," said Vlassitch. "I read aloud to her an excellent article on the question of emigration. You must read it, brother! You really must. It's remarkable for its lofty tone. I could not resist writing a letter to the editor to be forwarded to the author. I wrote only a single line: 'I thank you and warmly press your noble hand.'"

Pyotr Mihalitch was tempted to say, "Don't meddle in what does not concern you," but he held his tongue.

Vlassitch walked by his right stirrup and Zina by the left; both seemed to have forgotten that they had to go home. It was damp, and they had almost reached Koltovitch's copse. Pyotr Mihalitch felt that they were expecting something from him, though they hardly knew what it was, and he felt unbearably sorry for them. Now as they walked by the horse with submissive faces, lost in thought, he had a deep conviction that they were unhappy, and could not be happy, and their love seemed to him a melancholy, irreparable mistake. Pity and the sense that he could do nothing to help them reduced him to that state of spiritual softening when he was ready to make any sacrifice to get rid of the painful feeling of sympathy.

Neighbours

" I'll come over sometimes for a night," he said.

But it sounded as though he were making a concession, and did not satisfy him. When they
stopped near Koltovitch's copse to say good-bye, he
bent down to Zina, touched her shoulder, and said:
" You are right, Zina! You have done well."
To avoid saying more and bursting into tears, he
lashed his horse and galloped into the wood. As
he rode into the darkness, he looked round and saw
Vlassitch and Zina walking home along the road —
he taking long strides, while she walked with a
hurried, jerky step beside him — talking eagerly
about something.

" I am an old woman! " thought Pyotr Mihalitch. " I went to solve the question and I have only
made it more complicated — there it is! "

He was heavy at heart. When he got out of the
copse he rode at a walk and then stopped his horse
near the pond. He wanted to sit and think without
moving. The moon was rising and was reflected
in a streak of red on the other side of the pond.
There were low rumbles of thunder in the distance.
Pyotr Mihalitch looked steadily at the water and
imagined his sister's despair, her martyr-like pallor,
the tearless eyes with which she would conceal her
humiliation from others. He imagined her with
child, imagined the death of their mother, her
funeral, Zina's horror. . . . The proud, supersti-
tious old woman would be sure to die of grief. Terrible pictures of the future rose before him on the

background of smooth, dark water, and among pale feminine figures he saw himself, a weak, cowardly man with a guilty face.

A hundred paces off on the right bank of the pond, something dark was standing motionless: was it a man or a tall post? Pyotr Mihalitch thought of the divinity student who had been killed and thrown into the pond.

"Olivier behaved inhumanly, but one way or another he did settle the question, while I have settled nothing and have only made it worse," he thought, gazing at the dark figure that looked like a ghost. "He said and did what he thought right while I say and do what I don't think right; and I don't know really what I do think. . . ."

He rode up to the dark figure: it was an old rotten post, the relic of some shed.

From Koltovitch's copse and garden there came a strong fragrant scent of lilies of the valley and honey-laden flowers. Pyotr Mihalitch rode along the bank of the pond and looked mournfully into the water. And thinking about his life, he came to the conclusion he had never said or acted upon what he really thought, and other people had repaid him in the same way. And so the whole of life seemed to him as dark as this water in which the night sky was reflected and water-weeds grew in a tangle. And it seemed to him that nothing could ever set it right.

1892

WARD NO. 6

I

In the hospital yard there stands a small lodge surrounded by a perfect forest of burdocks, nettles, and wild hemp. Its roof is rusty, the chimney is tumbling down, the steps at the front-door are rotting away and overgrown with grass, and there are only traces left of the stucco. The front of the lodge faces the hospital; at the back it looks out into the open country, from which it is separated by the grey hospital fence with nails on it. These nails, with their points upwards, and the fence, and the lodge itself, have that peculiar, desolate, God-forsaken look which is only found in our hospital and prison buildings.

If you are not afraid of being stung by the nettles, come by the narrow footpath that leads to the lodge, and let us see what is going on inside. Opening the first door, we walk into the entry. Here along the walls and by the stove every sort of hospital rubbish lies littered about. Mattresses, old tattered dressing-gowns, trousers, blue striped shirts, boots and shoes no good for anything—all these remnants are piled up in heaps, mixed up and crumpled, mouldering and giving out a sickly smell.

The porter, Nikita, an old soldier wearing rusty

good-conduct stripes, is always lying on the litter with a pipe between his teeth. He has a grim, surly, battered-looking face, overhanging eyebrows which give him the expression of a sheep-dog of the steppes, and a red nose; he is short and looks thin and scraggy, but he is of imposing deportment and his fists are vigorous. He belongs to the class of simple-hearted, practical, and dull-witted people, prompt in carrying out orders, who like discipline better than anything in the world, and so are convinced that it is their duty to beat people. He showers blows on the face, on the chest, on the back, on whatever comes first, and is convinced that there would be no order in the place if he did not.

Next you come into a big, spacious room which fills up the whole lodge except for the entry. Here the walls are painted a dirty blue, the ceiling is as sooty as in a hut without a chimney—it is evident that in the winter the stove smokes and the room is full of fumes. The windows are disfigured by iron gratings on the inside. The wooden floor is grey and full of splinters. There is a stench of sour cabbage, of smouldering wicks, of bugs, and of ammonia, and for the first minute this stench gives you the impression of having walked into a menagerie. . . .

There are bedsteads screwed to the floor. Men in blue hospital dressing-gowns, and wearing nightcaps in the old style, are sitting and lying on them. These are the lunatics.

There are five of them in all here. Only one is of the upper class, the rest are all artisans. The one nearest the door—a tall, lean workman with

shining red whiskers and tear-stained eyes—sits
with his head propped on his hand, staring at the
same point. Day and night he grieves, shaking his
head, sighing and smiling bitterly. He rarely takes
a part in conversation and usually makes no answer
to questions; he eats and drinks mechanically when
food is offered him. From his agonizing, throbbing
cough, his thinness, and the flush on his cheeks, one
may judge that he is in the first stage of consumption. Next him is a little, alert, very lively old man,
with a pointed beard and curly black hair like a
negro's. By day he walks up and down the ward
from window to window, or sits on his bed, cross-
legged like a Turk, and, ceaselessly as a bullfinch
whistles, softly sings and titters. He shows his
childish gaiety and lively character at night also
when he gets up to say his prayers—that is, to beat
himself on the chest with his fists, and to scratch
with his fingers at the door. This is the Jew Moiseika, an imbecile, who went crazy twenty years ago
when his hat factory was burnt down.

And of all the inhabitants of Ward No. 6, he is
the only one who is allowed to go out of the lodge,
and even out of the yard into the street. He has
enjoyed this privilege for years, probably because
he is an old inhabitant of the hospital—a quiet, harmless imbecile, the buffoon of the town, where people
are used to seeing him surrounded by boys and dogs.
In his wretched gown, in his absurd night-cap, and
in slippers, sometimes with bare legs and even without trousers, he walks about the streets, stopping at
the gates and little shops, and begging for a copper.
In one place they will give him some kvass, in an-

other some bread, in another a copper, so that he generally goes back to the ward feeling rich and well fed. Everything that he brings back Nikita takes from him for his own benefit. The soldier does this roughly, angrily turning the Jew's pockets inside out, and calling God to witness that he will not let him go into the street again, and that breach of the regulations is worse to him than anything in the world.

Moiseika likes to make himself useful. He gives his companions water, and covers them up when they are asleep; he promises each of them to bring him back a kopeck, and to make him a new cap; he feeds with a spoon his neighbour on the left, who is paralyzed. He acts in this way, not from compassion nor from any considerations of a humane kind, but through imitation, unconsciously dominated by Gromov, his neighbour on the right hand.

Ivan Dmitritch Gromov, a man of thirty-three, who is a gentleman by birth, and has been a court usher and provincial secretary, suffers from the mania of persecution. He either lies curled up in bed, or walks from corner to corner as though for exercise; he very rarely sits down. He is always excited, agitated, and overwrought by a sort of vague, undefined expectation. The faintest rustle in the entry or shout in the yard is enough to make him raise his head and begin listening: whether they are coming for him, whether they are looking for him. And at such times his face expresses the utmost uneasiness and repulsion.

I like his broad face with its high cheek-bones, always pale and unhappy, and reflecting, as though in a mirror, a soul tormented by conflict and long-continued terror. His grimaces are strange and abnormal, but the delicate lines traced on his face by profound, genuine suffering show intelligence and sense, and there is a warm and healthy light in his eyes. I like the man himself, courteous, anxious to be of use, and extraordinarily gentle to everyone except Nikita. When anyone drops a button or a spoon, he jumps up from his bed quickly and picks it up; every day he says good-morning to his companions, and when he goes to bed he wishes them good-night.

Besides his continually overwrought condition and his grimaces, his madness shows itself in the following way also. Sometimes in the evenings he wraps himself in his dressing-gown, and, trembling all over, with his teeth chattering, begins walking rapidly from corner to corner and between the bedsteads. It seems as though he is in a violent fever. From the way he suddenly stops and glances at his companions, it can be seen that he is longing to say something very important, but, apparently reflecting that they would not listen, or would not understand him, he shakes his head impatiently and goes on pacing up and down. But soon the desire to speak gets the upper hand of every consideration, and he will let himself go and speak fervently and passionately. His talk is disordered and feverish like delirium, disconnected, and not always intelligible, but, on the other hand, something extremely fine may be felt in it, both in the words and the voice. When he talks you recognize in him the lunatic and the man. It is difficult to reproduce on paper his insane talk.

He speaks of the baseness of mankind, of violence trampling on justice, of the glorious life which will one day be upon earth, of the window-gratings, which remind him every minute of the stupidity and cruelty of oppressors. It makes a disorderly, incoherent potpourri of themes old but not yet out of date.

II

Some twelve or fifteen years ago an official called Gromov, a highly respectable and prosperous person, was living in his own house in the principal street of the town. He had two sons, Sergey and Ivan. When Sergey was a student in his fourth year he was taken ill with galloping consumption and died, and his death was, as it were, the first of a whole series of calamities which suddenly showered on the Gromov family. Within a week of Sergey's funeral the old father was put on his trial for fraud and misappropriation, and he died of typhoid in the prison hospital soon afterwards. The house, with all their belongings, was sold by auction, and Ivan Dmitritch and his mother were left entirely without means.

Hitherto in his father's lifetime, Ivan Dmitritch, who was studying in the University of Petersburg, had received an allowance of sixty or seventy roubles a month, and had had no conception of poverty; now he had to make an abrupt change in his life. He had to spend his time from morning to night giving lessons for next to nothing, to work at copying, and with all that to go hungry, as all his earnings were sent to keep his mother. Ivan Dmitritch could not stand such a life; he lost heart and strength, and, giving up the university, went home.

Here, through interest, he obtained the post of teacher in the district school, but could not get on with his colleagues, was not liked by the boys, and soon gave up the post. His mother died. He was for six months without work, living on nothing but bread and water; then he became a court usher. He kept this post until he was dismissed owing to his illness.

He had never even in his young student days given the impression of being perfectly healthy. He had always been pale, thin, and given to catching cold; he ate little and slept badly. A single glass of wine went to his head and made him hysterical. He always had a craving for society, but, owing to his irritable temperament and suspiciousness, he never became very intimate with anyone, and had no friends. He always spoke with contempt of his fellow-townsmen, saying that their coarse ignorance and sleepy animal existence seemed to him loathsome and horrible. He spoke in a loud tenor, with heat, and invariably either with scorn and indignation, or with wonder and enthusiasm, and always with perfect sincerity. Whatever one talked to him about he always brought it round to the same subject: that life was dull and stifling in the town; that the townspeople had no lofty interests, but lived a dingy, meaningless life, diversified by violence, coarse profligacy, and hypocrisy; that scoundrels were well fed and clothed, while honest men lived from hand to mouth; that they needed schools, a progressive local paper, a theatre, public lectures, the co-ordination of the intellectual elements; that society must see its failings and be horrified. In his criticisms of people he laid on the colours thick, using only black and white, and no fine shades; mankind was divided for him into honest men and scoundrels: there was nothing in between. He always spoke with passion and enthusiasm of women and of love, but he had never been in love.

In spite of the severity of his judgments and his nervousness, he was liked, and behind his back was spoken of affectionately as Vanya. His innate refinement and readiness to be of service, his good breeding, his moral purity, and his shabby coat, his frail appearance and family misfortunes, aroused a kind, warm, sorrowful feeling. Moreover, he was well educated and well read; according to the townspeople's notions, he knew everything, and was in their eyes something like a walking encyclopædia.

He had read a great deal. He would sit at the club, nervously pulling at his beard and looking through the magazines and books; and from his face one could see that he was not reading, but devouring the pages without giving himself time to digest what he read. It must be supposed that reading was one of his morbid habits, as he fell upon anything that came into his hands with equal avidity, even last year's newspapers and calendars. At home he always read lying down.

III.

One autumn morning Ivan Dmitritch, turning up the collar of his greatcoat and splashing through the mud, made his way by side-streets and back lanes to see some artisan, and to collect some payment that was owing. He was in a gloomy mood, as he always was in the morning. In one of the side-streets he was met by two convicts in fetters and four soldiers with rifles in charge of them. Ivan Dmitritch had very often met convicts before, and they had always excited feelings of compassion and discomfort in him; but now this meeting made a peculiar, strange impression on him. It suddenly seemed to him for some reason that he, too, might be put into fetters and led through the mud to prison like that. After visiting the artisan, on the way home he met near the post office a police superintendent of his acquaintance, who greeted him and walked a few paces along the street with him, and for some reason this seemed to him suspicious. At home he could not get the convicts or the soldiers with their rifles out of his head all day, and an unaccountable inward agitation prevented him from reading or concentrating his mind. In the evening he did not light his lamp, and at night he could not sleep, but kept thinking that he might be arrested, put into fetters, and thrown into prison. He did not know of any harm he had done, and could be certain that he would never be guilty of murder, arson, or theft in the future either; but was it not easy to commit a crime by accident, unconsciously, and was not false witness always possible, and, indeed, miscarriage of justice? It was not without good reason that the agelong experience of the simple people teaches that beggary and prison are ills none can be safe from. A judicial mistake is very possible as legal proceedings are conducted nowadays, and there is nothing to be wondered at in it. People who have an official, professional relation to other men's sufferings—for instance, judges, police officers, doctors—in course of time, through habit, grow so callous that they cannot, even if they wish it, take any but a formal attitude to their clients; in this respect they are not different from the peasant who slaughters sheep and calves in the back-yard, and does not notice the blood. With this formal, soulless attitude to human personality the judge needs but one thing—time—in order to deprive an innocent man of all rights of property, and to condemn him to penal servitude. Only the time spent on performing certain formalities for which the judge is paid his salary, and then—it is all over. Then you may look in vain for justice and protection in this dirty, wretched little town a hundred and fifty miles from a railway station! And, indeed, is it not absurd even to think of justice when every kind of violence is accepted by society as a rational and consistent necessity, and every act of mercy—for instance, a verdict of acquittal—calls forth a perfect outburst of dissatisfied and revengeful feeling?

In the morning Ivan Dmitritch got up from his bed in a state of horror, with cold perspiration on his forehead, completely convinced that he might be arrested any minute. Since his gloomy thoughts of yesterday had haunted him so long, he thought, it must be that there was some truth in them. They could not, indeed, have come into his mind without any grounds whatever.

A policeman walking slowly passed by the windows: that was not for nothing. Here were two men standing still and silent near the house. Why were they silent? And agonizing days and nights followed for Ivan Dmitritch. Everyone who passed by the windows or came into the yard seemed to him a spy or a detective. At midday the chief of the police usually drove down the street with a pair of horses; he was going from his estate near the town to the police department; but Ivan Dmitritch fancied every time that he was driving especially quickly, and that he had a peculiar expression: it was evident that he was in haste to announce that there was a very important criminal in the town. Ivan Dmitritch started at every ring at the bell and knock at the gate, and was agitated whenever he came upon anyone new at his landlady's; when he met police officers and gendarmes he smiled and began whistling so as to seem unconcerned. He could not sleep for whole nights in succession expecting to be arrested, but he snored loudly and sighed as though in deep sleep, that his landlady might think he was asleep; for if he could not sleep it meant that he was tormented by the stings of conscience—what a piece of evidence! Facts and common sense persuaded him that all these terrors were nonsense and morbidity, that if one looked at the matter more broadly there was nothing really terrible in arrest and imprisonment—so long as the conscience is at ease; but the more sensibly and logically he reasoned, the more acute and agonizing his mental distress became. It might be compared with the story of a hermit who tried to cut a dwelling-place for himself in a virgin forest; the more zealously he worked with his axe, the thicker the forest grew. In the end

Ivan Dmitritch, seeing it was useless, gave up reasoning altogether, and abandoned himself entirely to despair and terror.

He began to avoid people and to seek solitude. His official work had been distasteful to him before: now it became unbearable to him. He was afraid they would somehow get him into trouble, would put a bribe in his pocket unnoticed and then denounce him, or that he would accidentally make a mistake in official papers that would appear to be fraudulent, or would lose other people's money. It is strange that his imagination had never at other times been so agile and inventive as now, when every day he thought of thousands of different reasons for being seriously anxious over his freedom and honour; but, on the other hand, his interest in the outer world, in books in particular, grew sensibly fainter, and his memory began to fail him.

In the spring when the snow melted there were found in the ravine near the cemetery two half-decomposed corpses—the bodies of an old woman and a boy bearing the traces of death by violence. Nothing was talked of but these bodies and their unknown murderers. That people might not think he had been guilty of the crime, Ivan Dmitritch walked about the streets, smiling, and when he met acquaintances he turned pale, flushed, and began declaring that there was no greater crime than the murder of the weak and defenceless. But this duplicity soon exhausted him, and after some reflection he decided that in his position the best thing to do was to hide in his landlady's cellar. He sat in the cellar all day and then all night, then another day, was fearfully cold, and waiting till dusk, stole secretly like a thief back to his room. He stood in the middle of the room till daybreak, listening without stirring. Very early in the morning, before sunrise, some workmen came into the house. Ivan Dmitritch knew perfectly well that they had come to mend the stove in the kitchen, but terror told him that they were police officers disguised as workmen. He slipped stealthily out of the flat, and, overcome by terror, ran along the street without his cap and coat. Dogs raced after him barking, a peasant shouted somewhere behind him, the wind whistled in his ears, and it seemed to Ivan Dmitritch that the force and violence of the whole world was massed together behind his back and was chasing after him.

He was stopped and brought home, and his landlady sent for a doctor. Doctor Andrey Yefimitch, of whom we shall have more to say hereafter, prescribed cold compresses on his head and laurel drops, shook his head, and went away, telling the landlady he should not come again, as one should not interfere with people who are going out of their minds. As he had not the means to live at home and be nursed, Ivan Dmitritch was soon sent to the hospital, and was there put into the ward for venereal patients. He could not sleep at night, was full of whims and fancies, and disturbed the patients, and was soon afterwards, by Andrey Yefimitch's orders, transferred to Ward No. 6.

Within a year Ivan Dmitritch was completely forgotten in the town, and his books, heaped up by his landlady in a sledge in the shed, were pulled to pieces by boys.

IV

Ivan Dmitritch's neighbour on the left hand is, as I have said already, the Jew Moiseika; his neighbour on the right hand is a peasant so rolling in fat that he is almost spherical, with a blankly stupid face, utterly devoid of thought. This is a motionless, gluttonous, unclean animal who has long ago lost all powers of thought or feeling. An acrid, stifling stench always comes from him.

Nikita, who has to clean up after him, beats him terribly with all his might, not sparing his fists; and what is dreadful is not his being beaten—that one can get used to—but the fact that this stupefied creature does not respond to the blows with a sound or a movement, nor by a look in the eyes, but only sways a little like a heavy barrel.

The fifth and last inhabitant of Ward No. 6 is a man of the artisan class who has once been a sorter in the post office, a thinnish, fair little man with a good-natured but rather sly face. To judge from the clear, cheerful look in his calm and intelligent eyes, he has some pleasant idea in his mind, and has some very important and agreeable secret. He has under his pillow and under his mattress something that he never shows anyone, not from fear of its being taken from him and stolen, but from modesty. Sometimes he goes to the window, and turning his back to his companions, puts something on his breast, and bending his head, looks at it; if you go up to him at such a moment, he is overcome with confusion and snatches something off his breast. But it is not difficult to guess his secret.

"Congratulate me," he often says to Ivan Dmitritch; "I have been presented with the Stanislav order of the second degree with the star. The second degree with the star is only given to foreigners, but for some reason they want to make an exception for me," he says with a smile, shrugging his shoulders in perplexity. "That I must confess I did not expect."

"I don't understand anything about that," Ivan Dmitritch replies morosely.

"But do you know what I shall attain to sooner or later?" the former sorter persists, screwing up his eyes slily. "I shall certainly get the Swedish 'Polar Star.' That's an order it is worth working for, a white cross with a black ribbon. It's very beautiful."

Probably in no other place is life so monotonous as in this ward. In the morning the patients, except the paralytic and the fat peasant, wash in the entry at a big tub and wipe themselves with the skirts of their dressing-gowns; after that they drink tea out of tin mugs which Nikita brings them out of the main building. Everyone is allowed one mugful. At midday they have soup made out of sour cabbage and boiled grain, in the evening their supper consists of grain left from dinner. In the intervals they lie down, sleep, look out of window, and walk from one corner to the other. And so every day. Even the former sorter always talks of the same orders.

Fresh faces are rarely seen in Ward No. 6. The doctor has not taken in any new mental cases for a long time, and the people who are fond of visiting lunatic asylums are few in this world. Once every two months Semyon Lazaritch, the barber, appears in the ward. How he cuts the patients' hair, and how Nikita helps him to do it, and what a trepidation the lunatics are always thrown into by the arrival of the drunken, smiling barber, we will not describe.

No one even looks into the ward except the barber. The patients are condemned to see day after day no one but Nikita.

A rather strange rumour has, however, been circulating in the hospital of late.

It is rumoured that the doctor has begun to visit Ward No. 6.

V

A strange rumour!

Dr. Andrey Yefimitch Ragin is a strange man in his way. They say that when he was young he was very religious, and prepared himself for a clerical career, and that when he had finished his studies at the high school in 1863 he intended to enter a theological academy, but that his father, a surgeon and doctor of medicine, jeered at him and declared point-blank that he would disown him if he became a priest. How far this is true I don't know, but Andrey Yefimitch himself has more than once confessed that he has never had a natural bent for medicine or science in general.

However that may have been, when he finished his studies in the medical faculty he did not enter the priesthood. He showed no special devoutness, and was no more like a priest at the beginning of his medical career than he is now.

His exterior is heavy, coarse like a peasant's, his face, his beard, his flat hair, and his coarse, clumsy figure, suggest an overfed, intemperate, and harsh innkeeper on the highroad. His face is surly-looking and covered with blue veins, his eyes are little and his nose is red. With his height and broad shoulders he has huge hands and feet; one would think that a blow from his fist would knock the life out of anyone, but his step is soft, and his walk is cautious and insinuating; when he meets anyone in a narrow passage he is always the first to stop and make way, and to say, not in a bass, as one would expect, but in a high, soft tenor: " I beg your pardon! " He has a little swelling on his neck which prevents him from wearing stiff starched collars, and so he always goes about in soft linen or cotton shirts. Altogether he does not dress like a doctor. He wears the same suit for ten years, and the new clothes, which he usually buys at a Jewish shop, look as shabby and crumpled on him as his old ones; he sees patients and dines and pays visits all in the same coat; but this is not due to niggardliness, but to complete carelessness about his appearance.

When Andrey Yefimitch came to the town to take up his duties the " institution founded to the glory of God " was in a terrible condition. One could hardly breathe for the stench in the wards, in the passages, and in the courtyards of the hospital. The hospital servants, the nurses, and their children slept in the wards together with the patients. They complained that there was no living for beetles, bugs,

and mice. The surgical wards were never free from
erysipelas. There were only two scalpels and not
one thermometer in the whole hospital; potatoes
were kept in the baths. The superintendent, the
housekeeper, and the medical assistant robbed the
patients, and of the old doctor, Andrey Yefimitch's
predecessor, people declared that he secretly sold
the hospital alcohol, and that he kept a regular ha-
rem consisting of nurses and female patients. These
disorderly proceedings were perfectly well known
in the town, and were even exaggerated, but people
took them calmly; some justified them on the ground
that there were only peasants and working men in
the hospital, who could not be dissatisfied, since
they were much worse off at home than in the hospital—they couldn't be fed on woodcocks! Others
said in excuse that the town alone, without help from
the Zemstvo, was not equal to maintaining a good
hospital; thank God for having one at all, even a
poor one. And the newly formed Zemstvo did not
open infirmaries either in the town or the neighbour-
hood, relying on the fact that the town already had
its hospital.

After looking over the hospital Andrey Yefimitch
came to the conclusion that it was an immoral institution and extremely prejudicial to the health of the
townspeople. In his opinion the most sensible thing
that could be done was to let out the patients and
close the hospital. But he reflected that his will
alone was not enough to do this, and that it would
be useless; if physical and moral impurity were driven
out of one place, they would only move to another;
one must wait for it to wither away of itself. Be-

sides, if people open a hospital and put up with having it, it must be because they need it; superstition and all the nastiness and abominations of daily life were necessary, since in process of time they worked out to something sensible, just as manure turns into black earth. There was nothing on earth so good that it had not something nasty about its first origin.

When Andrey Yefimitch undertook his duties he was apparently not greatly concerned about the irregularities at the hospital. He only asked the attendants and nurses not to sleep in the wards, and had two cupboards of instruments put up; the superintendent, the housekeeper, the medical assistant, and the erysipelas remained unchanged.

Andrey Yefimitch loved intelligence and honesty intensely, but he had no strength of will nor belief in his right to organize an intelligent and honest life about him. He was absolutely unable to give orders, to forbid things, and to insist. It seemed as though he had taken a vow never to raise his voice and never to make use of the imperative. It was difficult for him to say " Fetch " or " Bring "; when he wanted his meals he would cough hesitatingly and say to the cook: " How about tea? . . ." or " How about dinner? . . ." To dismiss the superintendent or to tell him to leave off stealing, or to abolish the unnecessary parasitic post altogether, was absolutely beyond his powers. When Andrey Yefimitch was deceived or flattered, or accounts he knew to be cooked were brought him to sign, he would turn as red as a crab and feel guilty, but yet he would sign the accounts. When the patients complained to him of being hungry or of the roughness of the nurses, he would be confused and mutter guiltily: " Very well, very well, I will go into it later. . . . Most likely there is some misunderstanding. . . ."

At first Andrey Yefimitch worked very zealously. He saw patients every day from morning till dinner-time, performed operations, and even attended confinements. The ladies said of him that he was attentive and clever at diagnosing diseases, especially those of women and children. But in process of time the work unmistakably wearied him by its monotony and obvious uselessness. To-day one sees thirty patients, and to-morrow they have increased to thirty-five, the next day forty, and so on from day to day, from year to year, while the mortality in the town did not decrease and the patients did not leave off coming. To be any real help to forty patients between morning and dinner was not physically possible, so it could but lead to deception. If twelve thousand patients were seen in a year it meant, if one looked at it simply, that twelve thousand men were deceived. To put those who were seriously ill into wards, and to treat them according to the principles of science, was impossible, too, because though there were principles there was no science; if he were to put aside philosophy and pedantically follow the rules as other doctors did, the things above all necessary were cleanliness and ventilation instead of dirt, wholesome nourishment instead of broth made of stinking, sour cabbage, and good assistants instead of thieves; and, indeed, why hinder people dying if death is the normal and legitimate end of everyone?

What is gained if some shopkeeper or clerk lives an extra five or ten years? If the aim of medicine is by drugs to alleviate suffering, the question forces itself on one: why alleviate it? In the first place, they say that suffering leads man to perfection; and in the second, if mankind really learns to alleviate its sufferings with pills and drops, it will completely abandon religion and philosophy, in which it has hitherto found not merely protection from all sorts of trouble, but even happiness. Pushkin suffered terrible agonies before his death, poor Heine lay paralyzed for several years; why, then, should not some Andrey Yefimitch or Matryona Savishna be ill, since their lives had nothing of importance in them, and would have been entirely empty and like the life of an amœba except for suffering?

Oppressed by such reflections, Andrey Yefimitch relaxed his efforts and gave up visiting the hospital every day.

VI

His life was passed like this. As a rule he got up at eight o'clock in the morning, dressed, and drank his tea. Then he sat down in his study to read, or went to the hospital. At the hospital the out-patients were sitting in the dark, narrow little corridor waiting to be seen by the doctor. The nurses and the attendants, tramping with their boots over the brick floors, ran by them; gaunt-looking patients in dressing-gowns passed; dead bodies and vessels full of filth were carried by; the children were crying, and there was a cold draught. Andrey Yefimitch

knew that such surroundings were torture to feverish, consumptive, and impressionable patients; but
what could be done? In the consulting-room he was
met by his assistant, Sergey Sergeyitch—a fat little
man with a plump, well-washed shaven face, with
soft, smooth manners, wearing a new loosely cut
suit, and looking more like a senator than a medical
assistant. He had an immense practice in the town,
wore a white tie, and considered himself more pro-
ficient than the doctor, who had no practice. In the
corner of the consulting-room there stood a huge
ikon in a shrine with a heavy lamp in front of it, and
near it a candle-stand with a white cover on it. On
the walls hung portraits of bishops, a view of the
Svyatogorsky Monastery, and wreaths of dried corn-
flowers. Sergey Sergeyitch was religious, and liked
solemnity and decorum. The ikon had been put up
at his expense; at his instructions some one of the
patients read the hymns of praise in the consulting-
room on Sundays, and after the reading Sergey
Sergeyitch himself went through the wards with a
censer and burned incense.

There were a great many patients, but the time
was short, and so the work was confined to the asking of a few brief questions and the administration
of some drugs, such as castor-oil or volatile oint-
ment. Andrey Yefimitch would sit with his cheek
resting in his hand, lost in thought and asking questions mechanically. Sergey Sergeyitch sat down too,
rubbing his hands, and from time to time putting in
his word.

"We suffer pain and poverty," he would say,

"because we do not pray to the merciful God as we should. Yes!"

Andrey Yefimitch never performed any operations when he was seeing patients; he had long ago given up doing so, and the sight of blood upset him. When he had to open a child's mouth in order to look at its throat, and the child cried and tried to defend itself with its little hands, the noise in his ears made his head go round and brought tears into his eyes. He would make haste to prescribe a drug, and motion to the woman to take the child away.

He was soon wearied by the timidity of the patients and their incoherence, by the proximity of the pious Sergey Sergeyitch, by the portraits on the walls, and by his own questions which he had asked over and over again for twenty years. And he would go away after seeing five or six patients. The rest would be seen by his assistant in his absence.

With the agreeable thought that, thank God, he had no private practice now, and that no one would interrupt him, Andrey Yefimitch sat down to the table immediately on reaching home and took up a book. He read a great deal and always with enjoyment. Half his salary went on buying books, and of the six rooms that made up his abode three were heaped up with books and old magazines. He liked best of all works on history and philosophy; the only medical publication to which he subscribed was *The Doctor,* of which he always read the last pages first. He would always go on reading for several hours without a break and without being weary. He did not read as rapidly and impulsively as Ivan Dmitritch had done in the past, but slowly and with concentration, often pausing over a passage which he liked or did not find intelligible. Near the books there always stood a decanter of vodka, and a salted cucumber or a pickled apple lay beside it, not on a plate, but on the baize table-cloth. Every half-hour he would pour himself out a glass of vodka and drink it without taking his eyes off the book. Then without looking at it he would feel for the cucumber and bite off a bit.

At three o'clock he would go cautiously to the kitchen door, cough, and say: " Daryushka, what about dinner? . . ."

After his dinner—a rather poor and untidily served one—Andrey Yefimitch would walk up and down his rooms with his arms folded, thinking. The clock would strike four, then five, and still he would be walking up and down thinking. Occasionally the kitchen door would creak, and the red and sleepy face of Daryushka would appear.

" Andrey Yefimitch, isn't it time for you to have your beer? " she would ask anxiously.

" No, it is not time yet . . ." he would answer. " I'll wait a little. . . . I'll wait a little. . . ."

Towards the evening the postmaster, Mihail Averyanitch, the only man in the town whose society did not bore Andrey Yefimitch, would come in. Mihail Averyanitch had once been a very rich land-owner, and had served in the cavalry, but had come to ruin, and was forced by poverty to take a job in the post office late in life. He had a hale and hearty appearance, luxuriant grey whiskers, the manners of a well-bred man, and a loud, pleasant voice. He was good-natured and emotional, but hot-tempered.

Ward No. 6

When anyone in the post office made a protest, expressed disagreement, or even began to argue, Mihail Averyanitch would turn crimson, shake all over, and shout in a voice of thunder, "Hold your tongue!" so that the post office had long enjoyed the reputation of an institution which it was terrible to visit. Mihail Averyanitch liked and respected Andrey Yefimitch for his culture and the loftiness of his soul; he treated the other inhabitants of the town superciliously, as though they were his subordinates.

"Here I am," he would say, going in to Andrey Yefimitch. "Good-evening, my dear fellow! I'll be bound, you are getting sick of me, aren't you?"

"On the contrary, I am delighted," said the doctor. "I am always glad to see you."

The friends would sit down on the sofa in the study and for some time would smoke in silence.

"Daryushka, what about the beer?" Andrey Yefimitch would say.

They would drink their first bottle still in silence, the doctor brooding and Mihail Averyanitch with a gay and animated face, like a man who has something very interesting to tell. The doctor was always the one to begin the conversation.

"What a pity," he would say quietly and slowly, not looking his friend in the face (he never looked anyone in the face)—"what a great pity it is that there are no people in our town who are capable of carrying on intelligent and interesting conversation, or care to do so. It is an immense privation for us. Even the educated class do not rise above vulgarity; the level of their development, I assure you, is not a bit higher than that of the lower orders."

" Perfectly true. I agree."

" You know, of course," the doctor went on quietly and deliberately, " that everything in this world is insignificant and uninteresting except the higher spiritual manifestations of the human mind. Intellect draws a sharp line between the animals and man, suggests the divinity of the latter, and to some extent even takes the place of the immortality which does not exist. Consequently the intellect is the only possible source of enjoyment. We see and hear of no trace of intellect about us, so we are deprived of enjoyment. We have books, it is true, but that is not at all the same as living talk and converse. If you will allow me to make a not quite apt comparison: books are the printed score, while talk is the singing."

" Perfectly true."

A silence would follow. Daryushka would come out of the kitchen and with an expression of blank dejection would stand in the doorway to listen, with her face propped on her fist.

" Eh! " Mihail Averyanitch would sigh. " To expect intelligence of this generation! "

And he would describe how wholesome, entertaining, and interesting life had been in the past. How intelligent the educated class in Russia used to be, and what lofty ideas it had of honour and friendship; how they used to lend money without an IOU, and it was thought a disgrace not to give a helping hand to a comrade in need; and what campaigns, what adventures, what skirmishes, what comrades, what women! And the Caucasus, what a marvellous country! The wife of a battalion commander, a queer woman, used to put on an officer's uniform and drive off into the mountains in the evening, alone, without a guide. It was said that she had a love affair with some princeling in the native village.

"Queen of Heaven, Holy Mother . . ." Daryushka would sigh.

"And how we drank! And how we ate! And what desperate liberals we were!"

Andrey Yefimitch would listen without hearing; he was musing as he sipped his beer.

"I often dream of intellectual people and conversation with them," he said suddenly, interrupting Mihail Averyanitch. "My father gave me an excellent education, but under the influence of the ideas of the sixties made me become a doctor. I believe if I had not obeyed him then, by now I should have been in the very centre of the intellectual movement. Most likely I should have become a member of some university. Of course, intellect, too, is transient and not eternal, but you know why I cherish a partiality for it. Life is a vexatious trap; when a thinking man reaches maturity and attains to full consciousness he cannot help feeling that he is in a trap from which there is no escape. Indeed, he is summoned without his choice by fortuitous circumstances from non-existence into life . . . what for? He tries to find out the meaning and object of his existence; he is told nothing, or he is told absurdities; he knocks and it is not opened to him; death comes to him— also without his choice. And so, just as in prison men held together by common misfortune feel more at ease when they are together, so one does not notice the trap in life when people with a bent for analysis and generalization meet together and pass their time in the interchange of proud and free ideas. In that sense the intellect is the source of an enjoyment nothing can replace."

" Perfectly true."

Not looking his friend in the face, Andrey Yefimitch would go on, quietly and with pauses, talking about intellectual people and conversation with them, and Mihail Averyanitch would listen attentively and agree: " Perfectly true."

" And you do not believe in the immortality of the soul?" he would ask suddenly.

" No, honoured Mihail Averyanitch; I do not believe it, and have no grounds for believing it."

" I must own I doubt it too. And yet I have a feeling as though I should never die. Oh, I think to myself: ' Old fogey, it is time you were dead!' But there is a little voice in my soul says: ' Don't believe it; you won't die.' "

Soon after nine o'clock Mihail Averyanitch would go away. As he put on his fur coat in the entry he would say with a sigh:

" What a wilderness fate has carried us to, though, really! What's most vexatious of all is to have to die here. Ech! . . ."

VII

After seeing his friend out Andrey Yefimitch would sit down at the table and begin reading again. The stillness of the evening, and afterwards of the night, was not broken by a single sound, and it seemed as though time were standing still and brooding with the doctor over the book, and as though there were nothing in existence but the books and the lamp with the green shade. The doctor's coarse peasant-like face was gradually lighted up by a smile of delight and enthusiasm over the progress of the human intellect. Oh, why is not man immortal? he thought. What is the good of the brain centres and convolutions, what is the good of sight, speech, self-consciousness, genius, if it is all destined to depart into the soil, and in the end to grow cold together with the earth's crust, and then for millions of years to fly with the earth round the sun with no meaning and no object? To do that there was no need at all to draw man with his lofty, almost godlike intellect out of non-existence, and then, as though in mockery, to turn him into clay. The transmutation of substances! But what cowardice to comfort oneself with that cheap substitute for immortality! The unconscious processes that take place in nature are lower even than the stupidity of man, since in stupidity there is, anyway, consciousness and will, while in those processes there is absolutely nothing. Only the coward who has more fear of death than dignity can comfort himself with the fact that his body will in time live again in the grass, in the stones, in the toad. To find one's immortality in the transmutation of substances is as strange as to prophesy a brilliant future for the case after a precious violin has been broken and become useless.

When the clock struck, Andrey Yefimitch would sink back into his chair and close his eyes to think a little. And under the influence of the fine ideas of which he had been reading he would, unawares, recall his past and his present. The past was hateful—better not to think of it. And it was the same in the present as in the past. He knew that at the very time when his thoughts were floating together with the cooling earth round the sun, in the main building beside his abode people were suffering in sickness and physical impurity: someone perhaps could not sleep and was making war upon the insects, someone was being infected by erysipelas, or moaning over too tight a bandage; perhaps the patients were playing cards with the nurses and drinking vodka. According to the yearly return, twelve thousand people had been deceived; the whole hospital rested as it had done twenty years ago on thieving, filth, scandals, gossip, on gross quackery, and, as before, it was an immoral institution extremely injurious to the health of the inhabitants. He knew that Nikita knocked the patients about behind the barred windows of Ward No. 6, and that Moiseika went about the town every day begging alms.

On the other hand, he knew very well that a magical change had taken place in medicine during the last twenty-five years. When he was studying at the university he had fancied that medicine would soon be overtaken by the fate of alchemy and metaphysics; but now when he was reading at night the science of medicine touched him and excited his wonder, and even enthusiasm. What unexpected brilliance, what a revolution! Thanks to the antiseptic system operations were performed such as the great Pirogov had considered impossible even *in spe*. Ordinary Zemstvo doctors were venturing to perform the resection of the kneecap; of abdominal operations only one per cent. was fatal; while stone was considered such a trifle that they did not even write about it. A radical cure for syphilis had been discovered. And the theory of heredity, hypnotism, the discoveries of Pasteur and of Koch, hygiene based on statistics, and the work of our Zemstvo doctors!

Psychiatry with its modern classification of mental diseases, methods of diagnosis, and treatment, was a perfect Elborus in comparison with what had been in the past. They no longer poured cold water on the heads of lunatics nor put strait-waistcoats upon them; they treated them with humanity, and even, so it was stated in the papers, got up balls and entertainments for them. Andrey Yefimitch knew that with modern tastes and views such an abomination as Ward No. 6 was possible only a hundred and fifty miles from a railway in a little town where the mayor and all the town council were half-illiterate tradesmen who looked upon the doctor as an oracle who must be believed without any criticism even if he had poured molten lead into their mouths; in any other place the public and the newspapers would long ago have torn this little Bastille to pieces.

"But, after all, what of it?" Andrey Yefimitch would ask himself, opening his eyes. "There is the antiseptic system, there is Koch, there is Pasteur, but the essential reality is not altered a bit; ill-health and mortality are still the same. They get up balls and entertainments for the mad, but still they don't let them go free; so it's all nonsense and vanity, and there is no difference in reality between the best

Vienna clinic and my hospital." But depression and a feeling akin to envy prevented him from feeling indifferent; it must have been owing to exhaustion. His heavy head sank on to the book, he put his hands under his face to make it softer, and thought: " I serve in a pernicious institution and receive a salary from people whom I am deceiving. I am not honest, but then, I of myself am nothing, I am only part of an inevitable social evil: all local officials are pernicious and receive their salary for doing nothing. . . . And so for my dishonesty it is not I who am to blame, but the times. . . . If I had been born two hundred years later I should have been different. . . ."

When it struck three he would put out his lamp and go into his bedroom; he was not sleepy.

VIII

Two years before, the Zemstvo in a liberal mood had decided to allow three hundred roubles a year to pay for additional medical service in the town till the Zemstvo hospital should be opened, and the district doctor, Yevgeny Fyodoritch Hobotov, was invited to the town to assist Andrey Yefimitch. He was a very young man—not yet thirty—tall and dark, with broad cheek-bones and little eyes; his forefathers had probably come from one of the many alien races of Russia. He arrived in the town without a farthing, with a small portmanteau, and a plain young woman whom he called his cook. This woman had a baby at the breast. Yevgeny Fyodoritch used to go about in a cap with a peak, and in high boots, and in the winter wore a sheepskin. He made great friends with Sergey Sergeyitch, the medical assistant, and with the treasurer, but held aloof from the other officials, and for some reason called them aristocrats. He had only one book in his lodgings, " The Latest Prescriptions of the Vienna Clinic for 1881." When he went to a patient he always took this book with him. He played billiards in the evening at the club: he did not like cards. He was very fond of using in conversation such expressions as " endless bobbery," " canting soft soap," " shut up with your finicking. . . ."

He visited the hospital twice a week, made the round of the wards, and saw out-patients. The complete absence of antiseptic treatment and the cupping roused his indignation, but he did not introduce any new system, being afraid of offending Andrey Yefimitch. He regarded his colleague as a sly old rascal, suspected him of being a man of large means, and secretly envied him. He would have been very glad to have his post.

IX

On a spring evening towards the end of March, when there was no snow left on the ground and the starlings were singing in the hospital garden, the doctor went out to see his friend the postmaster as far as the gate. At that very moment the Jew Moiseika, returning with his booty, came into the yard. He had no cap on, and his bare feet were thrust into goloshes; in his hand he had a little bag of coppers.

" Give me a kopeck! " he said to the doctor, smiling, and shivering with cold. Andrey Yefimitch, who could never refuse anyone anything, gave him a ten-kopeck piece.

" How bad that is! " he thought, looking at the Jew's bare feet with their thin red ankles. " Why, it's wet."

And stirred by a feeling akin both to pity and disgust, he went into the lodge behind the Jew, looking now at his bald head, now at his ankles. As the doctor went in, Nikita jumped up from his heap of litter and stood at attention.

" Good-day, Nikita," Andrey Yefimitch said mildly. " That Jew should be provided with boots or something, he will catch cold."

" Certainly, your honour. I'll inform the superintendent."

" Please do; ask him in my name. Tell him that I asked."

The door into the ward was open. Ivan Dmitritch, lying propped on his elbow on the bed, listened in alarm to the unfamiliar voice, and suddenly recognized the doctor. He trembled all over with anger, jumped up, and with a red and wrathful face, with his eyes starting out of his head, ran out into the middle of the road.

" The doctor has come! " he shouted, and broke into a laugh. " At last! Gentlemen, I congratulate you. The doctor is honouring us with a visit! Cursed reptile! " he shrieked, and stamped in a frenzy such as had never been seen in the ward before. " Kill the reptile! No, killing's too good. Drown him in the midden-pit! "

Andrey Yefimitch, hearing this, looked into the ward from the entry and asked gently: "What for?"

"What for?" shouted Ivan Dmitritch, going up to him with a menacing air and convulsively wrapping himself in his dressing-gown. "What for? Thief!" he said with a look of repulsion, moving his lips as though he would spit at him. "Quack! hangman!"

"Calm yourself," said Andrey Yefimitch, smiling guiltily. "I assure you I have never stolen anything; and as to the rest, most likely you greatly exaggerate. I see you are angry with me. Calm yourself, I beg, if you can, and tell me coolly what are you angry for?"

"What are you keeping me here for?"

"Because you are ill."

"Yes, I am ill. But you know dozens, hundreds of madmen are walking about in freedom because your ignorance is incapable of distinguishing them from the sane. Why am I and these poor wretches to be shut up here like scapegoats for all the rest? You, your assistant, the superintendent, and all your hospital rabble, are immeasurably inferior to every one of us morally; why then are we shut up and you not? Where's the logic of it?"

"Morality and logic don't come in, it all depends on chance. If anyone is shut up he has to stay, and if anyone is not shut up he can walk about, that's all. There is neither morality nor logic in my being a doctor and your being a mental patient, there is nothing but idle chance."

"That twaddle I don't understand . . ." Ivan

Dmitritch brought out in a hollow voice, and he sat down on his bed.

Moiseika, whom Nikita did not venture to search in the presence of the doctor, laid out on his bed pieces of bread, bits of paper, and little bones, and, still shivering with cold, began rapidly in a singsong voice saying something in Yiddish. He most likely imagined that he had opened a shop.

" Let me out," said Ivan Dmitritch, and his voice quivered.

" I cannot."

" But why, why? "

" Because it is not in my power. Think, what use will it be to you if I do let you out? Go. The townspeople or the police will detain you or bring you back."

" Yes, yes, that's true," said Ivan Dmitritch, and he rubbed his forehead. " It's awful! But what am I to do, what? "

Andrey Yefimitch liked Ivan Dmitritch's voice and his intelligent young face with its grimaces. He longed to be kind to the young man and soothe him; he sat down on the bed beside him, thought, and said:

" You ask me what to do. The very best thing in your position would be to run away. But, unhappily, that is useless. You would be taken up. When society protects itself from the criminal, mentally deranged, or otherwise inconvenient people, it is invincible. There is only one thing left for you: to resign yourself to the thought that your presence here is inevitable."

" It is no use to anyone."

Ward No. 6

" So long as prisons and madhouses exist someone must be shut up in them. If not you, I. If not I, some third person. Wait till in the distant future prisons and madhouses no longer exist, and there will be neither bars on the windows nor hospital gowns. Of course, that time will come sooner or later."

Ivan Dmitritch smiled ironically.

" You are jesting," he said, screwing up his eyes. " Such gentlemen as you and your assistant Nikita have nothing to do with the future, but you may be sure, sir, better days will come! I may express myself cheaply, you may laugh, but the dawn of a new life is at hand; truth and justice will triumph, and—our turn will come! I shall not live to see it, I shall perish, but some people's great-grandsons will see it. I greet them with all my heart and rejoice, rejoice with them! Onward! God be your help, friends!"

With shining eyes Ivan Dmitritch got up, and stretching his hands towards the window, went on with emotion in his voice:

" From behind these bars I bless you! Hurrah for truth and justice! I rejoice!"

" I see no particular reason to rejoice," said Andrey Yefimitch, who thought Ivan Dmitritch's movement theatrical, though he was delighted by it. " Prisons and madhouses there will not be, and truth, as you have just expressed it, will triumph; but the reality of things, you know, will not change, the laws of nature will still remain the same. People will suffer pain, grow old, and die just as they do now. However magnificent a dawn lighted up your

127

life, you would yet in the end be nailed up in a coffin and thrown into a hole."

" And immortality? "

" Oh, come, now! "

" You don't believe in it, but I do. Somebody in Dostoevsky or Voltaire said that if there had not been a God men would have invented him. And I firmly believe that if there is no immortality the great intellect of man will sooner or later invent it."

" Well said," observed Andrey Yefimitch, smiling with pleasure; " it's a good thing you have faith. With such a belief one may live happily even shut up within walls. You have studied somewhere, I presume? "

" Yes, I have been at the university, but did not complete my studies."

" You are a reflecting and a thoughtful man. In any surroundings you can find tranquillity in yourself. Free and deep thinking which strives for the comprehension of life, and complete contempt for the foolish bustle of the world—those are two blessings beyond any that man has ever known. And you can possess them even though you lived behind threefold bars. Diogenes lived in a tub, yet he was happier than all the kings of the earth."

" Your Diogenes was a blockhead," said Ivan Dmitritch morosely. " Why do you talk to me about Diogenes and some foolish comprehension of life? " he cried, growing suddenly angry and leaping up. " I love life; I love it passionately. I have the mania of persecution, a continual agonizing terror; but I have moments when I am overwhelmed by the thirst for life, and then I am afraid of going mad. I want dreadfully to live, dreadfully!"

He walked up and down the ward in agitation, and said, dropping his voice:

"When I dream I am haunted by phantoms. People come to me, I hear voices and music, and I fancy I am walking through woods or by the seashore, and I long so passionately for movement, for interests. . . . Come, tell me, what news is there?" asked Ivan Dmitritch; "what's happening?"

"Do you wish to know about the town or in general?"

"Well, tell me first about the town, and then in general."

"Well, in the town it is appallingly dull. . . . There's no one to say a word to, no one to listen to. There are no new people. A young doctor called Hobotov has come here recently."

"He had come in my time. Well, he is a low cad, isn't he?"

"Yes, he is a man of no culture. It's strange, you know. . . . Judging by every sign, there is no intellectual stagnation in our capital cities; there is a movement—so there must be real people there too; but for some reason they always send us such men as I would rather not see. It's an unlucky town!"

"Yes, it is an unlucky town," sighed Ivan Dmitritch, and he laughed. "And how are things in general? What are they writing in the papers and reviews?"

It was by now dark in the ward. The doctor got up, and, standing, began to describe what was being written abroad and in Russia, and the tendency of thought that could be noticed now. Ivan Dmitritch listened attentively and put questions, but suddenly, as though recalling something terrible, clutched at his head and lay down on the bed with his back to the doctor.

" What's the matter? " asked Andrey Yefimitch.

" You will not hear another word from me," said Ivan Dmitritch rudely. "Leave me alone."

" Why so? "

" I tell you, leave me alone. Why the devil do you persist? "

Andrey Yefimitch shrugged his shoulders, heaved a sigh, and went out. As he crossed the entry he said: " You might clear up here, Nikita . . . there's an awfully stuffy smell."

" Certainly, your honour."

" What an agreeable young man! " thought Andrey Yefimitch, going back to his flat. " In all the years I have been living here I do believe he is the first I have met with whom one can talk. He is capable of reasoning and is interested in just the right things."

While he was reading, and afterwards, while he was going to bed, he kept thinking about Ivan Dmitritch, and when he woke next morning he remembered that he had the day before made the acquaintance of an intelligent and interesting man, and determined to visit him again as soon as possible.

X

Ivan Dmitritch was lying in the same position as on the previous day, with his head clutched in both hands and his legs drawn up. His face was not visible.

"Good-day, my friend," said Andrey Yefimitch. "You are not asleep, are you?"

"In the first place, I am not your friend," Ivan Dmitritch articulated into the pillow; "and in the second, your efforts are useless; you will not get one word out of me."

"Strange," muttered Andrey Yefimitch in confusion. "Yesterday we talked peacefully, but suddenly for some reason you took offence and broke off all at once. . . . Probably I expressed myself awkwardly, or perhaps gave utterance to some idea which did not fit in with your convictions. . . ."

"Yes, a likely idea!" said Ivan Dmitritch, sitting up and looking at the doctor with irony and uneasiness. His eyes were red. "You can go and spy and probe somewhere else, it's no use your doing it here. I knew yesterday what you had come for."

"A strange fancy," laughed the doctor. "So you suppose me to be a spy?"

"Yes, I do. . . . A spy or a doctor who has been charged to test me—it's all the same——"

"Oh, excuse me, what a queer fellow you are really!"

The doctor sat down on the stool near the bed and shook his head reproachfully.

"But let us suppose you are right," he said, "let us suppose that I am treacherously trying to trap you into saying something so as to betray you to the police. You would be arrested and then tried. But would you be any worse off being tried and in prison than you are here? If you are banished to a settlement, or even sent to penal servitude, would it be worse than being shut up in this ward? I imagine it would be no worse. . . . What, then, are you afraid of?"

These words evidently had an effect on Ivan Dmitritch. He sat down quietly.

It was between four and five in the afternoon—the time when Andrey Yefimitch usually walked up and down his rooms, and Daryushka asked whether it was not time for his beer. It was a still, bright day.

"I came out for a walk after dinner, and here I have come, as you see," said the doctor. "It is quite spring."

"What month is it? March?" asked Ivan Dmitritch.

"Yes, the end of March."

"Is it very muddy?"

"No, not very. There are already paths in the garden."

"It would be nice now to drive in an open carriage somewhere into the country," said Ivan Dmitritch, rubbing his red eyes as though he were just awake, "then to come home to a warm, snug study, and . . . and to have a decent doctor to cure one's headache. . . . It's so long since I have lived like a human being. It's disgusting here! Insufferably disgusting!"

After his excitement of the previous day he was exhausted and listless, and spoke unwillingly. His fingers twitched, and from his face it could be seen that he had a splitting headache.

"There is no real difference between a warm,

snug study and this ward," said Andrey Yefimitch.
" A man's peace and contentment do not lie outside
a man, but in himself."

" What do you mean? "

" The ordinary man looks for good and evil in
external things—that is, in carriages, in studies—
but a thinking man looks for it in himself."

" You should go and preach that philosophy in
Greece, where it's warm and fragrant with the scent
of pomegranates, but here it is not suited to the
climate. With whom was it I was talking of
Diogenes? Was it with you? "

" Yes, with me yesterday."

" Diogenes did not need a study or a warm habita-
tion; it's hot there without. You can lie in your tub
and eat oranges and olives. But bring him to Russia to live: he'd be begging to be let indoors in May,
let alone December. He'd be doubled up with the
cold."

" No. One can be insensible to cold as to every
other pain. Marcus Aurelius says: ' A pain is a
vivid idea of pain; make an effort of will to change
that idea, dismiss it, cease to complain, and the pain
will disappear.' That is true. The wise man, or
simply the reflecting, thoughtful man, is distinguished
precisely by his contempt for suffering; he is always
contented and surprised at nothing."

" Then I am an idiot, since I suffer and am dis-
contented and surprised at the baseness of mankind."

" You are wrong in that; if you will reflect more
on the subject you will understand how insignificant
is all that external world that agitates us. One

must strive for the comprehension of life, and in that is true happiness."

" Comprehension . . ." repeated Ivan Dmitritch frowning. " External, internal. . . . Excuse me, but I don't understand it. I only know," he said, getting up and looking angrily at the doctor—" I only know that God has created me of warm blood and nerves, yes, indeed! If organic tissue is capable of life it must react to every stimulus. And I do! To pain I respond with tears and outcries, to baseness with indignation, to filth with loathing. To my mind, that is just what is called life. The lower the organism, the less sensitive it is, and the more feebly it reacts to stimulus; and the higher it is, the more responsively and vigorously it reacts to reality. How is it you don't know that? A doctor, and not know such trifles! To despise suffering, to be always contented, and to be surprised at nothing, one must reach this condition "—and Ivan Dmitritch pointed to the peasant who was a mass of fat—" or to harden oneself by suffering to such a point that one loses all sensibility to it—that is, in other words, to cease to live. You must excuse me, I am not a sage or a philosopher," Ivan Dmitritch continued with irritation, " and I don't understand anything about it. I am not capable of reasoning."

" On the contrary, your reasoning is excellent."

" The Stoics, whom you are parodying, were remarkable people, but their doctrine crystallized two thousand years ago and has not advanced, and will not advance, an inch forward, since it is not practical or living. It had a success only with the minority which spends its life in savouring all sorts of theories and ruminating over them; the majority did not understand it. A doctrine which advocates indifference to wealth and to the comforts of life, and a contempt for suffering and death, is quite unintelligible to the vast majority of men, since that majority has never known wealth or the comforts of life; and to despise suffering would mean to it despising life itself, since the whole existence of man is made up of the sensations of hunger, cold, injury, loss, and a Hamlet-like dread of death. The whole of life lies in these sensations; one may be oppressed by it, one may hate it, but one cannot despise it. Yes, so, I repeat, the doctrine of the Stoics can never have a future; from the beginning of time up to to-day you see continually increasing the struggle, the sensibility to pain, the capacity of responding to stimulus."

Ivan Dmitritch suddenly lost the thread of his thoughts, stopped, and rubbed his forehead with vexation.

" I meant to say something important, but I have lost it," he said. " What was I saying? Oh, yes! This is what I mean: one of the Stoics sold himself into slavery to redeem his neighbour, so, you see, even a Stoic did react to stimulus, since, for such a generous act as the destruction of oneself for the sake of one's neighbour, he must have had a soul capable of pity and indignation. Here in prison I have forgotten everything I have learned, or else I could have recalled something else. Take Christ, for instance: Christ responded to reality by weeping, smiling, being sorrowful and moved to wrath, even overcome by misery. He did not go to meet

His sufferings with a smile, He did not despise death, but prayed in the Garden of Gethsemane that this cup might pass Him by."

Ivan Dmitritch laughed and sat down.

"Granted that a man's peace and contentment lie not outside but in himself," he said, "granted that one must despise suffering and not be surprised at anything, yet on what ground do you preach the theory? Are you a sage? A philosopher?"

"No, I am not a philosopher, but everyone ought to preach it because it is reasonable."

"No, I want to know how it is that you consider yourself competent to judge of 'comprehension,' contempt for suffering, and so on. Have you ever suffered? Have you any idea of suffering? Allow me to ask you, were you ever thrashed in your childhood?"

"No, my parents had an aversion for corporal punishment."

"My father used to flog me cruelly; my father was a harsh, sickly Government clerk with a long nose and a yellow neck. But let us talk of you. No one has laid a finger on you all your life, no one has scared you nor beaten you; you are as strong as a bull. You grew up under your father's wing and studied at his expense, and then you dropped at once into a sinecure. For more than twenty years you have lived rent free with heating, lighting, and service all provided, and had the right to work how you pleased and as much as you pleased, even to do nothing. You were naturally a flabby, lazy man, and so you have tried to arrange your life so that nothing should disturb you or make you move. You have handed over your work to the assistant and the rest of the rabble while you sit in peace and warmth, save money, read, amuse yourself with reflections, with all sorts of lofty nonsense, and " (Ivan Dmitritch looked at the doctor's red nose) " with boozing; in fact, you have seen nothing of life, you know absolutely nothing of it, and are only theoretically acquainted with reality; you despise suffering and are surprised at nothing for a very simple reason: vanity of vanities, the external and the internal, contempt for life, for suffering and for death, comprehension, true happiness— that's the philosophy that suits the Russian sluggard best. You see a peasant beating his wife, for instance. Why interfere? Let him beat her, they will both die sooner or later, anyway; and, besides, he who beats injures by his blows, not the person he is beating, but himself. To get drunk is stupid and unseemly, but if you drink you die, and if you don't drink you die. A peasant woman comes with toothache . . . well, what of it? Pain is the idea of pain, and besides ' there is no living in this world without illness; we shall all die, and so, go away, woman, don't hinder me from thinking and drinking vodka.' A young man asks advice, what he is to do, how he is to live; anyone else would think before answering, but you have got the answer ready: strive for ' comprehension ' or for true happiness. And what is that fantastic ' true happiness '? There's no answer, of course. We are kept here behind barred windows, tortured, left to rot; but that is very good and reasonable, because there is no difference at all between this ward and a warm, snug study.

A convenient philosophy. You can do nothing, and your conscience is clear, and you feel you are wise. . . . No, sir, it is not philosophy, it's not thinking, it's not breadth of vision, but laziness, fakirism, drowsy stupefaction. Yes," cried Ivan Dmitritch, getting angry again, " you despise suffering, but I'll be bound if you pinch your finger in the door you will howl at the top of your voice."

" And perhaps I shouldn't howl," said Andrey Yefimitch, with a gentle smile.

" Oh, I dare say! Well, if you had a stroke of paralysis, or supposing some fool or bully took advantage of his position and rank to insult you in public, and if you knew he could do it with impunity, then you would understand what it means to put people off with comprehension and true happiness."

" That's original," said Andrey Yefimitch, laughing with pleasure and rubbing his hands. "I am agreeably struck by your inclination for drawing generalizations, and the sketch of my character you have just drawn is simply brilliant. I must confess that talking to you gives me great pleasure. Well, I've listened to you, and now you must graciously listen to me."

XI

The conversation went on for about an hour longer, and apparently made a deep impression an Andrey Yefimitch. He began going to the ward every day. He went there in the mornings and after dinner, and often the dusk of evening found

him in conversation with Ivan Dmitritch. At first
Ivan Dmitritch held aloof from him, suspected him
of evil designs, and openly expressed his hostility.
But afterwards he got used to him, and his abrupt
manner changed to one of condescending irony.

Soon it was all over the hospital that the doctor,
Andrey Yefimitch, had taken to visiting Ward No.
6. No one—neither Sergey Sergeyitch, nor Nikita,
nor the nurses—could conceive why he went there,
why he stayed there for hours together, what he
was talking about, and why he did not write prescriptions. His actions seemed strange. Often Mihail
Averyanitch did not find him at home, which had
never happened in the past, and Daryushka was
greatly perturbed, for the doctor drank his beer now
at no definite time, and sometimes was even late for
dinner.

One day—it was at the end of June—Dr.
Hobotov went to see Andrey Yefimitch about something. Not finding him at home, he proceeded to
look for him in the yard; there he was told that
the old doctor had gone to see the mental patients.
Going into the lodge and stopping in the entry,
Hobotov heard the following conversation:

" We shall never agree, and you will not succeed
in converting me to your faith," Ivan Dmitritch was
saying irritably; " you are utterly ignorant of reality,
and you have never known suffering, but have only
like a leech fed beside the sufferings of others, while
I have been in continual suffering from the day of my
birth till to-day. For that reason, I tell you frankly,
I consider myself superior to you and more com-

petent in every respect. It's not for you to teach me."

"I have absolutely no ambition to convert you to my faith," said Andrey Yefimitch gently, and with regret that the other refused to understand him. "And that is not what matters, my friend; what matters is not that you have suffered and I have not. Joy and suffering are passing; let us leave them, never mind them. What matters is that you and I think; we see in each other people who are capable of thinking and reasoning, and that is a common bond between us however different our views. If you knew, my friend, how sick I am of the universal senselessness, ineptitude, stupidity, and with what delight I always talk with you! You are an intelligent man, and I enjoy your company."

Hobotov opened the door an inch and glanced into the ward; Ivan Dmitritch in his night-cap and the doctor Andrey Yefimitch were sitting side by side on the bed. The madman was grimacing, twitching, and convulsively wrapping himself in his gown, while the doctor sat motionless with bowed head, and his face was red and look helpless and sorrowful. Hobotov shrugged his shoulders, grinned, and glanced at Nikita. Nikita shrugged his shoulders too.

Next day Hobotov went to the lodge, accompanied by the assistant. Both stood in the entry and listened.

"I fancy our old man has gone clean off his chump!" said Hobotov as he came out of the lodge.

"Lord have mercy upon us sinners!" sighed the

decorous Sergey Sergeyitch, scrupulously avoiding the puddles that he might not muddy his polished boots. " I must own, honoured Yevgeny Fyodoritch, I have been expecting it for a long time."

XII

After this Andrey Yefimitch began to notice a mysterious air in all around him. The attendants, the nurses, and the patients looked at him inquisitively when they met him, and then whispered together. The superintendent's little daughter Masha, whom he liked to meet in the hospital garden, for some reason ran away from him now when he went up with a smile to stroke her on the head. The postmaster no longer said, " Perfectly true," as he listened to him, but in unaccountable confusion muttered, " Yes, yes, yes . . ." and looked at him with a grieved and thoughtful expression; for some reason he took to advising his friend to give up vodka and beer, but as a man of delicate feeling he did not say this directly, but hinted it, telling him first about the commanding officer of his battalion, an excellent man, and then about the priest of the regiment, a capital fellow, both of whom drank and fell ill, but on giving up drinking completely regained their health. On two or three occasions Andrey Yefimitch was visited by his colleague Hobotov, who also advised him to give up spirituous liquors, and for no apparent reason recommended him to take bromide.

In August Andrey Yefimitch got a letter from the mayor of the town asking him to come on very important business. On arriving at the town hall at the time fixed, Andrey Yefimitch found there the military commander, the superintendent of the district school, a member of the town council, Hobotov, and a plump, fair gentleman who was introduced to him as a doctor. This doctor, with a Polish surname difficult to pronounce, lived at a pedigree stud-farm twenty miles away, and was now on a visit to the town.

" There's something that concerns you," said the member of the town council, addressing Andrey Yefimitch after they had all greeted one another and sat down to the table. " Here Yevgeny Fyodoritch says that there is not room for the dispensary in the main building, and that it ought to be transferred to one of the lodges. That's of no consequence—of course it can be transferred, but the point is that the lodge wants doing up."

" Yes, it would have to be done up," said Andrey Yefimitch after a moment's thought. " If the corner lodge, for instance, were fitted up as a dispensary, I imagine it would cost at least five hundred roubles. An unproductive expenditure ! "

Everyone was silent for a space.

" I had the honour of submitting to you ten years ago," Andrey Yefimitch went on in a low voice, " that the hospital in its present form is a luxury for the town beyond its means. It was built in the forties, but things were different then. The town spends too much on unnecessary buildings and superfluous staff. I believe with a different system two model hospitals might be maintained for the same money."

" Well, let us have a different system, then ! " the member of the town council said briskly.

" I have already had the honour of submitting to you that the medical department should be transferred to the supervision of the Zemstvo."

" Yes, transfer the money to the Zemstvo and they will steal it," laughed the fair-haired doctor.

" That's what it always comes to," the member of the council assented, and he also laughed.

Andrey Yefimitch looked with apathetic, lustreless eyes at the fair-haired doctor and said: " One should be just."

Again there was silence. Tea was brought in. The military commander, for some reason much embarrassed, touched Andrey Yefimitch's hand across the table and said: "You have quite forgotten us, doctor. But of course you are a hermit: you don't play cards and don't like women. You would be dull with fellows like us."

They all began saying how boring it was for a decent person to live in such a town. No theatre, no music, and at the last dance at the club there had been about twenty ladies and only two gentlemen. The young men did not dance, but spent all the time crowding round the refreshment bar or playing cards.

Not looking at anyone and speaking slowly in a low voice, Andrey Yefimitch began saying what a pity, what a terrible pity it was that the townspeople should waste their vital energy, their hearts, and their minds on cards and gossip, and should have neither the power nor the inclination to spend their time in interesting conversation and reading, and should refuse to take advantage of the enjoyments of the mind. The mind alone was interesting and worthy of attention, all the rest was low and petty. Hobotov listened to his colleague attentively and suddenly asked:

"Andrey Yefimitch, what day of the month is it?"

Having received an answer, the fair-haired doctor and he, in the tone of examiners conscious of their lack of skill, began asking Andrey Yefimitch what was the day of the week, how many days there were in the year, and whether it was true that there was a remarkable prophet living in Ward No. 6.

In response to the last question Andrey Yefimitch turned rather red and said: "Yes, he is mentally deranged, but he is an interesting young man."

They asked him no other questions.

When he was putting on his overcoat in the entry, the military commander laid a hand on his shoulder and said with a sigh:

"It's time for us old fellows to rest!"

As he came out of the hall, Andrey Yefimitch understood that it had been a committee appointed to enquire into his mental condition. He recalled the questions that had been asked him, flushed crimson, and for some reason, for the first time in his life, felt bitterly grieved for medical science.

"My God . . ." he thought, remembering how these doctors had just examined him; "why, they have only lately been hearing lectures on mental pathology; they had passed an examination—what's the explanation of this crass ignorance? They have not a conception of mental pathology!"

And for the first time in his life he felt insulted and moved to anger.

In the evening of the same day Mihail Averya-nitch came to see him. The postmaster went up to him without waiting to greet him, took him by both hands, and said in an agitated voice:

" My dear fellow, my dear friend, show me that you believe in my genuine affection and look on me as your friend! " And preventing Andrey Yefimitch from speaking, he went on, growing excited: " I love you for your culture and nobility of soul. Listen to me, my dear fellow. The rules of their profession compel the doctors to conceal the truth from you, but I blurt out the plain truth like a soldier. You are not well! Excuse me, my dear fellow, but it is the truth; everyone about you has been noticing it for a long time. Dr. Yevgeny Fyodoritch has just told me that it is essential for you to rest and distract your mind for the sake of your health. Perfectly true! Excellent! In a day or two I am taking a holiday and am going away for a sniff of a different atmosphere. Show that you are a friend to me, let us go together! Let us go for a jaunt as in the good old days."

" I feel perfectly well," said Andrey Yefimitch after a moment's thought. " I can't go away. Allow me to show you my friendship in some other way."

To go off with no object, without his books, without his Daryushka, without his beer, to break abruptly through the routine of life, established for twenty years—the idea for the first minute struck him as wild and fantastic, but he remembered the conversation at the Zemstvo committee and the depressing feelings with which he had returned home, and the thought of a brief absence from the town in which stupid people looked on him as a madman was pleasant to him.

"And where precisely do you intend to go?" he asked.

"To Moscow, to Petersburg, to Warsaw. . . . I spent the five happiest years of my life in Warsaw. What a marvellous town! Let us go, my dear fellow!"

XIII

A week later it was suggested to Andrey Yefimitch that he should have a rest—that is, send in his resignation—a suggestion he received with indifference, and a week later still, Mihail Averyanitch and he were sitting in a posting carriage driving to the nearest railway station. The days were cool and bright, with a blue sky and a transparent distance. They were two days driving the hundred and fifty miles to the railway station, and stayed two nights on the way. When at the posting station the glasses given them for their tea had not been properly washed, or the drivers were slow in harnessing the horses, Mihail Averyanitch would turn crimson, and quivering all over would shout:

"Hold your tongue! Don't argue!"

And in the carriage he talked without ceasing for a moment, describing his campaigns in the Caucasus and in Poland. What adventures he had had, what meetings! He talked loudly and opened his eyes so wide with wonder that he might well be thought to be lying. Moreover, as he talked he breathed in Andrey Yefimitch's face and laughed into his ear. This bothered the doctor and prevented him from thinking or concentrating his mind.

In the train they travelled, from motives of economy, third-class in a non-smoking compartment. Half the passengers were decent people. Mihail Averyanitch soon made friends with everyone, and moving from one seat to another, kept saying loudly that they ought not to travel by these appalling lines. It was a regular swindle! A very different thing riding on a good horse: one could do over seventy miles a day and feel fresh and well after it. And our bad harvests were due to the draining of the Pinsk marshes; altogether, the way things were done was dreadful. He got excited, talked loudly, and would not let others speak. This endless chatter to the accompaniment of loud laughter and expressive gestures wearied Andrey Yefimitch.

"Which of us is the madman?" he thought with vexation. "I, who try not to disturb my fellow-passengers in any way, or this egoist who thinks that he is cleverer and more interesting than anyone here, and so will leave no one in peace?"

In Moscow Mihail Averyanitch put on a military coat without epaulettes and trousers with red braid on them. He wore a military cap and overcoat in the street, and soldiers saluted him. It seemed to Andrey Yefimitch, now, that his companion was a man who had flung away all that was good and kept only what was bad of all the characteristics of a country gentleman that he had once possessed. He liked to be waited on even when it was quite unnecessary. The matches would be lying before him on the table, and he would see them and shout to the waiter to give him the matches; he did not hesitate to appear before a maidservant in nothing but his underclothes; he used the familiar mode of address to all footmen indiscriminately, even old men, and when he was angry called them fools and blockheads. This, Andrey Yefimitch thought, was like a gentleman, but disgusting.

First of all Mihail Averyanitch led his friend to the Iversky Madonna. He prayed fervently, shedding tears and bowing down to the earth, and when he had finished, heaved a deep sigh and said:

"Even though one does not believe it makes one somehow easier when one prays a little. Kiss the ikon, my dear fellow."

Andrey Yefimitch was embarrassed and he kissed the image, while Mihail Averyanitch pursed up his lips and prayed in a whisper, and again tears came into his eyes. Then they went to the Kremlin and looked there at the Tsar-cannon and the Tsar-bell, and even touched them with their fingers, admired the view over the river, visited St. Saviour's and the Rumyantsev museum.

They dined at Tyestov's. Mihail Averyanitch looked a long time at the menu, stroking his whiskers, and said in the tone of a gourmand accustomed to dine in restaurants:

"We shall see what you give us to eat to-day, angel!"

XIV

The doctor walked about, looked at things, ate and drank, but he had all the while one feeling: an-

noyance with Mihail Averyanitch. He longed to have
a rest from his friend, to get away from him, to
hide himself, while the friend thought it his duty
not to let the doctor move a step away from him,
and to provide him with as many distractions as
possible. When there was nothing to look at he
entertained him with conversation. For two days
Andrey Yefimitch endured it, but on the third he
announced to his friend that he was ill and wanted
to stay at home for the whole day; his friend replied
that in that case he would stay too—that really
he needed rest, for he was run off his legs already.
Andrey Yefimitch lay on the sofa, with his face to
the back, and clenching his teeth, listened to his
friend, who assured him with heat that sooner or
later France would certainly thrash Germany, that
there were a great many scoundrels in Moscow, and
that it was impossible to judge of a horse's quality
by its outward appearance. The doctor began to
have a buzzing in his ears and palpitations of the
heart, but out of delicacy could not bring himself
to beg his friend to go away or hold his tongue.
Fortunately Mihail Averyanitch grew weary of
sitting in the hotel room, and after dinner he went
out for a walk.

As soon as he was alone Andrey Yefimitch abandoned himself to a feeling of relief. How pleasant
to lie motionless on the sofa and to know that one
is alone in the room! Real happiness is impossible
without solitude. The fallen angel betrayed God
probably because he longed for solitude, of which
the angels know nothing. Andrey Yefimitch wanted
to think about what he had seen and heard during

the last few days, but he could not get Mihail Averyanitch out of his head.

" Why, he has taken a holiday and come with me out of friendship, out of generosity," thought the doctor with vexation; " nothing could be worse than this friendly supervision. I suppose he is good-natured and generous and a lively fellow, but he is a bore. An insufferable bore. In the same way there are people who never say anything but what is clever and good, yet one feels that they are dull-witted people."

For the following days Andrey Yefimitch declared himself ill and would not leave the hotel room; he lay with his face to the back of the sofa, and suffered agonies of weariness when his friend entertained him with conversation, or rested when his friend was absent. He was vexed with himself for having come, and with his friend, who grew every day more talkative and more free-and-easy; he could not succeed in attuning his thoughts to a serious and lofty level.

" This is what I get from the real life Ivan Dmitritch talked about," he thought, angry at his own pettiness. " It's of no consequence, though. . . . I shall go home, and everything will go on as before. . . ."

It was the same thing in Petersburg too; for whole days together he did not leave the hotel room, but lay on the sofa and only got up to drink beer.

Mihail Averyanitch was all haste to get to Warsaw.

" My dear man, what should I go there for? "

said Andrey Yefimitch in an imploring voice. "You go alone and let me get home! I entreat you!"

"On no account," protested Mihail Averyanitch. "It's a marvellous town."

Andrey Yefimitch had not the strength of will to insist on his own way, and much against his inclination went to Warsaw. There he did not leave the hotel room, but lay on the sofa, furious with himself, with his friend, and with the waiters, who obstinately refused to understand Russian; while Mihail Averyanitch, healthy, hearty, and full of spirits as usual, went about the town from morning to night, looking for his old acquaintances. Several times he did not return home at night. After one night spent in some unknown haunt he returned home early in the morning, in a violently excited condition, with a red face and tousled hair. For a long time he walked up and down the rooms muttering something to himself, then stopped and said:

"Honour before everything."

After walking up and down a little longer he clutched his head in both hands and pronounced in a tragic voice: "Yes, honour before everything! Accursed be the moment when the idea first entered my head to visit this Babylon! My dear friend," he added, addressing the doctor, "you may despise me, I have played and lost; lend me five hundred roubles!"

Andrey Yefimitch counted out five hundred roubles and gave them to his friend without a word. The latter, still crimson with shame and anger, incoherently articulated some useless vow, put on his cap, and went out. Returning two hours later he flopped into an easy-chair, heaved a loud sigh, and said:

"My honour is saved. Let us go, my friend; I do not care to remain another hour in this accursed town. Scoundrels! Austrian spies!"

By the time the friends were back in their own town it was November, and deep snow was lying in the streets. Dr. Hobotov had Andrey Yefimitch's post; he was still living in his old lodgings, waiting for Andrey Yefimitch to arrive and clear out of the hospital apartments. The plain woman whom he called his cook was already established in one of the lodges.

Fresh scandals about the hospital were going the round of the town. It was said that the plain woman had quarrelled with the superintendent, and that the latter had crawled on his knees before her begging forgiveness. On the very first day he arrived Andrey Yefimitch had to look out for lodgings.

"My friend," the postmaster said to him timidly, "excuse an indiscreet question: what means have you at your disposal?"

Andrey Yefimitch, without a word, counted out his money and said: "Eighty-six roubles."

"I don't mean that," Mihail Averyanitch brought out in confusion, misunderstanding him; "I mean, what have you to live on?"

"I tell you, eighty-six roubles . . . I have nothing else."

Mihail Averyanitch looked upon the doctor as an honourable man, yet he suspected that he had accumulated a fortune of at least twenty thousand. Now learning that Andrey Yefimitch was a beggar, that he had nothing to live on he was for some reason suddenly moved to tears and embraced his friend.

XV

Andrey Yefimitch now lodged in a little house with three windows. There were only three rooms besides the kitchen in the little house. The doctor lived in two of them which looked into the street, while Daryushka and the landlady with her three children lived in the third room and the kitchen. Sometimes the landlady's lover, a drunken peasant who was rowdy and reduced the children and Daryushka to terror, would come for the night. When he arrived and established himself in the kitchen and demanded vodka, they all felt very uncomfortable, and the doctor would be moved by pity to take the crying children into his room and let them lie on his floor, and this gave him great satisfaction.

He got up as before at eight o'clock, and after his morning tea sat down to read his old books and magazines: he had no money for new ones. Either because the books were old, or perhaps because of the change in his surroundings, reading exhausted him, and did not grip his attention as before. That he might not spend his time in idleness he made a detailed catalogue of his books and gummed little labels on their backs, and this mechanical, tedious work seemed to him more interesting than reading. The monotonous, tedious work lulled his thoughts to sleep in some unaccountable way, and the time passed quickly while he thought of nothing. Even sitting in the kitchen, peeling potatoes with Daryushka or picking over the buckwheat grain, seemed to him interesting. On Saturdays and Sundays he went to church. Standing near the wall and half closing his eyes, he listened to the singing and thought of his father, of his mother, of the university, of the religions of the world; he felt calm and melancholy, and as he went out of the church afterwards he regretted that the service was so soon over. He went twice to the hospital to talk to Ivan Dmitritch. But on both occasions Ivan Dmitritch was unusually excited and ill-humoured; he bade the doctor leave him in peace, as he had long been sick of empty chatter, and declared, to make up for all his sufferings, he asked from the damned scoundrels only one favour—solitary confinement. Surely they would not refuse him even that? On both occasions when Andrey Yefimitch was taking leave of him and wishing him good-night, he answered rudely and said:

" Go to hell! "

And Andrey Yefimitch did not know now whether to go to him for the third time or not. He longed to go.

In old days Andrey Yefimitch used to walk about his rooms and think in the interval after dinner, but now from dinner-time till evening tea he lay on the sofa with his face to the back and gave himself up to trivial thoughts which he could not struggle against. He was mortified that after more than twenty years of service he had been given neither a pension nor any assistance. It is true that he had not done his work honestly, but, then, all who are in the Service get a pension without distinction whether they are honest or not. Contemporary justice lies precisely in the bestowal of grades, orders, and pensions, not for moral qualities or capacities, but for service whatever it may have been like. Why was he alone to be an exception? He had no money at all. He was ashamed to pass by the shop and look at the woman who owned it. He owed thirty-two roubles for beer already. There was money owing to the landlady also. Daryushka sold old clothes and books on the sly, and told lies to the landlady, saying that the doctor was just going to receive a large sum of money.

He was angry with himself for having wasted on travelling the thousand roubles he had saved up. How useful that thousand roubles would have been now! He was vexed that people would not leave him in peace. Hobotov thought it his duty to look in on his sick colleague from time to time. Everything about him was revolting to Andrey Yefimitch —his well-fed face and vulgar, condescending tone, and his use of the word " colleague," and his high top-boots; the most revolting thing was that he thought it was his duty to treat Andrey Yefimitch, and thought that he really was treating him. On every visit he brought a bottle of bromide and rhubarb pills.

Mihail Averyanitch, too, thought it his duty to visit his friend and entertain him. Every time he went in to Andrey Yefimitch with an affectation of ease, laughed constrainedly, and began assuring him that he was looking very well to-day, and that, thank

God, he was on the highroad to recovery, and from this it might be concluded that he looked on his friend's condition as hopeless. He had not yet repaid his Warsaw debt, and was overwhelmed by shame; he was constrained, and so tried to laugh louder and talk more amusingly. His anecdotes and descriptions seemed endless now, and were an agony both to Andrey Yefimitch and himself.

In his presence Andrey Yefimitch usually lay on the sofa with his face to the wall, and listened with his teeth clenched; his soul was oppressed with rankling disgust, and after every visit from his friend he felt as though this disgust had risen higher, and was mounting into his throat.

To stifle petty thoughts he made haste to reflect that he himself, and Hobotov, and Mihail Averyanitch, would all sooner or later perish without leaving any trace on the world. If one imagined some spirit flying by the earthly globe in space in a million years he would see nothing but clay and bare rocks. Everything—culture and the moral law—would pass away and not even a burdock would grow out of them. Of what consequence was shame in the presence of a shopkeeper, of what consequence was the insignificant Hobotov or the wearisome friendship of Mihail Averyanitch? It was all trivial and nonsensical.

But such reflections did not help him now. Scarcely had he imagined the earthly globe in a million years, when Hobotov in his high top-boots or Mihail Averyanitch with his forced laugh would appear from behind a bare rock, and he even heard the shamefaced whisper: " The Warsaw debt. . . .

I will repay it in a day or two, my dear fellow, without fail. . . ."

XVI

One day Mihail Averyanitch came after dinner when Andrey Yefimitch was lying on the sofa. It so happened that Hobotov arrived at the same time with his bromide. Andrey Yefimitch got up heavily and sat down, leaning both arms on the sofa.

"You have a much better colour to-day than you had yesterday, my dear man," began Mihail Averyanitch. "Yes, you look jolly. Upon my soul, you do!"

"It's high time you were well, colleague," said Hobotov, yawning. "I'll be bound, you are sick of this bobbery."

"And we shall recover," said Mihail Averyanitch cheerfully. "We shall live another hundred years! To be sure!"

"Not a hundred years, but another twenty," Hobotov said reassuringly. "It's all right, all right, colleague; don't lose heart. . . . Don't go piling it on!"

"We'll show what we can do," laughed Mihail Averyanitch, and he slapped his friend on the knee. "We'll show them yet! Next summer, please God, we shall be off to the Caucasus, and we will ride all over it on horseback—trot, trot, trot! And when we are back from the Caucasus I shouldn't wonder if we will all dance at the wedding." Mihail Averyanitch gave a sly wink. "We'll marry you, my dear boy, we'll marry you. . . ."

Andrey Yefimitch felt suddenly that the rising disgust had mounted to his throat, his heart began beating violently.

"That's vulgar," he said, getting up quickly and walking away to the window. "Don't you understand that you are talking vulgar nonsense?"

He meant to go on softly and politely, but against his will he suddenly clenched his fists and raised them above his head.

"Leave me alone," he shouted in a voice unlike his own, flushing crimson and shaking all over. "Go away, both of you!"

Mihail Averyanitch and Hobotov got up and stared at him first with amazement and then with alarm.

"Go away, both!" Andrey Yefimitch went on shouting. "Stupid people! Foolish people! I don't want either your friendship or your medicines, stupid man! Vulgar! Nasty!"

Hobotov and Mihail Averyanitch, looking at each other in bewilderment, staggered to the door and went out. Andrey Yefimitch snatched up the bottle of bromide and flung it after them; the bottle broke with a crash on the door-frame.

"Go to the devil!" he shouted in a tearful voice, running out into the passage. "To the devil!"

When his guests were gone Andrey Yefimitch lay down on the sofa, trembling as though in a fever, and went on for a long while repeating: "Stupid people! Foolish people!"

When he was calmer, what occurred to him first of all was the thought that poor Mihail Averyanitch must be feeling fearfully ashamed and depressed now, and that it was all dreadful. Nothing like this had ever happened to him before. Where was his intelligence and his tact? Where was his comprehension of things and his philosophical indifference?

The doctor could not sleep all night for shame and vexation with himself, and at ten o'clock next morning he went to the post office and apologized to the postmaster.

"We won't think again of what has happened," Mihail Averyanitch, greatly touched, said with a sigh, warmly pressing his hand. "Let bygones be bygones. Lyubavkin," he suddenly shouted so loud that all the postmen and other persons present started, "hand a chair; and you wait," he shouted to a peasant woman who was stretching out a registered letter to him through the grating. "Don't you see that I am busy? We will not remember the past," he went on, affectionately addressing Andrey Yefimitch; "sit down, I beg you, my dear fellow."

For a minute he stroked his knees in silence, and then said:

"I have never had a thought of taking offence. Illness is no joke, I understand. Your attack frightened the doctor and me yesterday, and we had a long talk about you afterwards. My dear friend, why won't you treat your illness seriously? You can't go on like this. . . . Excuse me speaking openly as a friend," whispered Mihail Averyanitch. "You live in the most unfavourable surroundings, in a crowd, in uncleanliness, no one to look after you, no money for proper treatment. . . . My dear friend, the doctor and I implore you with all our hearts, listen to our advice: go into the hospital! There you will have wholesome food and attendance and treatment. Though, between ourselves, Yevgeny Fyodoritch is *mauvais ton,* yet he does understand his work, you can fully rely upon him. He has promised me he will look after you."

Andrey Yefimitch was touched by the postmaster's genuine sympathy and the tears which suddenly glittered on his cheeks.

"My honoured friend, don't believe it!" he whispered, laying his hand on his heart; "don't believe them. It's all a sham. My illness is only that in twenty years I have only found one intelligent man in the whole town, and he is mad. I am not ill at all, it's simply that I have got into an enchanted circle which there is no getting out of. I don't care; I am ready for anything."

"Go into the hospital, my dear fellow."

"I don't care if it were into the pit."

"Give me your word, my dear man, that you will obey Yevgeny Fyodoritch in everything."

"Certainly I will give you my word. But I repeat, my honoured friend, I have got into an enchanted circle. Now everything, even the genuine sympathy of my friends, leads to the same thing— to my ruin. I am going to my ruin, and I have the manliness to recognize it."

"My dear fellow, you will recover."

"What's the use of saying that?" said Andrey Yefimitch, with irritation. "There are few men who at the end of their lives do not experience what I am experiencing now. When you are told that you have something such as diseased kidneys or enlarged heart, and you begin being treated for it, or are told you are mad or a criminal—that is, in fact, when people suddenly turn their attention to you— you may be sure you have got into an enchanted circle from which you will not escape. You will try to escape and make things worse. You had better give in, for no human efforts can save you. So it seems to me."

Meanwhile the public was crowding at the grating. That he might not be in their way, Andrey Yefimitch got up and began to take leave. Mihail Averyanitch made him promise on his honour once more, and escorted him to the outer door.

Towards evening on the same day Hobotov, in his sheepskin and his high top-boots, suddenly made his appearance, and said to Andrey Yefimitch in a tone as though nothing had happened the day before:

"I have come on business, colleague. I have come to ask you whether you would not join me in a consultation. Eh?"

Thinking that Hobotov wanted to distract his mind with an outing, or perhaps really to enable him to earn something, Andrey Yefimitch put on his coat and hat, and went out with him into the street. He was glad of the opportunity to smooth over his fault of the previous day and to be reconciled, and in his heart thanked Hobotov, who did not even allude to yesterday's scene and was evidently sparing him. One would never have expected such delicacy from this uncultured man.

" Where is your invalid? " asked Andrey Yefimitch.

" In the hospital. . . . I have long wanted to show him to you. A very interesting case."

They went into the hospital yard, and going round the main building, turned towards the lodge where the mental cases were kept, and all this, for some reason, in silence. When they went into the lodge Nikita as usual jumped up and stood at attention.

" One of the patients here has a lung complication," Hobotov said in an undertone, going into the ward with Andrey Yefimitch. " You wait here, I'll be back directly. I am going for a stethoscope."

And he went away.

XVII

It was getting dusk. Ivan Dmitritch was lying on his bed with his face thrust into his pillow; the paralytic was sitting motionless, crying quietly and moving his lips. The fat peasant and the former sorter were asleep. It was quiet.

Andrey Yefimitch sat down on Ivan Dmitritch's bed and waited. But half an hour passed, and instead of Hobotov, Nikita came into the ward with a dressing-gown, some underlinen, and a pair of slippers in a heap on his arm.

" Please change your things, your honour," he said softly. " Here is your bed; come this way," he added, pointing to an empty bedstead which had obviously been recently brought into the ward. " It's all right; please God, you will recover."

Andrey Yefimitch understood it all. Without

saying a word he crossed to the bed to which Nikita pointed and sat down; seeing that Nikita was standing waiting, he undressed entirely and he felt ashamed. Then he put on the hospital clothes; the drawers were very short, the shirt was long, and the dressing-gown smelt of smoked fish.

"Please God, you will recover," repeated Nikita, and he gathered up Andrey Yefimitch's clothes into his arms, went out, and shut the door after him.

"No matter . . ." thought Andrey Yefimitch, wrapping himself in his dressing-gown in a shame-faced way and feeling that he looked like a convict in his new costume. "It's no matter. . . . It does not matter whether it's a dress-coat or a uniform or this dressing-gown. . . ."

But how about his watch? And the notebook that was in the side-pocket? And his cigarettes? Where had Nikita taken his clothes? Now perhaps to the day of his death he would not put on trousers, a waistcoat, and high boots. It was all somehow strange and even incomprehensible at first. Andrey Yefimitch was even now convinced that there was no difference between his landlady's house and Ward No. 6, that everything in this world was nonsense and vanity of vanities. And yet his hands were trembling, his feet were cold, and he was filled with dread at the thought that soon Ivan Dmitritch would get up and see that he was in a dressing-gown. He got up and walked across the room and sat down again.

Here he had been sitting already half an hour, an hour, and he was miserably sick of it: was it really possible to live here a day, a week, and even years like these people? Why, he had been sitting here, had walked about and sat down again; he could get up and look out of window and walk from corner to corner again, and then what? Sit so all the time, like a post, and think? No, that was scarcely possible.

Andrey Yefimitch lay down, but at once got up, wiped the cold sweat from his brow with his sleeve, and felt that his whole face smelt of smoked fish. He walked about again.

"It's some misunderstanding . . ." he said, turning out the palms of his hands in perplexity. "It must be cleared up. There is a misunderstanding. . . ."

Meanwhile Ivan Dmitritch woke up; he sat up and propped his cheeks on his fists. He spat. Then he glanced lazily at the doctor, and apparently for the first minute did not understand; but soon his sleepy face grew malicious and mocking.

"Aha! so they have put you in here, too, old fellow?" he said in a voice husky from sleepiness, screwing up one eye. "Very glad to see you. You sucked the blood of others, and now they will suck yours. Excellent!"

"It's a misunderstanding . . ." Andrey Yefimitch brought out, frightened by Ivan Dmitritch's words; he shrugged his shoulders and repeated: "It's some misunderstanding. . . ."

Ivan Dmitritch spat again and lay down.

"Cursed life," he grumbled, "and what's bitter and insulting, this life will not end in compensation for our sufferings, it will not end with apotheosis as it would in an opera, but with death; peasants

will come and drag one's dead body by the arms
and the legs to the cellar. Ugh! Well, it does not
matter. . . . We shall have our good time in the
other world. . . . I shall come here as a ghost from
the other world and frighten these reptiles. I'll
turn their hair grey."

Moiseika returned, and, seeing the doctor, held
out his hand.

"Give me one little kopeck," he said.

XVIII

Andrey Yefimitch walked away to the window
and looked out into the open country. It was
getting dark, and on the horizon to the right a cold
crimson moon was mounting upwards. Not far
from the hospital fence, not much more than two
hundred yards away, stood a tall white house shut
in by a stone wall. This was the prison.

"So this is real life," thought Andrey Yefimitch,
and he felt frightened.

The moon and the prison, and the nails on the
fence, and the far-away flames at the bone-charring
factory were all terrible. Behind him there was
the sound of a sigh. Andrey Yefimitch looked
round and saw a man with glittering stars and
orders on his breast, who was smiling and slily winking. And this, too, seemed terrible.

Andrey Yefimitch assured himself that there was
nothing special about the moon or the prison, that
even sane persons wear orders, and that everything
in time will decay and turn to earth, but he was
suddenly overcome with despair; he clutched at the

grating with both hands and shook it with all his might. The strong grating did not yield.

Then that it might not be so dreadful he went to Ivan Dmitritch's bed and sat down.

" I have lost heart, my dear fellow," he muttered, trembling and wiping away the cold sweat, " I have lost heart."

" You should be philosophical," said Ivan Dmitritch ironically.

" My God, my God. . . . Yes, yes. . . . You were pleased to say once that there was no philosophy in Russia, but that all people, even the paltriest, talk philosophy. But you know the philosophizing of the paltriest does not harm anyone," said Andrey Yefimitch in a tone as if he wanted to cry and complain. " Why, then, that malignant laugh, my friend, and how can these paltry creatures help philosophizing if they are not satisfied? For an intelligent, educated man, made in God's image, proud and loving freedom, to have no alternative but to be a doctor in a filthy, stupid, wretched little town, and to spend his whole life among bottles, leeches, mustard plasters! Quackery, narrowness, vulgarity! Oh, my God!"

" You are talking nonsense. If you don't like being a doctor you should have gone in for being a statesman."

" I could not, I could not do anything. We are weak, my dear friend. . . . I used to be indifferent. I reasoned boldly and soundly, but at the first coarse touch of life upon me I have lost heart. . . . Prostration. . . . We are weak, we are poor creatures . . . and you, too, my dear friend, you are intelligent, generous, you drew in good impulses with your mother's milk, but you had hardly entered upon life when you were exhausted and fell ill. . . . Weak, weak! "

Andrey Yefimitch was all the while at the approach of evening tormented by another persistent sensation besides terror and the feeling of resentment. At last he realized that he was longing for a smoke and for beer.

" I am going out, my friend," he said. " I will tell them to bring a light; I can't put up with this. . . . I am not equal to it. . . ."

Andrey Yefimitch went to the door and opened it, but at once Nikita jumped up and barred his way.

" Where are you going? You can't, you can't! " he said. " It's bedtime."

" But I'm only going out for a minute to walk about the yard," said Andrey Yefimitch.

" You can't, you can't; it's forbidden. You know that yourself."

" But what difference will it make to anyone if I do go out? " asked Andrey Yefimitch, shrugging his shoulders. " I don't understand. Nikita, I must go out! " he said in a trembling voice. " I must."

" Don't be disorderly, it's not right," Nikita said peremptorily.

" This is beyond everything," Ivan Dmitritch cried suddenly, and he jumped up. " What right has he not to let you out? How dare they keep us here? I believe it is clearly laid down in the law that no one can be deprived of freedom without trial! It's an outrage! It's tyranny! "

" Of course it's tyranny," said Andrey Yefimitch,

encouraged by Ivan Dmitritch's outburst. "I must go out, I want to. He has no right! Open, I tell you."

"Do you hear, you dull-witted brute?" cried Ivan Dmitritch, and he banged on the door with his fist. "Open the door, or I will break it open! Torturer!"

"Open the door," cried Andrey Yefimitch, trembling all over; "I insist!"

"Talk away!" Nikita answered through the door, "talk away. . . ."

"Anyhow, go and call Yevgeny Fyodoritch! Say that I beg him to come for a minute!"

"His honour will come of himself to-morrow."

"They will never let us out," Ivan Dmitritch was going on meanwhile. "They will leave us to rot here! Oh, Lord, can there really be no hell in the next world, and will these wretches be forgiven? Where is justice? Open the door, you wretch! I am choking!" he cried in a hoarse voice, and flung himself upon the door. "I'll dash out my brains, murderers!"

Nikita opened the door quickly, and roughly with both his hands and his knee shoved Andrey Yefimitch back, then swung his arm and punched him in the face with his fist. It seemed to Andrey Yefimitch as though a huge salt wave enveloped him from his head downwards and dragged him to the bed; there really was a salt taste in his mouth: most likely the blood was running from his teeth. He waved his arms as though he were trying to swim out and clutched at a bedstead, and at the same moment felt Nikita hit him twice on the back.

Ivan Dmitritch gave a loud scream. He must have been beaten too.

Then all was still, the faint moonlight came through the grating, and a shadow like a net lay on the floor. It was terrible. Andrey Yefimitch lay and held his breath: he was expecting with horror to be struck again. He felt as though someone had taken a sickle, thrust it into him, and turned it round several times in his breast and bowels. He bit the pillow from pain and clenched his teeth, and all at once through the chaos in his brain there flashed the terrible unbearable thought that these people, who seemed now like black shadows in the moonlight, had to endure such pain day by day for years. How could it have happened that for more than twenty years he had not known it and had refused to know it? He knew nothing of pain, had no conception of it, so he was not to blame, but his conscience, as inexorable and as rough as Nikita, made him turn cold from the crown of his head to his heels. He leaped up, tried to cry out with all his might, and to run in haste to kill Nikita, and then Hobotov, the superintendent and the assistant, and then himself; but no sound came from his chest, and his legs would not obey him. Gasping for breath, he tore at the dressing-gown and the shirt on his breast, rent them, and fell senseless on the bed.

XIX

Next morning his head ached, there was a droning in his ears and a feeling of utter weakness all over.

He was not ashamed at recalling his weakness the day before. He had been cowardly, had even been afraid of the moon, had openly expressed thoughts and feelings such as he had not expected in himself before; for instance, the thought that the paltry people who philosophized were really dissatisfied. But now nothing mattered to him.

He ate nothing, he drank nothing. He lay motionless and silent.

"It is all the same to me," he thought when they asked him questions. "I am not going to answer. . . . It's all the same to me."

After dinner Mihail Averyanitch brought him a quarter of a pound of tea and a pound of fruit pastilles. Daryushka came too and stood for a whole hour by the bed with an expression of dull grief on her face. Dr. Hobotov visited him. He brought a bottle of bromide and told Nikita to fumigate the ward with something.

Towards evening Andrey Yefimitch died of an apoplectic stroke. At first he had a violent shivering fit and a feeling of sickness; something revolting as it seemed, penetrating through his whole body, even to his finger-tips, strained from his stomach to his head and flooded his eyes and ears. There was a greenness before his eyes. Andrey Yefimitch understood that his end had come, and remembered that Ivan Dmitritch, Mihail Averyanitch, and millions of people believed in immortality. And what if it really existed? But he did not want immortality, and he thought of it only for one instant. A herd of deer, extraordinarily beautiful and graceful, of which he had been reading the day before, ran by him; then a peasant woman stretched out her hand to him with a registered letter. . . . Mihail Averyanitch said something, then it all vanished, and Andrey Yefimitch sank into oblivion for ever.

The hospital porters came, took him by his arms and his legs, and carried him away to the chapel.

There he lay on the table, with open eyes, and the moon shed its light upon him at night. In the morning Sergey Sergeyitch came, prayed piously before the crucifix, and closed his former chief's eyes.

Next day Andrey Yefimitch was buried. Mihail Averyanitch and Daryushka were the only people at the funeral.

1892

THE DARLING

OLENKA, the daughter of the retired collegiate asses-
sor, Plemyanniakov, was sitting in her back porch,
lost in thought. It was hot, the flies were persistent
and teasing, and it was pleasant to reflect that it
would soon be evening. Dark rainclouds were gathering from the east, and bringing from time to time
a breath of moisture in the air.

Kukin, who was the manager of an open-air theatre
called the Tivoli, and who lived in the lodge, was
standing in the middle of the garden looking at the
sky.

"Again!" he observed despairingly. "It's going to rain again! Rain every day, as though to
spite me. I might as well hang myself! It's ruin!
Fearful losses every day."

He flung up his hands, and went on, addressing
Olenka:

"There! that's the life we lead, Olga Semyonovna. It's enough to make one cry. One works
and does one's utmost; one wears oneself out, getting no sleep at night, and racks one's brain what

to do for the best. And then what happens? To begin with, one's public is ignorant, boorish. I give them the very best operetta, a dainty masque, first rate music-hall artists. But do you suppose that's what they want! They don't understand anything of that sort. They want a clown; what they ask for is vulgarity. And then look at the weather! Almost every evening it rains. It started on the tenth of May, and it's kept it up all May and June. It's simply awful! The public doesn't come, but I've to pay the rent just the same, and pay the artists."

The next evening the clouds would gather again, and Kukin would say with an hysterical laugh:

"Well, rain away, then! Flood the garden, drown me! Damn my luck in this world and the next! Let the artists have me up! Send me to prison! — to Siberia! — the scaffold! Ha, ha, ha!"

And next day the same thing.

Olenka listened to Kukin with silent gravity, and sometimes tears came into her eyes. In the end his misfortunes touched her; she grew to love him. He was a small thin man, with a yellow face, and curls combed forward on his forehead. He spoke in a thin tenor; as he talked his mouth worked on one side, and there was always an expression of despair on his face; yet he aroused a deep and genuine affection in her. She was always fond of some one, and could not exist without loving. In earlier days she had loved her papa, who now sat in a darkened room, breathing with difficulty; she had loved her aunt who used to come every other year from Bryansk; and before that, when she was at school, she had loved her French master. She was a gentle, soft-hearted, compassionate girl, with mild, tender eyes and very good health. At the sight of her full rosy cheeks, her soft white neck with a little dark mole on it, and the kind, naïve smile, which came into her face when she listened to anything pleasant, men thought, " Yes, not half bad," and smiled too, while lady visitors could not refrain from seizing her hand in the middle of a conversation, exclaiming in a gush of delight, " You darling! "

The house in which she had lived from her birth upwards, and which was left her in her father's will, was at the extreme end of the town, not far from the Tivoli. In the evenings and at night she could hear the band playing, and the crackling and banging of fireworks, and it seemed to her that it was Kukin struggling with his destiny, storming the entrenchments of his chief foe, the indifferent public; there was a sweet thrill at her heart, she had no desire to sleep, and when he returned home at daybreak, she tapped softly at her bedroom window, and showing him only her face and one shoulder through the curtain, she gave him a friendly smile. . . .

He proposed to her, and they were married. And when he had a closer view of her neck and her plump, fine shoulders, he threw up his hands, and said:

" You darling ! "

He was happy, but as it rained on the day and night of his wedding, his face still retained an expression of despair.

They got on very well together. She used to sit in his office, to look after things in the Tivoli, to put down the accounts and pay the wages. And her rosy cheeks, her sweet, naïve, radiant smile, were to be seen now at the office window, now in the refreshment bar or behind the scenes of the theatre. And already she used to say to her acquaintances that the theatre was the chief and most important thing in life, and that it was only through the drama that one could derive true enjoyment and become cultivated and humane.

" But do you suppose the public understands that ? " she used to say. " What they want is a clown. Yesterday we gave ' Faust Inside Out,' and almost all the boxes were empty ; but if Vanitchka and I had been producing some vulgar thing, I assure you the theatre would have been packed. Tomorrow Vanitchka and I are doing ' Orpheus in Hell.' Do come."

And what Kukin said about the theatre and the actors she repeated. Like him she despised the public for their ignorance and their indifference to art ; she took part in the rehearsals, she corrected the actors, she kept an eye on the behaviour of the musicians, and when there was an unfavourable no-

The Darling

tice in the local paper, she shed tears, and then went to the editor's office to set things right.

The actors were fond of her and used to call her " Vanitchka and I," and " the darling "; she was sorry for them and used to lend them small sums of money, and if they deceived her, she used to shed a few tears in private, but did not complain to her husband.

They got on well in the winter too. They took the theatre in the town for the whole winter, and let it for short terms to a Little Russian company, or to a conjurer, or to a local dramatic society. Olenka grew stouter, and was always beaming with satisfaction, while Kukin grew thinner and yellower, and continually complained of their terrible losses, although he had not done badly all the winter. He used to cough at night, and she used to give him hot raspberry tea or lime-flower water, to rub him with eau-de-Cologne and to wrap him in her warm shawls.

" You're such a sweet pet! " she used to say with perfect sincerity, stroking his hair. " You're such a pretty dear! "

Towards Lent he went to Moscow to collect a new troupe, and without him she could not sleep, but sat all night at her window, looking at the stars, and she compared herself with the hens, who are awake all night and uneasy when the cock is not in the hen-house. Kukin was detained in Moscow, and wrote that he would be back at Easter, adding some instructions about the Tivoli. But on the Sunday before Easter, late in the evening, came a sudden ominous knock at the gate; some one was hammering on the gate as though on a barrel — boom, boom, boom! The drowsy cook went flopping with her bare feet through the puddles, as she ran to open the gate.

" Please open," said some one outside in a thick bass. " There is a telegram for you."

Olenka had received telegrams from her husband before, but this time for some reason she felt numb with terror. With shaking hands she opened the telegram and read as follows:

" Ivan Petrovitch died suddenly to-day. Awaiting immate instructions fufuneral Tuesday."

That was how it was written in the telegram — " fufuneral," and the utterly incomprehensible word " immate." It was signed by the stage manager of the operatic company.

" My darling!" sobbed Olenka. " Vanitchka, my precious, my darling! Why did I ever meet you! Why did I know you and love you! Your poor heart-broken Olenka is all alone without you!"

Kukin's funeral took place on Tuesday in Moscow, Olenka returned home on Wednesday, and as soon as she got indoors she threw herself on her bed and sobbed so loudly that it could be heard next door, and in the street.

" Poor darling!" the neighbours said, as they

The Darling

crossed themselves. " Olga Semyonovna, poor darling! How she does take on!"

Three months later Olenka was coming home from mass, melancholy and in deep mourning. It happened that one of her neighbours, Vassily Andreitch Pustovalov, returning home from church, walked back beside her. He was the manager at Babakayev's, the timber merchant's. He wore a straw hat, a white waistcoat, and a gold watch-chain, and looked more like a country gentleman than a man in trade.

" Everything happens as it is ordained, Olga Semyonovna," he said gravely, with a sympathetic note in his voice; " and if any of our dear ones die, it must be because it is the will of God, so we ought to have fortitude and bear it submissively."

After seeing Olenka to her gate, he said good-bye and went on. All day afterwards she heard his sedately dignified voice, and whenever she shut her eyes she saw his dark beard. She liked him very much. And apparently she had made an impression on him too, for not long afterwards an elderly lady, with whom she was only slightly acquainted, came to drink coffee with her, and as soon as she was seated at table began to talk about Pustovalov, saying that he was an excellent man whom one could thoroughly depend upon, and that any girl would be glad to marry him. Three days later Pustovalov came himself. He did not stay long, only about ten minutes, and he did not say much, but when he left, Olenka loved him — loved him so much that she lay awake all night in a perfect fever, and in the morning she sent for the elderly lady. The match was quickly arranged, and then came the wedding.

Pustovalov and Olenka got on very well together when they were married.

Usually he sat in the office till dinner-time, then he went out on business, while Olenka took his place, and sat in the office till evening, making up accounts and booking orders.

" Timber gets dearer every year; the price rises twenty per cent," she would say to her customers and friends. " Only fancy we used to sell local timber, and now Vassitchka always has to go for wood to the Mogilev district. And the freight! " she would add, covering her cheeks with her hands in horror. " The freight! "

It seemed to her that she had been in the timber trade for ages and ages, and that the most important and necessary thing in life was timber; and there was something intimate and touching to her in the very sound of words such as " baulk," " post," " beam," " pole," " scantling," " batten," " lath," " plank," etc.

At night when she was asleep she dreamed of perfect mountains of planks and boards, and long strings of wagons, carting timber somewhere far away. She dreamed that a whole regiment of six-inch beams forty feet high, standing on end, was marching upon the timber-yard; that logs, beams, and boards knocked together with the resounding crash

The Darling

of dry wood, kept falling and getting up again, piling themselves on each other. Olenka cried out in her sleep, and Pustovalov said to her tenderly: "Olenka, what's the matter, darling? Cross yourself!"

Her husband's ideas were hers. If he thought the room was too hot, or that business was slack, she thought the same. Her husband did not care for entertainments, and on holidays he stayed at home. She did likewise.

"You are always at home or in the office," her friends said to her. "You should go to the theatre, darling, or to the circus."

"Vassitchka and I have no time to go to theatres," she would answer sedately. "We have no time for nonsense. What's the use of these theatres?"

On Saturdays Pustovalov and she used to go to the evening service; on holidays to early mass, and they walked side by side with softened faces as they came home from church. There was a pleasant fragrance about them both, and her silk dress rustled agreeably. At home they drank tea, with fancy bread and jams of various kinds, and afterwards they ate pie. Every day at twelve o'clock there was a savoury smell of beet-root soup and of mutton or duck in their yard, and on fast-days of fish, and no one could pass the gate without feeling hungry. In the office the samovar was always boiling, and customers were regaled with tea and cracknels. Once a week the couple went to the baths and returned side by side, both red in the face.

"Yes, we have nothing to complain of, thank God," Olenka used to say to her acquaintances. "I wish every one were as well off as Vassitchka and I."

When Pustovalov went away to buy wood in the Mogilev district, she missed him dreadfully, lay awake and cried. A young veterinary surgeon in the army, called Smirnin, to whom they had let their lodge, used sometimes to come in in the evening. He used to talk to her and play cards with her, and this entertained her in her husband's absence. She was particularly interested in what he told her of his home life. He was married and had a little boy, but was separated from his wife because she had been unfaithful to him, and now he hated her and used to send her forty roubles a month for the maintenance of their son. And hearing of all this, Olenka sighed and shook her head. She was sorry for him.

"Well, God keep you," she used to say to him at parting, as she lighted him down the stairs with a candle. "Thank you for coming to cheer me up, and may the Mother of God give you health."

And she always expressed herself with the same sedateness and dignity, the same reasonableness, in imitation of her husband. As the veterinary surgeon was disappearing behind the door below, she would say:

"You know, Vladimir Platonitch, you'd better

make it up with your wife. You should forgive her for the sake of your son. You may be sure the little fellow understands."

And when Pustovalov came back, she told him in a low voice about the veterinary surgeon and his unhappy home life, and both sighed and shook their heads and talked about the boy, who, no doubt, missed his father, and by some strange connection of ideas, they went up to the holy ikons, bowed to the ground before them and prayed that God would give them children.

And so the Pustovalovs lived for six years quietly and peaceably in love and complete harmony.

But behold! one winter day after drinking hot tea in the office, Vassily Andreitch went out into the yard without his cap on to see about sending off some timber, caught cold and was taken ill. He had the best doctors, but he grew worse and died after four months' illness. And Olenka was a widow once more.

" I've nobody, now you've left me, my darling," she sobbed, after her husband's funeral. " How can I live without you, in wretchedness and misery! Pity me, good people, all alone in the world!"

She went about dressed in black with long " weepers," and gave up wearing hat and gloves for good. She hardly ever went out, except to church, or to her husband's grave, and led the life of a nun. It was not till six months later that she took off the weepers and opened the shutters of the windows.

She was sometimes seen in the mornings, going with her cook to market for provisions, but what went on in her house and how she lived now could only be surmised. People guessed, from seeing her drinking tea in her garden with the veterinary surgeon, who read the newspaper aloud to her, and from the fact that, meeting a lady she knew at the post-office, she said to her:

" There is no proper veterinary inspection in our town, and that's the cause of all sorts of epidemics. One is always hearing of people's getting infection from the milk supply, or catching diseases from horses and cows. The health of domestic animals ought to be as well cared for as the health of human beings."

She repeated the veterinary surgeon's words, and was of the same opinion as he about everything. It was evident that she could not live a year without some attachment, and had found new happiness in the lodge. In any one else this would have been censured, but no one could think ill of Olenka; everything she did was so natural. Neither she nor the veterinary surgeon said anything to other people of the change in their relations, and tried, indeed, to conceal it, but without success, for Olenka could not keep a secret. When he had visitors, men serving in his regiment, and she poured out tea or served the supper, she would begin talking of the cattle plague, of the foot and mouth disease, and of the municipal slaughter-houses. He was dreadfully embarrassed, and when the guests had gone, he would seize her by the hand and hiss angrily:

"I've asked you before not to talk about what you don't understand. When we veterinary surgeons are talking among ourselves, please don't put your word in. It's really annoying."

And she would look at him with astonishment and dismay, and ask him in alarm: "But, Voloditchka, what *am* I to talk about?"

And with tears in her eyes she would embrace him, begging him not to be angry, and they were both happy.

But this happiness did not last long. The veterinary surgeon departed, departed for ever with his regiment, when it was transferred to a distant place — to Siberia, it may be. And Olenka was left alone.

Now she was absolutely alone. Her father had long been dead, and his armchair lay in the attic, covered with dust and lame of one leg. She got thinner and plainer, and when people met her in the street they did not look at her as they used to, and did not smile to her; evidently her best years were over and left behind, and now a new sort of life had begun for her, which did not bear thinking about. In the evening Olenka sat in the porch, and heard the band playing and the fireworks popping in the Tivoli, but now the sound stirred no response. She looked into her yard without interest, thought of nothing, wished for nothing, and afterwards, when night came on she went to bed and dreamed of her empty yard. She ate and drank as it were unwillingly.

And what was worst of all, she had no opinions of any sort. She saw the objects about her and understood what she saw, but could not form any opinion about them, and did not know what to talk about. And how awful it is not to have any opinions! One sees a bottle, for instance, or the rain, or a peasant driving in his cart, but what the bottle is for, or the rain, or the peasant, and what is the meaning of it, one can't say, and could not even for a thousand roubles. When she had Kukin, or Pustovalov, or the veterinary surgeon, Olenka could explain everything, and give her opinion about anything you like, but now there was the same emptiness in her brain and in her heart as there was in her yard outside. And it was as harsh and as bitter as wormwood in the mouth.

Little by little the town grew in all directions. The road became a street, and where the Tivoli and the timber-yard had been, there were new turnings and houses. How rapidly time passes! Olenka's house grew dingy, the roof got rusty, the shed sank on one side, and the whole yard was overgrown with docks and stinging-nettles. Olenka herself had grown plain and elderly; in summer she sat in the porch, and her soul, as before, was empty and dreary and full of bitterness. In winter she sat at her window and looked at the snow. When she caught the scent of spring, or heard the chime of the church bells, a sudden rush of memories from the past came over her, there was a tender ache in her heart, and her eyes brimmed over with tears; but this was only for a minute, and then came emptiness again and the sense of the futility of life. The black kitten, Briska, rubbed against her and purred softly, but Olenka was not touched by these feline caresses. That was not what she needed. She wanted a love that would absorb her whole being, her whole soul and reason — that would give her ideas and an object in life, and would warm her old blood. And she would shake the kitten off her skirt and say with vexation:

" Get along; I don't want you! "

And so it was, day after day and year after year, and no joy, and no opinions. Whatever Mavra, the cook, said she accepted.

One hot July day, towards evening, just as the cattle were being driven away, and the whole yard was full of dust, some one suddenly knocked at the gate. Olenka went to open it herself and was dumbfounded when she looked out: she saw Smirnin, the veterinary surgeon, grey-headed, and dressed as a civilian. She suddenly remembered everything. She could not help crying and letting her head fall on his breast without uttering a word, and in the violence of her feeling she did not notice how they both walked into the house and sat down to tea.

" My dear Vladimir Platonitch! What fate has

brought you?" she muttered, trembling with joy.

"I want to settle here for good, Olga Semyon-ovna," he told her. "I have resigned my post, and have come to settle down and try my luck on my own account. Besides, it's time for my boy to go to school. He's a big boy. I am reconciled with my wife, you know."

"Where is she?" asked Olenka.

"She's at the hotel with the boy, and I'm looking for lodgings."

"Good gracious, my dear soul! Lodgings? Why not have my house? Why shouldn't that suit you? Why, my goodness, I wouldn't take any rent!" cried Olenka in a flutter, beginning to cry again. "You live here, and the lodge will do nicely for me. Oh dear! how glad I am!"

Next day the roof was painted and the walls were whitewashed, and Olenka, with her arms akimbo, walked about the yard giving directions. Her face was beaming with her old smile, and she was brisk and alert as though she had waked from a long sleep. The veterinary's wife arrived — a thin, plain lady, with short hair and a peevish expression. With her was her little Sasha, a boy of ten, small for his age, blue-eyed, chubby, with dimples in his cheeks. And scarcely had the boy walked into the yard when he ran after the cat, and at once there was the sound of his gay, joyous laugh.

"Is that your puss, auntie?" he asked Olenka.

The Darling

"When she has little ones, do give us a kitten. Mamma is awfully afraid of mice."

Olenka talked to him, and gave him tea. Her heart warmed and there was a sweet ache in her bosom, as though the boy had been her own child. And when he sat at the table in the evening, going over his lessons, she looked at him with deep tenderness and pity as she murmured to herself:

"You pretty pet! . . . my precious! . . . Such a fair little thing, and so clever."

"'An island is a piece of land which is entirely surrounded by water,'" he read aloud.

"An island is a piece of land," she repeated, and this was the first opinion to which she gave utterance with positive conviction after so many years of silence and dearth of ideas.

Now she had opinions of her own, and at supper she talked to Sasha's parents, saying how difficult the lessons were at the high schools, but that yet the high-school was better than a commercial one, since with a high-school education all careers were open to one, such as being a doctor or an engineer.

Sasha began going to the high school. His mother departed to Harkov to her sister's and did not return; his father used to go off every day to inspect cattle, and would often be away from home for three days together, and it seemed to Olenka as though Sasha was entirely abandoned, that he was not wanted at home, that he was being starved, and she carried him off to her lodge and gave him a little room there.

And for six months Sasha had lived in the lodge with her. Every morning Olenka came into his bedroom and found him fast asleep, sleeping noiselessly with his hand under his cheek. She was sorry to wake him.

" Sashenka," she would say mournfully, " get up, darling. It's time for school."

He would get up, dress and say his prayers, and then sit down to breakfast, drink three glasses of tea, and eat two large cracknels and half a buttered roll. All this time he was hardly awake and a little ill-humoured in consequence.

" You don't quite know your fable, Sashenka," Olenka would say, looking at him as though he were about to set off on a long journey. " What a lot of trouble I have with you! You must work and do your best, darling, and obey your teachers."

" Oh, do leave me alone! " Sasha would say.

Then he would go down the street to school, a little figure, wearing a big cap and carrying a satchel on his shoulder. Olenka would follow him noiselessly.

" Sashenka! " she would call after him, and she would pop into his hand a date or a caramel. When he reached the street where the school was, he would feel ashamed of being followed by a tall, stout woman; he would turn round and say:

" You'd better go home, auntie. I can go the rest of the way alone."

The Darling

She would stand still and look after him fixedly till he had disappeared at the school-gate.

Ah, how she loved him! Of her former attachments not one had been so deep; never had her soul surrendered to any feeling so spontaneously, so disinterestedly, and so joyously as now that her maternal instincts were aroused. For this little boy with the dimple in his cheek and the big school cap, she would have given her whole life, she would have given it with joy and tears of tenderness. Why? Who can tell why?

When she had seen the last of Sasha, she returned home, contented and serene, brimming over with love; her face, which had grown younger during the last six months, smiled and beamed; people meeting her looked at her with pleasure.

" Good-morning, Olga Semyonovna, darling. How are you, darling? "

" The lessons at the high school are very difficult now," she would relate at the market. " It's too much; in the first class yesterday they gave him a fable to learn by heart, and a Latin translation and a problem. You know it's too much for a little chap."

And she would begin talking about the teachers, the lessons, and the school books, saying just what Sasha said.

At three o'clock they had dinner together: in the evening they learned their lessons together and cried. When she put him to bed, she would stay a long time making the Cross over him and murmuring a prayer;

then she would go to bed and dream of that far-away misty future when Sasha would finish his studies and become a doctor or an engineer, would have a big house of his own with horses and a carriage, would get married and have children. . . . She would fall asleep still thinking of the same thing, and tears would run down her cheeks from her closed eyes, while the black cat lay purring beside her: "Mrr, mrr, mrr."

Suddenly there would come a loud knock at the gate.

Olenka would wake up breathless with alarm, her heart throbbing. Half a minute later would come another knock.

"It must be a telegram from Harkov," she would think, beginning to tremble from head to foot. "Sasha's mother is sending for him from Harkov. . . . Oh, mercy on us!"

She was in despair. Her head, her hands, and her feet would turn chill, and she would feel that she was the most unhappy woman in the world. But another minute would pass, voices would be heard: it would turn out to be the veterinary surgeon coming home from the club.

"Well, thank God!" she would think.

And gradually the load in her heart would pass off, and she would feel at ease. She would go back to bed thinking of Sasha, who lay sound asleep in the next room, sometimes crying out in his sleep:

"I'll give it you! Get away! Shut up!"

1899

THE HUSBAND

IN the course of the manœuvres the N—— cavalry regiment halted for a night at the district town of K——. Such an event as the visit of officers always has the most exciting and inspiring effect on the inhabitants of provinicial towns. The shopkeepers dream of getting rid of the rusty sausages and " best brand " sardines that have been lying for ten years on their shelves; the inns and restaurants keep open all night; the Military Commandant, his secretary, and the local garrison put on their best uniforms; the police flit to and fro like mad, while the effect on the ladies is beyond all description.

The ladies of K——, hearing the regiment approaching, forsook their pans of boiling jam and ran into the street. Forgetting their morning *deshabille* and general untidiness, they rushed breathless with excitement to meet the regiment, and listened greedily to the band playing the march. Looking at their pale, ecstatic faces, one might have thought those strains came from some heavenly choir rather than from a military brass band.

" The regiment! " they cried joyfully. " The regiment is coming! "

What could this unknown regiment that came by chance to-day and would depart at dawn to-morrow mean to them?

Afterwards, when the officers were standing in the middle of the square, and, with their hands behind them, discussing the question of billets, all the ladies were gathered together at the examining magistrate's and vying with one another in their criticisms of the regiment. They already knew, goodness knows how, that the colonel was married, but not living with his wife; that the senior officer's wife had a baby born dead every year; that the adjutant was hopelessly in love with some countess, and had even once attempted suicide. They knew everything. When a pock-marked soldier in a red shirt darted past the windows, they knew for certain that it was Lieutenant Rymzov's orderly running about the town, trying to get some English bitter ale on tick for his master. They had only caught a passing glimpse of the officers' backs, but had already decided that there was not one handsome or interesting man among them. . . . Having talked to their hearts' content, they sent for the Military Commandant and the committee of the club, and instructed them at all costs to make arrangements for a dance.

Their wishes were carried out. At nine o'clock in the evening the military band was playing in the street before the club, while in the club itself the officers were dancing with the ladies of K——. The ladies felt as though they were on wings. Intoxicated by the dancing, the music, and the clank of spurs, they threw themselves heart and soul into making the acquaintance of their new partners, and quite forgot their old civilian friends. Their fathers and husbands, forced temporarily into the background, crowded round the meagre refreshment table in the entrance hall. All these government cashiers, secretaries, clerks, and superintendents — stale, sickly-looking, clumsy figures — were perfectly well aware of their inferiority. They did not even enter the ball-room, but contented themselves with watching their wives and daughters in the distance dancing with the accomplished and graceful officers.

Among the husbands was Shalikov, the tax-collector — a narrow, spiteful soul, given to drink, with a big, closely cropped head, and thick, protruding lips. He had had a university education; there had been a time when he used to read progressive literature and sing students' songs, but now, as he said of himself, he was a tax-collector and nothing more.

He stood leaning against the doorpost, his eyes fixed on his wife, Anna Pavlovna, a little brunette of thirty, with a long nose and a pointed chin. Tightly laced, with her face carefully powdered, she danced without pausing for breath — danced till she was ready to drop exhausted. But though she was exhausted in body, her spirit was inexhaustible. . . . One could see as she danced that her thoughts were with the past, that faraway past when she used to dance at the " College for Young Ladies," dreaming of a life of luxury and gaiety, and never doubting that her husband was to be a prince or, at the worst, a baron.

The tax-collector watched, scowling with spite. . . .

It was not jealousy he was feeling. He was ill-humoured — first, because the room was taken up with dancing and there was nowhere he could play a game of cards; secondly, because he could not endure the sound of wind instruments; and, thirdly, because he fancied the officers treated the civilians somewhat too casually and disdainfully. But what above everything revolted him and moved him to indignation was the expression of happiness on his wife's face.

"It makes me sick to look at her!" he muttered. "Going on for forty, and nothing to boast of at any time, and she must powder her face and lace herself up! And frizzing her hair! Flirting and making faces, and fancying she's doing the thing in style! Ugh! you're a pretty figure, upon my soul!"

Anna Pavlovna was so lost in the dance that she did not once glance at her husband.

"Of course not! Where do we poor country bumpkins come in!" sneered the tax-collector. "We are at a discount now. . . . We're clumsy seals, unpolished provincial bears, and she's the queen of the ball! She has kept enough of her looks to please even officers. . . . They'd not object to making love to her, I dare say!"

During the mazurka the tax-collector's face twitched with spite. A black-haired officer with prominent eyes and Tartar cheekbones danced the mazurka with Anna Pavlovna. Assuming a stern expression, he worked his legs with gravity and feeling, and so crooked his knees that he looked like a jack-a-dandy pulled by strings, while Anna Pavlovna, pale and thrilled, bending her figure languidly and turning her eyes up, tried to look as though she scarcely touched the floor, and evidently felt herself that she was not on earth, not at the local club, but somewhere far, far away — in the clouds. Not only her face but her whole figure was expressive of beatitude. . . . The tax-collector could endure it no longer; he felt a desire to jeer at that beatitude, to make Anna Pavlovna feel that she had forgotten herself, that life was by no means so delightful as she fancied now in her excitement. . . .

" You wait; I'll teach you to smile so blissfully," he muttered. " You are not a boarding-school miss, you are not a girl. An old fright ought to realise she is a fright! "

Petty feelings of envy, vexation, wounded vanity, of that small, provincial misanthropy engendered in petty officials by vodka and a sedentary life, swarmed in his heart like mice. Waiting for the end of the mazurka, he went into the hall and walked up to his wife. Anna Pavlovna was sitting with her partner, and, flirting her fan and coquettishly dropping her eyelids, was describing how she used to dance in Petersburg (her lips were pursed up like a rosebud, and she pronounced " at home in Pütürsburg ").

" Anyuta, let us go home," croaked the tax-collector.

Seeing her husband standing before her, Anna Pavlovna started as though recalling the fact that she had a husband; then she flushed all over: she felt ashamed that she had such a sickly-looking, ill-humoured, ordinary husband.

. " Let us go home," repeated the tax-collector.

" Why? It's quite early! "

" I beg you to come home!" said the tax-collector deliberately, with a spiteful expression.

"Why? Has anything happened?" Anna Pavlovna asked in a flutter.

"Nothing has happened, but I wish you to go home at once. . . . I wish it; that's enough, and without further talk, please."

Anna Pavlovna was not afraid of her husband, but she felt ashamed on account of her partner, who was looking at her husband with surprise and amusement. She got up and moved a little apart with her husband.

"What notion is this?" she began. "Why go home? Why, it's not eleven o'clock."

"I wish it, and that's enough. Come along, and that's all about it."

"Don't be silly! Go home alone if you want to."

"All right; then I shall make a scene."

The tax-collector saw the look of beatitude gradually vanish from his wife's face, saw how ashamed and miserable she was — and he felt a little happier.

"Why do you want me at once?" asked his wife.

"I don't want you, but I wish you to be at home. I wish it, that's all."

At first Anna Pavlovna refused to hear of it, then she began entreating her husband to let her stay just another half-hour; then, without knowing why, she began to apologise, to protest — and all in a whisper, with a smile, that the spectators might not suspect that she was having a tiff with her husband. She began assuring him she would not stay long, only another ten minutes, only five minutes; but the tax-collector stuck obstinately to his point.

"Stay if you like," he said, "but I'll make a scene if you do."

And as she talked to her husband Anna Pavlovna looked thinner, older, plainer. Pale, biting her lips, and almost crying, she went out to the entry and began putting on her things.

"You are not going?" asked the ladies in surprise. "Anna Pavlovna, you are not going, dear?"

"Her head aches," said the tax-collector for his wife.

Coming out of the club, the husband and wife walked all the way home in silence. The tax-collector walked behind his wife, and watching her downcast, sorrowful, humiliated little figure, he recalled the look of beatitude which had so irritated him at the club, and the consciousness that the beatitude was gone filled his soul with triumph. He was pleased and satisfied, and at the same time he felt the lack of something; he would have liked to go back to the club and make every one feel dreary and miserable, so that all might know how stale and worthless life is when you walk along the streets in the dark and hear the slush of the mud under your feet, and when you know that you will wake up next morning with nothing to look forward to but vodka and cards. Oh, how awful it is!

And Anna Pavlovna could scarcely walk. . . . She was still under the influence of the dancing, the music, the talk, the lights, and the noise; she asked herself as she walked along why God had thus afflicted her. She felt miserable, insulted, and choking with hate as she listened to her husband's heavy footsteps. She was silent, trying to think of the most offensive, biting, and venomous word she could hurl at her husband, and at the same time she was fully aware that no word could penetrate her tax-collector's hide. What did he care for words? Her bitterest enemy could not have contrived for her a more helpless position.

And meanwhile the band was playing and the darkness was full of the most rousing, intoxicating dance-tunes.

1886

ARIADNE

On the deck of a steamer sailing from Odessa to Sevastopol, a rather good-looking gentleman, with a little round beard, came up to me to smoke, and said:

"Notice those Germans sitting near the shelter? Whenever Germans or Englishmen get together, they talk about the crops, the price of wool, or their personal affairs. But for some reason or other when we Russians get together we never discuss anything but women and abstract subjects — but especially women."

This gentleman's face was familiar to me already. We had returned from abroad the evening before in the same train, and at Volotchisk when the luggage was being examined by the Customs, I saw him standing with a lady, his travelling companion, before a perfect mountain of trunks and baskets filled with ladies' clothes, and I noticed how embarrassed and downcast he was when he had to pay duty on some piece of silk frippery, and his companion protested and threatened to make a complaint. Afterwards, on the way to Odessa, I saw him carrying little pies and oranges to the ladies' compartment.

It was rather damp; the vessel swayed a little, and the ladies had retired to their cabins.

The gentleman with the little round beard sat down beside me and continued:

"Yes, when Russians come together they discuss nothing but abstract subjects and women. We are so intellectual, so solemn, that we utter nothing but truths and can discuss only questions of a lofty order. The Russian actor does not know how to be funny; he acts with profundity even in a farce. We're just the same: when we have got to talk of trifles we treat them only from an exalted point of view. It comes from a lack of boldness, sincerity, and simplicity. We talk so often about women, I fancy, because we are dissatisfied. We take too ideal a view of women, and make demands out of all proportion with what reality can give us; we get something utterly different from what we want, and the result is dissatisfaction, shattered hopes, and inward suffering, and if any one is suffering, he's bound to talk of it. It does not bore you to go on with this conversation?"

"No, not in the least."

"In that case, allow me to introduce myself," said my companion, rising from his seat a little: "Ivan Ilyitch Shamohin, a Moscow landowner of a sort. . . . You I know very well."

He sat down and went on, looking at me with a genuine and friendly expression:

"A mediocre philosopher, like Max Nordau, would explain these incessant conversations about women as a form of erotic madness, or would put it down to our having been slave-owners and so on; I take quite a different view of it. I repeat, we are dissatisfied because we are idealists. We want the creatures who bear us and our children to be superior to us and to everything in the world. When we are young we adore and poeticize those with whom we are in love: love and happiness with us are synonyms. Among us in Russia marriage without love it despised, sensuality is ridiculed and inspires repulsion, and the greatest success is enjoyed by those tales and novels in which women are beautiful, poetical, and exalted; and if the Russian has been for years in ecstasies over Raphael's Madonna, or is eager for the emancipation of women, I assure you there is no affectation about it. But the trouble is that when we have been married or been intimate with a woman for some two or three years, we begin to feel deceived and disillusioned: we pair off with others, and again — disappointment, again — repulsion, and in the long run we become convinced that women are lying, trivial, fussy, unfair, undeveloped, cruel — in fact, far from being superior, are immeasurably inferior to us men. And in our dissatisfaction and disappointment there is nothing left for us but to grumble and talk about what we've been so cruelly deceived in."

While Shamohin was talking I noticed that the Russian language and our Russian surroundings gave him great pleasure. This was probably because he had been very homesick abroad. Though he praised the Russians and ascribed to them a rare idealism, he did not disparage foreigners, and that I put down to his credit. It could be seen, too, that there was some uneasiness in his soul, that he wanted to talk more of himself than of women, and that I was in for a long story in the nature of a confession. And when we had asked for a bottle of wine and had each of us drunk a glass, this was how he did in fact begin:

"I remember in a novel of Weltmann's some one says, 'So that's the story!' and some one else answers, 'No, that's not the story — that's only the introduction to the story.' In the same way what I've said so far is only the introduction; what I really want to tell you is my own love story. Excuse me, I must ask you again; it won't bore you to listen?"

I told him it would not, and he went on:

The scene of my story is laid in the Moscow province in one of its northern districts. The scenery there, I must tell you, is exquisite. Our homestead is on the high bank of a rapid stream, where the water chatters noisily day and night: imagine a big old garden, neat flower-beds, beehives, a kitchen-garden, and below it a river with leafy willows, which, when there is a heavy dew on them, have a lustreless look as though they had turned grey; and on the other side a meadow, and beyond the meadow on the upland a terrible, dark pine forest. In that

forest delicious, reddish agarics grow in endless profusion, and elks still live in its deepest recesses.
When I am nailed up in my coffin I believe I shall
still dream of those early mornings, you know, when
the sun hurts your eyes: or the wonderful spring
evenings when the nightingales and the landrails call
in the garden and beyond the garden, and sounds of
the harmonica float across from the village, while
they play the piano indoors and the stream babbles
. . . when there is such music, in fact, that one
wants at the same time to cry and to sing aloud.

We have not much arable land, but our pasture
makes up for it, and with the forest yields about
two thousand roubles a year. I am the only son
of my father; we are both modest persons, and with
my father's pension that sum was amply sufficient
for us.

The first three years after finishing at the university I spent in the country, looking after the estate
and constantly expecting to be elected on some local
assembly; but what was most important, I was violently in love with an extraordinarily beautiful and
fascinating girl. She was the sister of our neighbour, Kotlovitch, a ruined landowner who had on
his estate pine-apples, marvellous peaches, lightning
conductors, a fountain in the courtyard, and at the
same time not a farthing in his pocket. He did
nothing and knew how to do nothing. He was as
flabby as though he had been made of boiled turnip;
he used to doctor the peasants by homœopathy and

was interested in spiritualism. He was, however, a man of great delicacy and mildness, and by no means a fool, but I have no fondness for these gentlemen who converse with spirits and cure peasant women by magnetism. In the first place, the ideas of people who are not intellectually free are always in a muddle, and it's extremely difficult to talk to them; and, secondly, they usually love no one, and have nothing to do with women, and their mysticism has an unpleasant effect on sensitive people. I did not care for his appearance either. He was tall, stout, white-skinned, with a little head, little shining eyes, and chubby white fingers. He did not shake hands, but kneaded one's hands in his. And he was always apologising. If he asked for anything it was " Excuse me "; if he gave you anything it was " Excuse me " too.

As for his sister, she was a character out of a different opera. I must explain that I had not been acquainted with the Kotlovitches in my childhood and early youth, for my father had been a professor at N., and we had for many years lived away. When I did make their acquaintance the girl was twenty-two, had left school long before, and had spent two or three years in Moscow with a wealthy aunt who brought her out into society. When I was introduced and first had to talk to her, what struck me most of all was her rare and beautiful name — Ariadne. It suited her so wonderfully! She was a brunette, very thin, very slender, supple, elegant, and extremely graceful, with refined and exceedingly noble features. Her eyes were shining, too, but her brother's shone with a cold sweetness, mawkish as sugar-candy, while hers had the glow of youth, proud and beautiful. She conquered me on the first day of our acquaintance, and indeed it was inevitable. My first impression was so overwhelming that to this day I cannot get rid of my illusions; I am still tempted to imagine that nature had some grand, marvellous design when she created that girl.

Ariadne's voice, her walk, her hat, even her footprints on the sandy bank where she used to angle for gudgeon, filled me with delight and a passionate hunger for life. I judged of her spiritual being from her lovely face and lovely figure, and every word, every smile of Ariadne's bewitched me, conquered me and forced me to believe in the loftiness of her soul. She was friendly, ready to talk, gay and simple in her manners. She had a poetic belief in God, made poetic reflections about death, and there was such a wealth of varying shades in her spiritual organisation that even her faults seemed in her to carry with them peculiar, charming qualities. Suppose she wanted a new horse and had no money — what did that matter? Something might be sold or pawned, or if the steward swore that nothing could possibly be sold or pawned, the iron roofs might be torn off the lodges and taken to the factory, or at the very busiest time the farm-horses might be driven to the market and sold there for next to nothing. These unbridled desires reduced the whole household to despair at times, but she expressed them with such refinement that everything was forgiven her; all things were permitted her as to a goddess or to Cæsar's wife. My love was pathetic and was soon noticed by every one — my father, the neighbours, and the peasants — and they all sympathised with me. When I stood the workmen vodka, they would bow and say: " May the Kotlovitch young lady be your bride, please God! "

And Ariadne herself knew that I loved her. She would often ride over on horseback or drive in the char-à-banc to see us, and would spend whole days with me and my father. She made great friends with the old man, and he even taught her to bicycle, which was his favourite amusement.

I remember helping her to get on the bicycle one evening, and she looked so lovely that I felt as though I were burning my hands when I touched her. I shuddered with rapture, and when the two of them, my old father and she, both looking so handsome and elegant, bicycled side by side along the main road, a black horse ridden by the steward dashed aside on meeting them, and it seemed to me that it dashed aside because it too was overcome by her beauty. My love, my worship, touched Ariadne and softened her; she had a passionate longing to be captivated like me and to respond with the same love. It was so poetical!

But she was incapable of really loving as I did,

for she was cold and already somewhat corrupted. There was a demon in her, whispering to her day and night that she was enchanting, adorable; and, having no definite idea for what object she was created, or for what purpose life had been given her, she never pictured herself in the future except as very wealthy and distinguished; she had visions of balls, races, liveries, of sumptuous drawing-rooms, of a salon of her own, and of a perfect swarm of counts, princes, ambassadors, celebrated painters and artists, all of them adoring her and in ecstasies over her beauty and her dresses. . . .

This thirst for personal success, and this continual concentration of the mind in one direction, makes people cold, and Ariadne was cold — to me, to nature, and to music. Meanwhile time was passing, and still there were no ambassadors on the scene. Ariadne went on living with her brother, the spiritualist: things went from bad to worse, so that she had nothing to buy hats and dresses with, and had to resort to all sorts of tricks and dodges to conceal her poverty.

As luck would have it, a certain Prince Maktuev, a wealthy man but an utterly insignificant person, had paid his addresses to her when she was living at her aunt's in Moscow. She had refused him, point-blank. But now she was fretted by the worm of repentance that she had refused him; just as a peasant pouts with repulsion at a mug of kvass with cockroaches in it but yet drinks it, so she frowned disdainfully at the recollection of the prince, and yet she would say to me: "Say what you like, there is something inexplicable, fascinating, in a title. . . ."

She dreamed of a title, of a brilliant position, and at the same time she did not want to let me go. However one may dream of ambassadors one's heart is not a stone, and one has wistful feelings for one's youth. Ariadne tried to fall in love, made a show of being in love, and even swore that she loved me. But I am a highly strung and sensitive man; when I am loved I feel it even at a distance, without vows and assurances; at once I felt as it were a coldness in the air, and when she talked to me of love, it seemed to me as though I were listening to the singing of a metal nightingale. Ariadne was herself aware that she was lacking in something. She was vexed and more than once I saw her cry. Another time — can you imagine it? — all of a sudden she embraced me and kissed me. It happened in the evening on the river-bank, and I saw by her eyes that she did not love me, but was embracing me from curiosity, to test herself and to see what came of it. And I felt dreadful. I took her hands and said to her in despair: "These caresses without love cause me suffering!"

"What a queer fellow you are!" she said with annoyance, and walked away.

Another year or two might have passed, and in all probability I should have married her, and so

my story would have ended, but fate was pleased
to arrange our romance differently. It happened
that a new personage appeared on our horizon.
Ariadne's brother had a visit from an old university
friend called Mihail Ivanitch Lubkov, a charming
man of whom coachmen and footmen used to say:
" An entertaining gentleman." He was a man of
medium height, lean and bald, with a face like a
good-natured bourgeois, not interesting, but pale
and presentable, with a stiff, well-kept moustache,
with a neck like gooseskin, and a big Adam's apple.
He used to wear pince-nez on a wide black ribbon,
lisped, and could not pronounce either *r* or *l*. He
was always in good spirits, everything amused
him.

He had made an exceedingly foolish marriage
at twenty, and had acquired two houses in Moscow
as part of his wife's dowry. He began doing them
up and building a bath-house, and was completely
ruined. Now his wife and four children lodged in
Oriental Buildings in great poverty, and he had to
support them — and this amused him. He was thir-
ty-six and his wife was by now forty-two, and that,
too, amused him. His mother, a conceited, sulky
personage, with aristocratic pretensions, despised his
wife and lived apart with a perfect menagerie of
cats and dogs, and he had to allow her seventy-five
roubles a month also; he was, too, a man of taste,
liked lunching at the Slavyansky Bazaar and dining
at the Hermitage; he needed a great deal of money,

but his uncle only allowed him two thousand roubles a year, which was not enough, and for days together he would run about Moscow with his tongue out, as the saying is, looking for some one to borrow from — and this, too, amused him. He had come to Kotlovitch to find in the lap of nature, as he said, a rest from family life. At dinner, at supper, and on our walks, he talked about his wife, about his mother, about his creditors, about the bailiffs, and laughed at them; he laughed at himself and assured us that, thanks to his talent for borrowing, he had made a great number of agreeable acquaintances. He laughed without ceasing and we laughed too. Moreover, in his company we spent our time differently. I was more inclined to quiet, so to say idyllic pleasures; I liked fishing, evening walks, gathering mushrooms; Lubkov preferred picnics, fireworks, hunting. He used to get up picnics three times a week, and Ariadne, with an earnest and inspired face, used to write a list of oysters, champagne, sweets, and used to send me into Moscow to get them, without inquiring, of course, whether I had money. And at the picnics there were toasts and laughter, and again mirthful descriptions of how old his wife was, what fat lap-dogs his mother had, and what charming people his creditors were. . . .

Lubkov was fond of nature, but he regarded it as something long familiar and at the same time, in reality, infinitely beneath himself and created for his pleasure. He would sometimes stand still before some magnificent landscape and say: "It would be nice to have tea here."

One day, seeing Ariadne walking in the distance with a parasol, he nodded towards her and said:

"She's thin, and that's what I like; I don't like fat women."

This made me wince. I asked him not to speak like that about women before me. He looked at me in surprise and said:

"What is there amiss in my liking thin women and not caring for fat ones?"

I made no answer. Afterwards, being in very good spirits and a trifle elevated, he said:

"I've noticed Ariadne Grigoryevna likes you. I can't understand why you don't go in and win."

His words made me feel uncomfortable, and with some embarrassment I told him how I looked at love and women.

"I don't know," he sighed; "to my thinking, a woman's a woman and a man's a man. Ariadne Grigoryevna may be poetical and exalted, as you say, but it doesn't follow that she must be superior to the laws of nature. You see for yourself that she has reached the age when she must have a husband or a lover. I respect women as much as you do, but I don't think certain relations exclude poetry. Poetry's one thing and love is another. It's just the same as it is in farming. The beauty of nature is one thing and the income from your forests or fields is quite another."

When Ariadne and I were fishing, Lubkov would lie on the sand close by and make fun of me, or lecture me on the conduct of life.

" I wonder, my dear sir, how you can live without a love affair," he would say. " You are young, handsome, interesting — in fact, you're a man not to be sniffed at, yet you live like a monk. Och! I can't stand these fellows who are old at twenty-eight! I'm nearly ten years older than you are, and yet which of us is the younger? Ariadne Grigoryevna, which? "

" You, of course," Ariadne answered him.

And when he was bored with our silence and the attention with which we stared at our floats he went home, and she said, looking at me angrily:

" You're really not a man, but a mush, God forgive me! A man ought to be able to be carried away by his feelings, he ought to be able to be mad, to make mistakes, to suffer! A woman will forgive you audacity and insolence, but she will never forgive your reasonableness! "

She was angry in earnest, and went on:

" To succeed, a man must be resolute and bold. Lubkov is not so handsome as you are, but he is more interesting. He will always succeed with women because he's not like you; he's a man. . . ."

And there was actually a note of exasperation in her voice.

One day at supper she began saying, not addressing, me that if she were a man she would not stag-

nate in the country, but would travel, would spend
the winter somewhere aboard — in Italy, for instance. Oh, Italy! At this point my father unconsciously poured oil on the flames; he began telling
us at length about Italy, how splendid it was there,
the exquisite scenery, the museums. Ariadne suddenly conceived a burning desire to go to Italy. She
positively brought her fist down on the table and
her eyes flashed as she said: " I must go! "

After that came conversations every day about
Italy: how splendid it would be in Italy — ah, Italy!
— oh, Italy! And when Ariadne looked at me over
her shoulder, from her cold and obstinate expression I saw that in her dreams she had already conquered Italy with all its salons, celebrated foreigners
and tourists, and there was no holding her back now.
I advised her to wait a little, to put off her tour for
a year or two, but she frowned disdainfully and said:
" You're as prudent as an old woman! "

Lubkov was in favour of the tour. He said it
could be done very cheaply, and he, too, would go
to Italy and have a rest there from family life.

I behaved, I confess, as naïvely as a schoolboy.
Not from jealousy, but from a foreboding of something terrible and extraordinary, I tried as far as
possible not to leave them alone together, and they
made fun of me. For instance, when I went in they
would pretend they had just been kissing one another, and so on.

But lo and behold, one fine morning, her plump,

white-skinned brother, the spiritualist, made his appearance and expressed his desire to speak to me alone.

He was a man without will; in spite of his education and his delicacy he could never resist reading another person's letter, if it lay before him on the table. And now he admitted that he had by chance read a letter of Lubkov's to Ariadne.

"From that letter I learned that she is very shortly going abroad. My dear fellow, I am very much upset! Explain it to me for goodness' sake. I can make nothing of it!"

As he said this he breathed hard, breathing straight in my face and smelling of boiled beef.

"Excuse me for revealing the secret of this letter to you, but you are Ariadne's friend, she respects you. Perhaps you know something of it. She wants to go away, but with whom? Mr. Lubkov is proposing to go with her. Excuse me, but this is very strange of Mr. Lubkov; he is a married man, he has children, and yet he is making a declaration of love; he is writing to Ariadne ' darling.' Excuse me, but it is so strange!"

I turned cold all over; my hands and feet went numb and I felt an ache in my chest, as if a three-cornered stone had been driven into it. Kotlovitch sank helplessly into an easy-chair, and his hands fell limply at his sides.

"What can I do?" I inquired.

"Persuade her. . . . Impress her mind. . . .

Ariadne

Just consider, what is Lubkov to her? Is he a match for her? Oh, good God! How awful it is, how awful it is!" he went on, clutching his head. " She has had such splendid offers — Prince Maktuev and . . . and others. The prince adores her, and only last Wednesday week his late grandfather, Ilarion, declared positively that Ariadne would be his wife — positively! His grandfather Ilarion is dead, but he is a wonderfully intelligent person; we call up his spirit every day."

After this conversation I lay awake all night and thought of shooting myself. In the morning I wrote five letters and tore them all up. Then I sobbed in the barn. Then I took a sum of money from my father and set off for the Caucasus without saying good-bye.

Of course, a woman's a woman and a man's a man, but can all that be as simple in our day as it was before the Flood, and can it be that I, a cultivated man endowed with a complex spiritual organisation, ought to explain the intense attraction I feel towards a woman simply by the fact that her bodily formation is different from mine? Oh, how awful that would be! I want to believe that in his struggle with nature the genius of man has struggled with physical love too, as with an enemy, and that, if he has not conquered it, he has at least succeeded in tangling it in a net-work of illusions of brother-hood and love; and for me, at any rate, it is no longer a simple instinct of my animal nature as with a dog or a toad, but is real love, and every embrace is spiritualised by a pure impulse of the heart and respect for the woman. In reality, a disgust for the animal instinct has been trained for ages in hundreds of generations; it is inherited by me in my blood and forms part of my nature, and if I poetize love, is not that as natural and inevitable in our day as my ears' not being able to move and my not being covered with fur? I fancy that's how the majority of civilised people look at it, so that the absence of the moral, poetical element in love is treated in these days as a phenomenon, as a sign of atavism; they say it is a symptom of degeneracy, of many forms of insanity. It is true that, in poetizing love, we assume in those we love qualities that are lacking in them, and that is a source of continual mistakes and continual miseries for us. But to my thinking it is better, even so; that is, it is better to suffer than to find complacency on the basis of woman being woman and man being man.

In Tiflis I received a letter from my father. He wrote that Ariadne Grigoryevna had on such a day gone abroad, intending to spend the whole winter away. A month later I returned home. It was by now autumn. Every week Ariadne sent my father extremely interesting letters on scented paper, written in an excellent literary style. It is my opinion that every woman can be a writer. Ariadne described in great detail how it had not been easy for her to make it up with her aunt and induce the latter to give her a thousand roubles for the journey, and what a long time she had spent in Moscow trying to find an old lady, a distant relation, in order to persuade her to go with her. Such a profusion of detail suggested fiction, and I realised, of course, that she had no chaperon with her.

Soon afterwards I, too, had a letter from her, also scented and literary. She wrote that she had missed me, missed my beautiful, intelligent, loving eyes. She reproached me affectionately for wasting my youth, for stagnating in the country when I might, like her, be living in paradise under the palms, breathing the fragrance of the orange-trees. And she signed herself " Your forsaken Ariadne." Two days later came another letter in the same style, signed " Your forgotten Ariadne." My mind was confused. I loved her passionately, I dreamed of her every night, and then this " your forsaken," " your forgotten "— what did it mean? What was it for? And then the dreariness of the country, the long evenings, the disquieting thoughts of Lubkov. . . . The uncertainty tortured me, and poisoned my days and nights; it became unendurable. I could not bear it and went abroad.

Ariadne summoned me to Abbazzia. I arrived there on a bright warm day after rain; the rain-drops were still hanging on the trees and glistening on the huge, barrack-like *dépendance* where Ariadne and Lubkov were living.

They were not at home. I went into the park;

wandered about the avenues, then sat down. An Austrian General, with his hands behind him, walked past me, with red stripes on his trousers such as our generals wear. A baby was wheeled by in a perambulator and the wheels squeaked on the damp sand. A decrepit old man with jaundice passed, then a crowd of Englishwomen, a Catholic priest, then the Austrian General again. A military band, only just arrived from Fiume, with glittering brass instruments, sauntered by to the bandstand — they began playing.

Have you ever been at Abbazzia? It's a filthy little Slav town with only one street, which stinks, and in which one can't walk after rain without goloshes. I had read so much and always with such intense feeling about this earthly paradise that when afterwards, holding up my trousers, I cautiously crossed the narrow street, and in my ennui bought some hard pears from an old peasant woman who, recognising me as a Russian, said: " Tcheeteery " for " tchetyry " (four) —" davadtsat " for " dvadtsat " (twenty), and when I wondered in perplexity where to go and what to do here, and when I inevitably met Russians as disappointed as I was, I began to feel vexed and ashamed. There is a calm bay there full of steamers and boats with coloured sails. From there I could see Fiume and the distant islands covered with lilac mist, and it would have been picturesque if the view over the bay had

not been hemmed in by the hotels and their *dépend-*
ances — buildings in an absurd, trivial style of archi-
tecture, with which the whole of that green shore
has been covered by greedy money grubbers, so that
for the most part you see nothing in this little paradise but windows, terraces, and little squares with
tables and waiters' black coats.   There is a park
such as you find now in every watering-place abroad.
And the dark, motionless, silent foliage of the palms,
and the bright yellow sand in the avenue, and the
bright green seats, and the glitter of the braying military horns — all this sickened me in ten minutes!
And yet one is obliged for some reason to spend ten
days, ten weeks, there!

Having been dragged reluctantly from one of
these watering-places to another, I have been more
and more struck by the inconvenient and niggardly
life led by the wealthy and well-fed, the dulness and
feebleness of their imagination, the lack of boldness
in their tastes and desires.   And how much happier
are those tourists, old and young, who, not having
the money to stay in hotels, live where they can,
admire the view of the sea from the tops of the
mountains, lying on the green grass, walk instead of
riding, see the forests and villages at close quarters,
observe the customs of the country, listen to its songs,
fall in love with its women. . . .

While I was sitting in the park, it began to get
dark, and in the twilight my Ariadne appeared, ele-

gant and dressed like a princess; after her walked
Lubkov, wearing a' new loose-fitting suit, bought
probably in Vienna.

"Why are you cross with me?" he was saying.
"What have I done to you?"

Seeing me, she uttered a cry of joy, and probably,
if we had not been in the park, would have thrown
herself on my neck. She pressed my hands warmly
and laughed; and I laughed too and almost cried
with emotion. Questions followed, of the village,
of my father, whether I had seen her brother, and
so on. She insisted on my looking her straight in
the face, and asked if I remembered the gudgeon,
our little quarrels, the picnics. . . .

"How nice it all was really!" she sighed. "But
we're not having a slow time here either. We have
a great many acquaintances, my dear, my best of
friends! To-morrow I will introduce you to a
Russian family here, but please buy yourself another
hat." She scrutinised me and frowned. "Abbazzia is not the country," she said; "here one must
be *comme il faut.*"

Then we went to the restaurant. Ariadne was
laughing and mischievous all the time; she kept calling me "dear," "good," "clever," and seemed as
though she could not believe her eyes that I was
with her. We sat on till eleven o'clock, and parted
very well satisfied both with the supper and with
each other.

Next day Ariadne presented me to the Russian

family as: "The son of a distinguished professor whose estate is next to ours."

She talked to this family about nothing but estates and crops, and kept appealing to me. She wanted to appear to be a very wealthy landowner, and did, in fact, succeed in doing so. Her manner was superb like that of a real aristocrat, which indeed she was by birth.

"But what a person my aunt is!" she said suddenly, looking at me with a smile. "We had a slight tiff, and she has bolted off to Meran. What do you say to that?"

Afterwards when we were walking in the park I asked her:

"What aunt were you talking of just now? What aunt is that?"

"That was a saving lie," laughed Ariadne. "They must not know I'm without a chaperon."

After a moment's silence she came closer to me and said:

"My dear, my dear, do be friends with Lubkov. He is so unhappy! His wife and mother are simply awful."

She used the formal mode of address in speaking to Lubkov, and when she was going up to bed she said good-night to him exactly as she did to me, and their rooms were on different floors. All this made me hope that it was all nonsense, and that there was no sort of love affair between them, and I felt at ease when I met him. And when one day he asked me for the loan of three hundred roubles, I gave it to him with the greatest pleasure.

Every day we spent in enjoying ourselves and in nothing but enjoying ourselves; we strolled in the park, we ate, we drank. Every day there were conversations with the Russian family. By degrees I got used to the fact that if I went into the park I should be sure to meet the old man with jaundice, the Catholic priest, and the Austrian General, who always carried a pack of little cards, and wherever it was possible sat down and played patience, nervously twitching his shoulders. And the band played the same thing over and over again.

At home in the country I used to feel ashamed to meet the peasants when I was fishing or on a picnic party on a working day; here too I was ashamed at the sight of the footmen, the coachmen, and the workmen who met us. It always seemed to me they were looking at me and thinking: "Why are you doing nothing?" And I was conscious of this feeling of shame every day from morning to night. It was a strange, unpleasant, monotonous time; it was only varied by Lubkov's borrowing from me now a hundred, now fifty guldens, and being suddenly revived by the money as a morphia-maniac is by morphia, beginning to laugh loudly at his wife, at himself, at his creditors.

At last it began to be rainy and cold. We went to Italy, and I telegraphed to my father begging him for mercy's sake to send me eight hundred roubles to Rome. We stayed in Venice, in Bologna, in Florence, and in every town invariably put up at an expensive hotel, where we were charged separately for lights, and for service, and for heating, and for bread at lunch, and for the right of having dinner by ourselves. We ate enormously. In the morning they gave us *café complet;* at one o'clock lunch: meat, fish, some sort of omelette, cheese, fruits, and wine. At six o'clock dinner of eight courses with long intervals, during which we drank beer and wine. At nine o'clock tea. At midnight Ariadne would declare she was hungry, and ask for ham and boiled eggs. We would eat to keep her company.

In the intervals between meals we used to rush about the museums and exhibitions in continual anxiety for fear we should be late for dinner or lunch. I was bored at the sight of the pictures; I longed to be at home to rest; I was exhausted, looked about for a chair and hypocritically repeated after other people: "How exquisite, what atmosphere!" Like overfed boa constrictors, we noticed only the most glaring objects. The shop windows hypnotised us; we went into ecstasies over imitation brooches and bought a mass of useless trumpery.

The same thing happened in Rome, where it rained and there was a cold wind. After a heavy lunch we went to look at St. Peter's, and thanks to our replete condition and perhaps the bad weather, it made no sort of impression on us, and detecting in each other an indifference to art, we almost quarrelled.

The money came from my father. I went to get it, I remember, in the morning. Lubkov went with me.

" The present cannot be full and happy when one has a past," said he. " I have heavy burdens left on me by the past. However, if only I get the money, it's no great matter, but if not, I'm in a fix. Would you believe it, I have only eight francs left, yet I must send my wife a hundred and my mother another. And we must live here too. Ariadne's like a child; she won't enter into the position, and flings away money like a duchess. Why did she buy a watch yesterday? And, tell me, what object is there in our going on playing at being good children? Why, our hiding our relations from the servants and our friends costs us from ten to fifteen francs a day, as I have to have a separate room. What's the object of it? "

I felt as though a sharp stone had been turned round in my chest. There was no uncertainty now; it was all clear to me. I turned cold all over, and at once made a resolution to give up seeing them, to run away from them, to go home at once. . . .

" To get on terms with a woman is easy enough," Lubkov went on. " You have only to undress her; but afterwards what a bore it is, what a silly business ! "

226

Ariadne

When I counted over the money I received he said:

"If you don't lend me a thousand francs, I am faced with complete ruin. Your money is the only resource left to me."

I gave him the money, and he at once revived and began laughing about his uncle, a queer fish, who could never keep his address secret from his wife. When I reached the hotel I packed and paid my bill. I had still to say good-bye to Ariadne.

I knocked at the door.

"Entrez!"

In her room was the usual morning disorder: tea-things on the table, an unfinished roll, an eggshell; a strong overpowering reek of scent. The bed had not been made, and it was evident that two had slept in it.

Ariadne herself had only just got out of bed and was now with her hair down in a flannel dressing-jacket.

I said good-morning to her, and then sat in silence for a minute while she tried to put her hair tidy, and then I asked her, trembling all over:

"Why . . . why . . . did you send for me here?"

Evidently she guessed what I was thinking; she took me by the hand and said:

"I want you to be here, you are so pure."

I felt ashamed of my emotion, of my trembling.

And I was afraid I might begin sobbing, too! I
went out without saying another word, and within
an hour I was sitting in the train. All the journey,
for some reason, I imagined Ariadne with child, and
she seemed disgusting to me, and all the women I
saw in the trains and at the stations looked to me,
for some reason, as if they too were with child, and
they too seemed disgusting and pitiable. I was in
the position of a greedy, passionate miser who
should suddenly discover that all his gold coins were
false. The pure, gracious images which my imagination, warmed by love, had cherished for so long,
my plans, my hopes, my memories, my ideas of love
and of woman — all now were jeering and putting
out their tongues at me. "Ariadne," I kept asking
with horror, "that young, intellectual, extraordinarily beautiful girl, the daughter of a senator,
carrying on an intrigue with such an ordinary, uninteresting vulgarian? But why should she not love
Lubkov?" I answered myself. "In what is he inferior to me? Oh, let her love any one she likes,
but why lie to me? But why is she bound to be open
with me?" And so I went on over and over again
till I was stupefied.

It was cold in the train; I was travelling first
class, but even so there were three on a side, there
were no double windows, the outer door opened
straight into the compartment, and I felt as though
I were in the stocks, cramped, abandoned, pitiful,
and my legs were fearfully numb, and at the same

time I kept recalling how fascinating she had been
that morning in her dressing-jacket and with her hair
down, and I was suddenly overcome by such acute
jealousy that I leapt up in anguish, so that my neighbours stared at me in wonder and positive alarm.

At home I found deep snow and twenty degrees
of frost. I'm fond of the winter; I'm fond of it
because at that time, even in the hardest frosts, it's
particularly snug at home. It's pleasant to put on
one's fur jacket and felt overboots on a clear frosty
day, to do something in the garden or in the yard,
or to read in a well warmed room, to sit in my father's study before the open fire, to wash in my country bath-house. . . . Only if there is no mother in
the house, no sister and no children, it is somehow
dreary on winter evenings, and they seem extraordinarily long and quiet. And the warmer and
snugger it is, the more acutely is this lack felt. In
the winter when I came back from abroad, the evenings were endlessly long, I was intensely depressed,
so depressed that I could not even read; in the day-
time I was coming and going, clearing away the snow
in the garden or feeding the chickens and the calves,
but in the evening it was all up with me.

I had never cared for visitors before, but now I
was glad of them, for I knew there was sure to be
talk of Ariadne. Kotlovitch, the spiritualist, used
often to come to talk about his sister, and sometimes
he brought with him his friend Prince Maktuev, who
was as much in love with Ariadne as I was. To

sit in Ariadne's room, to finger the keys of her piano, to look at her music was a necessity for the prince — he could not live without it; and the spirit of his grandfather Ilarion was still predicting that sooner or later she would be his wife. The prince usually stayed a long time with us, from lunch to midnight, saying nothing all the time; in silence he would drink two or three bottles of beer, and from time to time, to show that he too was taking part in the conversation, he would laugh an abrupt, melancholy, foolish laugh. Before going home he would always take me aside and ask me in an undertone: "When did you see Ariadne Grigoryevna last? Was she quite well? I suppose she's not tired of being out there?"

Spring came on. There was the harrowing to do and then the sowing of spring corn and clover. I was sad, but there was the feeling of spring. One longed to accept the inevitable. Working in the fields and listening to the larks, I asked myself: "Couldn't I have done with this question of personal happiness once and for all? Couldn't I lay aside my fancy and marry a simple peasant girl?"

Suddenly when we were at our very busiest, I got a letter with the Italian stamp, and the clover and the beehives and the calves and the peasant girl all floated away like smoke. This time Ariadne wrote that she was profoundly, infinitely unhappy. She reproached me for not holding out a helping hand to her, for looking down upon her from the heights of my virtue and deserting her at the moment of danger. All this was written in a large, nervous handwriting with blots and smudges, and it was evident that she wrote in haste and distress. In conclusion she besought me to come and save her. Again my anchor was hauled up and I was carried away. Ariadne was in Rome. I arrived late in the evening, and when she saw me, she sobbed and threw herself on my neck. She had not changed at all that winter, and was just as young and charming. We had supper together and afterwards drove about Rome until dawn, and all the time she kept telling me about her doings. I asked where Lubkov was.

" Don't remind me of that creature ! " she cried. " He is loathsome and disgusting to me ! "

" But I thought you loved him," I said.

" Never," she said. " At first he struck me as original and aroused my pity, that was all. He is insolent and takes a woman by storm. And that's attractive. But we won't talk about him. That is a melancholy page in my life. He has gone to Russia to get money. Serve him right ! I told him not to dare to come back."

She was living then, not at an hotel, but in a private lodging of two rooms which she had decorated in her own taste, frigidly and luxuriously. After Lubkov had gone away she had borrowed from her acquaintances about five thousand francs, and my arrival certainly was the one salvation for her. I had reckoned on taking her back to the country, but I did not succeed in that. She was homesick for her native place, but her recollections of the poverty she had been through there, of privations, of the rusty roof on her brother's house, roused a shudder of disgust, and when I suggested going home to her, she squeezed my hands convulsively and said:

"No, no, I shall die of boredom there!"

Then my love entered upon its final phase.

"Be the darling that you used to be; love me a little," said Ariadne, bending over to me. "You're sulky and prudent, you're afraid to yield to impulse, and keep thinking of consequences, and that's dull. Come, I beg you, I beseech you, be nice to me!... My pure one, my holy one, my dear one, I love you so!"

I became her lover. For a month anyway I was like a madman, conscious of nothing but rapture. To hold in one's arms a young and lovely body, with bliss to feel her warmth every time one waked up from sleep, and to remember that she was there — she, my Ariadne! — oh, it was not easy to get used to that! But yet I did get used to it, and by degrees became capable of reflecting on. my new position. First of all, I realised, as before, that Ariadne did not love me. But she wanted to be really in love, she was afraid of solitude, and, above all, I was healthy, young, vigorous; she was sensual, like all cold people, as a rule — and we both made a show of being united by a passionate, mutual love. Afterwards I realised something else, too.

Ariadne

We stayed in Rome, in Naples, in Florence; we went to Paris, but there we thought it cold and went back to Italy. We introduced ourselves everywhere as husband and wife, wealthy landowners. People readily made our acquaintance and Ariadne had great social success everywhere. As she took lessons in painting, she was called an artist, and only imagine, that quite suited her, though she had not the slightest trace of talent.

She would sleep every day till two or three o'clock; she had her coffee and lunch in bed. At dinner she would eat soup, lobster, fish, meat, asparagus, game, and after she had gone to bed I used to bring up something, for instance roast beef, and she would eat it with a melancholy, careworn expression, and if she waked in the night she would eat apples and oranges.

The chief, so to say fundamental, characteristic of the woman was an amazing duplicity. She was continually deceitful every minute, apparently apart from any necessity, as it were by instinct, by an impulse such as makes the sparrow chirrup and the cockroach waggle its antennæ. She was deceitful with me, with the footman, with the porter, with the tradesmen in the shops, with her acquaintances; not one conversation, not one meeting, took place without affectation and pretence. A man had only to come into our room — whoever it might be, a waiter, or a baron — for her eyes, her expression, her voice to change, even the contour of her figure was transformed. At the very first glance at her then, you would have said there were no more wealthy and fashionable people in Italy than we. She never met an artist or a musician without telling him all sorts of lies about his remarkable talent.

"You have such a talent!" she would say, in honeyed cadences, "I'm really afraid of you. I think you must see right through people."

And all this simply in order to please, to be successful, to be fascinating! She waked up every morning with the one thought of "pleasing"! It was the aim and object of her life. If I had told her that in such a house, in such a street, there lived a man who was not attracted by her, it would have caused her real suffering. She wanted every day to enchant, to captivate, to drive men crazy. The fact that I was in her power and reduced to a complete nonentity before her charms gave her the same sort of satisfaction that visitors used to feel in tournaments. My subjection was not enough, and at nights, stretched out like a tigress, uncovered — she was always too hot — she would read the letters sent her by Lubkov; he besought her to return to Russia, vowing if she did not he would rob or murder some one to get the money to come to her. She hated him, but his passionate, slavish letters excited her. She had an extraordinary opinion of her own charms; she imagined that if somewhere, in some great assembly, men could have seen how beautifully she was made and the colour of her skin, she would have

vanquished all Italy, the whole world. Her talk
of her figure, of her skin, offended me, and observing
this, she would, when she was angry, to vex me, say
all sorts of vulgar things, taunting me. One day
when we were at the summer villa of a lady of our
acquaintance, and she lost her temper, she even went
so far as to say: " If you don't leave off boring
me with your sermons, I'll undress this minute and
lie naked here on these flowers."

Often looking at her asleep, or eating, or trying
to assume a naïve expression, I wondered why that
extraordinary beauty, grace, and intelligence had
been given her by God. Could it simply be for
lolling in bed, eating and lying, lying endlessly?
And was she intelligent really? She was afraid of
three candles in a row, of the number thirteen, was
terrified of spells and bad dreams. She argued
about free love and freedom in general like a big-
oted old woman, declared that Boleslav Markevitch
was a better writer than Turgenev. But she was
diabolically cunning and sharp, and knew how to
seem a highly educated, advanced person in company.

Even at a good-humoured moment, she could always insult a servant or kill an insect without a pang;
she liked bull-fights, liked to read about murders,
and was angry when prisoners were acquitted.

For the life Ariadne and I were leading, we had
to have a great deal of money. My poor father
sent me his pension, all the little sums he received,

borrowed for me wherever he could, and when one day he answered me: "Non habeo," I sent him a desperate telegram in which I besought him to mortgage the estate. A little later I begged him to get money somehow on a second mortgage. He did this too without a murmur and sent me every farthing. Ariadne despised the practical side of life; all this was no concern of hers, and when flinging away thousands of francs to satisfy her mad desires I groaned like an old tree, she would be singing "Addio bella Napoli" with a light heart.

Little by little I grew cold to her and began to be ashamed of our tie. I am not fond of pregnancy and confinements, but now I sometimes dreamed of a child who would have been at least a formal justification of our life. That I might not be completely disgusted with myself, I began reading and visiting museums and galleries, gave up drinking and took to eating very little. If one keeps oneself well in hand from morning to night, one's heart seems lighter. I began to bore Ariadne too. The people with whom she won her triumphs were, by the way, all of the middling sort; as before, there were no ambassadors, there was no salon, the money did not run to it, and this mortified her and made her sob, and she announced to me at last that perhaps she would not be against our returning to Russia.

And here we are on our way. For the last few months she has been zealously corresponding with her brother; she evidently has some secret projects, but what they are — God knows! I am sick of trying to fathom her underhand schemes! But we're going, not to the country, but to Yalta and afterwards to the Caucasus. She can only exist now at watering-places, and if you knew how I hate all these watering-places, how suffocated and ashamed I am in them. If I could be in the country now! If I could only be working now, earning my bread by the sweat of my brow, atoning for my follies. I am conscious of a superabundance of energy and I believe that if I were to put that energy to work I could redeem my estate in five years. But now, as you see, there is a complication. Here we're not abroad, but in mother Russia; we shall have to think of lawful wedlock. Of course, all attraction is over; there is no trace left of my old love, but, however that may be, I am bound in honour to marry her.

.   .   .   .

Shamohin, excited by his story, went below with me and we continued talking about women. It was late. It appeared that he and I were in the same cabin.

" So far it is only in the village that woman has not fallen behind man," said Shamohin. " There she thinks and feels just as man does, and struggles with nature in the name of culture as zealously as he. In the towns the woman of the bourgeois or intellectual class has long since fallen behind, and is returning to her primitive condition. She is half a human beast already, and, thanks to her, a great deal of what had been won by human genius has been lost again; the woman gradually disappears and in her place is the primitive female. This dropping-back on the part of the educated woman is a real danger to culture; in her retrogressive movement she tries to drag man after her and prevents him from moving forward. That is incontestable."

I asked: "Why generalise? Why judge of all women from Ariadne alone? The very struggle of women for education and sexual equality, which I look upon as a struggle for justice, precludes any hypothesis of a retrograde movement."

But Shamohin scarcely listened to me and he smiled distrustfully. He was a passionate, convinced misogynist, and it was impossible to alter his convictions.

"Oh, nonsense!" he interrupted. "When once a woman sees in me, not a man, not an equal, but a male, and her one anxiety all her life is to attract me — that is, to take possession of me — how can one talk of their rights? Oh, don't you believe them; they are very, very cunning! We men make a great stir about their emancipation, but they don't care about their emancipation at all, they only pretend to care about it; they are horribly cunning things, horribly cunning!"

I began to feel sleepy and weary of discussion. I turned over with my face to the wall.

"Yes," I heard as I fell asleep —"yes, and it's our education that's at fault, sir. In our towns, the

height, came back. The women — the sisters-in-law Marya and Fyokla — who had been working on the landowner's estate beyond the river, arrived home, too. Marya, the wife of Nikolay's brother Kiryak, had six children, and Fyokla, the wife of Nikolay's brother Denis — who had gone for a soldier — had two; and when Nikolay, going into the hut, saw all the family, all those bodies big and little moving about on the lockers, in the hanging cradles and in all the corners, and when he saw the greed with which the old father and the women ate the black bread, dipping it in water, he realized he had made a mistake in coming here, sick, penniless, and with a family, too — a great mistake!

" And where is Kiryak? " he asked after they had exchanged greetings.

" He is in service at the merchant's," answered his father; " a keeper in the woods. He is not a bad peasant, but too fond of his glass."

" He is no great help! " said the old woman tearfully. " Our men are a grievous lot; they bring nothing into the house, but take plenty out. Kiryak drinks, and so does the old man; it is no use hiding a sin; he knows his way to the tavern. The Heavenly Mother is wroth."

In honour of the visitors they brought out the samovar. The tea smelt of fish; the sugar was grey and looked as though it had been nibbled; cockroaches ran to and fro over the bread and among the crockery. It was disgusting to drink, and the conversation was disgusting, too — about nothing but poverty and illnesses. But before they had time

red, lay piled up in heaps, and below there stretched a broad, level, bright green meadow, from which the hay had been already carried, and in which the peasants' cattle were wandering. The river, three-quarters of a mile from the village, ran twisting and turning, with beautiful leafy banks; beyond it was again a broad meadow, a herd of cattle, long strings of white geese; then, just as on the near side, a steep ascent uphill, and on the top of the hill a hamlet, and a church with five domes, and at a little distance the manor-house.

"It's lovely here in your parts!" said Olga, crossing herself at the sight of the church. "What space, oh Lord!"

Just at that moment the bell began ringing for service (it was Saturday evening). Two little girls, down below, who were dragging up a pail of water, looked round at the church to listen to the bell.

"At this time they are serving the dinners at the Slavyansky Bazaar," said Nikolay dreamily.

Sitting on the edge of the slope, Nikolay and Olga watched the sun setting, watched the gold and crimson sky reflected in the river, in the church windows, and in the whole air — which was soft and still and unutterably pure as it never was in Moscow. And when the sun had set the flocks and herds passed, bleating and lowing; geese flew across from the further side of the river, and all sank into silence; the soft light died away in the air, and the dusk of evening began quickly moving down upon them.

Meanwhile Nikolay's father and mother, two gaunt, bent, toothless old people, just of the same

ualist! Now I understand what she was writing to him about! Oh, Lord!" he went on, gazing up to heaven, and pressing his parcels to his bosom. "If she hits it off with the prince, it means freedom, then I can go back to the country with my father!"

And he ran on.

"I begin to believe in spirits," he called to me, looking back. "The spirit of grandfather Ilarion seems to have prophesied the truth! Oh, if only it is so!"

The day after this meeting I left Yalta and how Shamohin's story ended I don't know.

1895

put on my coat or hands me a glass of water ——"

I heard no more, for I fell asleep.

Next morning when we were approaching Sevastopol, it was damp, unpleasant weather; the ship rocked. Shamohin sat on deck with me, brooding and silent. When the bell rang for tea, men with their coat-collars turned up and ladies with pale, sleepy faces began going below; a young and very beautiful lady, the one who had been so angry with the Customs officers at Volotchisk, stopped before Shamohin and said with the expression of a naughty, fretful child:

"Jean, your birdie's been sea-sick."

Afterwards when I was at Yalta I saw the same beautiful lady dashing about on horseback with a couple of officers hardly able to keep up with her. And one morning I saw her in an overall and a Phrygian cap, sketching on the sea-front with a great crowd admiring her a little way off. I too was introduced to her. She pressed my hand with great warmth, and looking at me ecstatically, thanked me in honeyed cadences for the pleasure I had given her by my writings.

"Don't you believe her," Shamohin whispered to me, "she has never read a word of them."

When I was walking on the sea-front in the early evening Shamohin met me with his arms full of big parcels of fruits and dainties.

"Prince Maktuev is here!" he said joyfully. "He came yesterday with her brother, the spirit-

whole education and bringing up of women in its essence tends to develop her into the human beast — that is, to make her attractive to the male and able to vanquish him. Yes, indeed "— Shamohin sighed —" little girls ought to be taught and brought up with boys, so that they might be always together. A woman ought to be trained so that she may be able, like a man, to recognise when she's wrong, or she always thinks she's in the right. Instil into a little girl from her cradle that a man is not first of all a cavalier or a possible lover, but her neighbour, her equal in everything. Train her to think logically, to generalise, and do not assure her that her brain weighs less than a man's and that therefore she can be indifferent to the sciences, to the arts, to the tasks of culture in general. The apprentice to the shoemaker or the house painter has a brain of smaller size than the grown-up man too, yet he works, suffers, takes his part in the general struggle for existence. We must give up our attitude to the physiological aspect, too — to pregnancy and childbirth, seeing that in the first place women don't have babies every month; secondly, not all women have babies; and, thirdly, a normal countrywoman works in the fields up to the day of her confinement and it does her no harm. Then there ought to be absolute equality in everyday life. If a man gives a lady his chair or picks up the handkerchief she has dropped, let her repay him in the same way. I have no objection if a girl of good family helps me to

Sasha lay down on the floor, while Olga went with the other women into the barn.

"Aye, aye, dearie," she said, lying down on the hay beside Marya; "you won't mend your trouble with tears. Bear it in patience, that is all. It is written in the Scriptures: 'If anyone smite thee on the right cheek, offer him the left one also.' . . . Aye, aye, dearie."

Then in a low singsong murmur she told them about Moscow, about her own life, how she had been a servant in furnished lodgings.

"And in Moscow the houses are big, built of brick," she said; "and there are ever so many churches, forty times forty, dearie; and they are all gentry in the houses, so handsome and so proper!"

Marya told her that she had not only never been in Moscow, but had not even been in their own district town; she could not read or write, and knew no prayers, not even "Our Father." Both she and Fyokla, the other sister-in-law, who was sitting a little way off listening, were extremely ignorant and could understand nothing. They both disliked their husbands; Marya was afraid of Kiryak, and whenever he stayed with her she was shaking with fear, and always got a headache from the fumes of vodka and tobacco with which he reeked. And in answer to the question whether she did not miss her husband, Fyokla answered with vexation:

"Miss him!"

They talked a little and sank into silence.

It was cool, and a cock crowed at the top of his

voice near the barn, preventing them from sleeping. When the bluish morning light was already peeping through all the crevices, Fyokla got up stealthily and went out, and then they heard the sound of her bare feet running off somewhere.

II

Olga went to church, and took Marya with her. As they went down the path towards the meadow both were in good spirits. Olga liked the wide view, and Marya felt that in her sister-in-law she had someone near and akin to her. The sun was rising. Low down over the meadow floated a drowsy hawk. The river looked gloomy; there was a haze hovering over it here and there, but on the further bank a streak of light already stretched across the hill. The church was gleaming, and in the manor garden the rooks were cawing furiously.

" The old man is all right," Marya told her, " but Granny is strict; she is continually nagging. Our own grain lasted till Carnival. We buy flour now at the tavern. She is angry about it; she says we eat too much."

" Aye, aye, dearie! Bear it in patience, that is all. It is written: ' Come unto Me, all ye that labour and are heavy laden.' "

Olga spoke sedately, rhythmically, and she walked like a pilgrim woman, with a rapid, anxious step. Every day she read the gospel, read it aloud like a deacon; a great deal of it she did not understand, but the words of the gospel moved her to tears, and words like " forasmuch as " and " verily " she pronounced with a sweet flutter at her heart. She believed in God, in the Holy Mother, in the Saints; she believed one must not offend anyone in the world — not simple folks, nor Germans, nor gypsies, nor Jews — and woe even to those who have no compassion on the beasts. She believed this was written in the Holy Scriptures; and so, when she pronounced phrases from Holy Writ, even though she did not understand them, her face grew softened, compassionate, and radiant.

" What part do you come from? " Marya asked her.

" I am from Vladimir. Only I was taken to Moscow long ago, when I was eight years old."

They reached the river. On the further side a woman was standing at the water's edge, undressing.

" It's our Fyokla," said Marya, recognizing her. " She has been over the river to the manor yard. To the stewards. She is a shameless hussy and foul-mouthed — fearfully! "

Fyokla, young and vigorous as a girl, with her black eyebrows and her loose hair, jumped off the bank and began splashing the water with her feet, and waves ran in all directions from her.

" Shameless — dreadfully! " repeated Marya.

The river was crossed by a rickety little bridge of logs, and exactly below it in the clear, limpid water was a shoal of broad-headed mullets. The dew was glistening on the green bushes that looked into the water. There was a feeling of warmth; it was comforting! What a lovely morning! And how lovely life would have been in this world, in all likelihood, if it were not for poverty, horrible, hopeless poverty, from which one can find no refuge! One had only to look round at the village to remember vividly all that had happened the day before, and the illusion of happiness which seemed to surround them vanished instantly.

They reached the church. Marya stood at the entrance, and did not dare to go farther. She did not dare to sit down either. Though they only began ringing for mass between eight and nine, she remained standing the whole time.

While the gospel was being read the crowd suddenly parted to make way for the family from the great house. Two young girls in white frocks and wide-brimmed hats walked in; with them a chubby, rosy boy in a sailor suit. Their appearance touched Olga; she made up her mind from the first glance that they were refined, well-educated, handsome people. Marya looked at them from under her brows, sullenly, dejectedly, as though they were not human beings coming in, but monsters who might crush her if she did not make way for them.

And every time the deacon boomed out something in his bass voice she fancied she heard " Ma-arya ! " and she shuddered.

III

The arrival of the visitors was already known in the village, and directly after mass a number of people gathered together in the hut. The Leonytchevs and Matvyeitchevs and the Ilyitchovs came to inquire about their relations who were in service in Moscow. All the lads of Zhukovo who could read and write were packed off to Moscow and hired out as butlers or waiters (while from the village on the other side of the river the boys all became bakers), and that had been the custom from the days of serfdom long ago when a certain Luka Ivanitch, a peasant from Zhukovo, now a legendary figure, who had been a waiter in one of the Moscow clubs, would take none but his fellow-villagers into his service, and found jobs for them in taverns and restaurants; and from that time the village of Zhukovo was always called among the inhabitants of the surrounding districts Slaveytown. Nikolay had been taken to Moscow when he was eleven, and Ivan Makaritch, one of the Matvyeitchevs, at that time a head-waiter in the " Hermitage " garden, had put him into a situation. And now, addressing the Matvyeitchevs, Nikolay said emphatically:

" Ivan Makaritch was my benefactor, and I am bound to pray for him day and night, as it is owing to him I have become a good man."

" My good soul! " a tall old woman, the sister of Ivan Makaritch, said tearfully, " and not a word have we heard about him, poor dear."

" In the winter he was in service at Omon's, and this season there was a rumour he was somewhere out of town, in gardens. . . . He has aged! In old days he would bring home as much as ten roubles a day in the summer-time, but now things are very quiet everywhere. The old man frets."

The women looked at Nikolay's feet, shod in felt boots, and at his pale face, and said mournfully:

" You are not one to get on, Nikolay Osipitch; you are not one to get on! No, indeed! "

And they all made much of Sasha. She was ten years old, but she was little and very thin, and might have been taken for no more than seven. Among the other little girls, with their sunburnt faces and roughly cropped hair, dressed in long faded smocks, she with her white little face, with her big dark eyes, with a red ribbon in her hair, looked funny, as though she were some little wild creature that had been caught and brought into the hut.

" She can read, too," Olga said in her praise, looking tenderly at her daughter. " Read a little, child! " she said, taking the gospel from the corner. " You read, and the good Christian people will listen."

The testament was an old and heavy one in leather binding, with dog's-eared edges, and it exhaled a smell as though monks had come into the hut. Sasha raised her eyebrows and began in a loud rhythmic chant:

" ' And the angel of the Lord . . . appeared unto Joseph, saying unto him: Rise up, and take the Babe and His mother.' "

" The Babe and His mother," Olga repeated, and flushed all over with emotion.

" ' And flee into Egypt, . . . and tarry there until such time as . . .' "

At the word " tarry " Olga could not refrain from tears. Looking at her, Marya began to whimper,

254

and after her Ivan Makaritch's sister. The old father cleared his throat, and bustled about to find something to give his grand-daughter, but, finding nothing, gave it up with a wave of his hand. And when the reading was over the neighbours dispersed to their homes, feeling touched and very much pleased with Olga and Sasha.

As it was a holiday, the family spent the whole day at home. The old woman, whom her husband, her daughters-in-law, her grandchildren all alike called Granny, tried to do everything herself; she heated the stove and set the samovar with her own hands, even waited at the midday meal, and then complained that she was worn out with work. And all the time she was uneasy for fear someone should eat a piece too much, or that her husband and daughters-in-law would sit idle. At one time she would hear the tavern-keeper's geese going at the back of the huts to her kitchen-garden, and she would run out of the hut with a long stick and spend half an hour screaming shrilly by her cabbages, which were as gaunt and scraggy as herself; at another time she fancied that a crow had designs on her chickens, and she rushed to attack it with loud words of abuse. She was cross and grumbling from morning till night. And often she raised such an outcry that passers-by stopped in the street.

She was not affectionate towards the old man, reviling him as a lazy-bones and a plague. He was not a responsible, reliable peasant, and perhaps if she had not been continually nagging at him he would not have worked at all, but would have simply sat

255

on the stove and talked. He talked to his son at great length about certain enemies of his, complained of the insults he said he had to put up with every day from the neighbours, and it was tedious to listen to him.

"Yes," he would say, standing with his arms akimbo, "yes. . . . A week after the Exaltation of the Cross I sold my hay willingly at thirty kopecks a pood. . . . Well and good. . . . So you see I was taking the hay in the morning with a good will; I was interfering with no one. In an unlucky hour I see the village elder, Antip Syedelnikov, coming out of the tavern. 'Where are you taking it, you ruffian?' says he, and takes me by the ear."

Kiryak had a fearful headache after his drinking bout, and was ashamed to face his brother.

"What vodka does! Ah, my God!" he muttered, shaking his aching head. "For Christ's sake, forgive me, brother and sister; I'm not happy myself."

As it was a holiday, they bought a herring at the tavern and made a soup of the herring's head. At midday they all sat down to drink tea, and went on drinking it for a long time, till they were all perspiring; they looked positively swollen from the tea-drinking, and after it began sipping the broth from the herring's head, all helping themselves out of one bowl. But the herring itself Granny had hidden.

In the evening a potter began firing pots on the ravine. In the meadow below the girls got up a choral dance and sang songs. They played the concertina. And on the other side of the river a kiln for baking pots was lighted, too, and the girls sang songs, and in the distance the singing sounded soft and musical. The peasants were noisy in and about the tavern. They were singing with drunken voices, each on his own account, and swearing at one another, so that Olga could only shudder and say:

" Oh, holy Saints! "

She was amazed that the abuse was incessant, and those who were loudest and most persistent in this foul language were the old men who were so near their end. And the girls and children heard the swearing, and were not in the least disturbed by it, and it was evident that they were used to it from their cradles.

It was past midnight, the kilns on both sides of the river were put out, but in the meadow below and in the tavern the merrymaking still went on. The old father and Kiryak, both drunk, walking arm-in-arm and jostling against each other's shoulders, went to the barn where Olga and Marya were lying.

" Let her alone," the old man persuaded him; " let her alone. . . . She is a harmless woman. . . . It's a sin. . . ."

" Ma-arya! " shouted Kiryak.

" Let her be. . . . It's a sin. . . . She is not a bad woman."

Both stopped by the barn and went on.

" I lo-ove the flowers of the fi-ield," the old man began singing suddenly in a high, piercing tenor. " I lo-ove to gather them in the meadows! "

Then he spat, and with a filthy oath went into the hut.

257

IV

Granny put Sasha by her kitchen-garden and told her to keep watch that the geese did not go in. It was a hot August day. The tavernkeeper's geese could make their way into the kitchen-garden by the backs of the huts, but now they were busily engaged picking up oats by the tavern, peacefully conversing together, and only the gander craned his head high as though trying to see whether the old woman were coming with her stick. The other geese might come up from below, but they were now grazing far away the other side of the river, stretched out in a long white garland about the meadow. Sasha stood about a little, grew weary, and, seeing that the geese were not coming, went away to the ravine.

There she saw Marya's eldest daughter Motka, who was standing motionless on a big stone, staring at the church. Marya had given birth to thirteen children, but she only had six living, all girls, not one boy, and the eldest was eight. Motka in a long smock was standing barefooted in the full sunshine; the sun was blazing down right on her head, but she did not notice that, and seemed as though turned to stone. Sasha stood beside her and said, looking at the church:

" God lives in the church. Men have lamps and candles, but God has little green and red and blue lamps like little eyes. At night God walks about the church, and with Him the Holy Mother of God and Saint Nikolay, thud, thud, thud! . . . And the watchman is terrified, terrified! Aye, aye, dearie," she added, imitating her mother. " And when the end of the world comes all the churches will be carried up to heaven."

" With the-ir be-ells? " Motka asked in her deep voice, drawling every syllable.

" With their bells. And when the end of the world comes the good will go to Paradise, but the angry will burn in fire eternal and unquenchable, dearie. To my mother as well as to Marya God will say: ' You never offended anyone, and for that go to the right to Paradise'; but to Kiryak and Granny He will say: ' You go to the left into the fire.' And anyone who has eaten meat in Lent will go into the fire, too."

She looked upwards at the sky, opening wide her eyes, and said:

" Look at the sky without winking, you will see angels."

Motka began looking at the sky, too, and a minute passed in silence.

" Do you see them? " asked Sasha.

" I don't," said Motka in her deep voice.

" But I do. Little angels are flying about the sky and flap, flap with their little wings as though they were gnats."

Motka thought for a little, with her eyes on the ground, and asked:

" Will Granny burn? "

" She will, dearie."

From the stone an even gentle slope ran down to the bottom, covered with soft green grass, which one

longed to lie down on or to touch with one's hands.
. . . Sasha lay down and rolled to the bottom.
Motka with a grave, severe face, taking a deep
breath, lay down, too, and rolled to the bottom, and
in doing so tore her smock from the hem to the
shoulder.

"What fun it is!" said Sasha, delighted.

They walked up to the top to roll down again, but
at that moment they heard a shrill, familiar voice.
Oh, how awful it was! Granny, a toothless, bony,
hunchbacked figure, with short grey hair which was
fluttering in the wind, was driving the geese out of
the kitchen-garden with a long stick, shouting.

"They have trampled all the cabbages, the
damned brutes! I'd cut your throats, thrice accursed
plagues! Bad luck to you!"

She saw the little girls, flung down the stick and
picked up a switch, and, seizing Sasha by the neck
with her fingers, thin and hard as the gnarled
branches of a tree, began whipping her. Sasha cried
with pain and terror, while the gander, waddling and
stretching his neck, went up to the old woman and
hissed at her, and when he went back to his flock
all the geese greeted him approvingly with "Ga-
ga-ga!" Then Granny proceeded to whip Motka,
and in this Motka's smock was torn again. Feeling in despair, and crying loudly, Sasha went to the
hut to complain. Motka followed her; she, too,
was crying on a deeper note, without wiping her
tears, and her face was as wet as though it had been
dipped in water.

Peasants

"Holy Saints!" cried Olga, aghast, as the two came into the hut. "Queen of Heaven!"

Sasha began telling her story, while at the same time Granny walked in with a storm of shrill cries and abuse; then Fyokla flew into a rage, and there was an uproar in the hut.

"Never mind, never mind!" Olga, pale and upset, tried to comfort them, stroking Sasha's head. "She is your grandmother; it's a sin to be angry with her. Never mind, my child."

Nikolay, who was worn out already by the everlasting hubbub, hunger, stifling fumes, filth, who hated and despised the poverty, who was ashamed for his wife and daughter to see his father and mother, swung his legs off the stove and said in an irritable, tearful voice, addressing his mother:

"You must not beat her! You have no right to beat her!"

"You lie rotting on the stove, you wretched creature!" Fyokla shouted at him spitefully. "The devil brought you all on us, eating us out of house and home."

Sasha and Motka and all the little girls in the hut huddled on the stove in the corner behind Nikolay's back, and from that refuge listened in silent terror, and the beating of their little hearts could be distinctly heard. Whenever there is someone in a family who has long been ill, and hopelessly ill, there come painful moments when all timidly, secretly, at the bottom of their hearts long for his death; and only the children fear the death of someone near them, and always feel horrified at the thought of it. And now the children, with bated breath, with a mournful look on their faces, gazed at Nikolay and thought that he was soon to die; and they wanted to cry and to say something friendly and compassionate to him.

He pressed close to Olga, as though seeking protection, and said to her softly in a quavering voice: " Olya darling, I can't stay here longer. It's more than I can bear. For God's sake, for Christ's sake, write to your sister Klavdia Abramovna. Let her sell and pawn everything she has; let her send us the money. We will go away from here. Oh, Lord," he went on miserably, " to have one peep at Moscow! If I could see it in my dreams, the dear place ! "

And when the evening came on, and it was dark in the hut, it was so dismal that it was hard to utter a word. Granny, very ill-tempered, soaked some crusts of rye bread in a cup, and was a long time, a whole hour, sucking at them. Marya, after milking the cow, brought in a pail of milk and set it on a bench; then Granny poured it from the pail into a jug just as slowly and deliberately, evidently pleased that it was now the Fast of the Assumption, so that no one would drink milk and it would be left untouched. And she only poured out a very little in a saucer for Fyokla's baby. When Marya and she carried the jug down to the cellar Motka suddenly stirred, clambered down from the stove, and going to the bench where stood the wooden cup full of crusts, sprinkled into it some milk from the saucer.

Granny, coming back into the hut, sat down to her soaked crusts again, while Sasha and Motka, sitting on the stove, gazed at her, and they were glad that she had broken her fast and now would go to hell. They were comforted and lay down to sleep, and Sasha as she dozed off to sleep imagined the Day of Judgment: a huge fire was burning, somewhat like a potter's kiln, and the Evil One, with horns like a cow's, and black all over, was driving Granny into the fire with a long stick, just as Granny herself had been driving the geese.

V

On the day of the Feast of the Assumption, between ten and eleven in the evening, the girls and lads who were merrymaking in the meadow suddenly raised a clamour and outcry, and ran in the direction of the village; and those who were above on the edge of the ravine could not for the first moment make out what was the matter.

"Fire! Fire!" they heard desperate shouts from below. "The village is on fire!"

Those who were sitting above looked round, and a terrible and extraordinary spectacle met their eyes. On the thatched roof of one of the end cottages stood a column of flame, seven feet high, which curled round and scattered sparks in all directions as though it were a fountain. And all at once the whole roof burst into bright flame, and the crackling of the fire was audible.

The light of the moon was dimmed, and the whole village was by now bathed in a red quivering glow: black shadows moved over the ground, there was a smell of burning, and those who ran up from below were all gasping and could not speak for trembling; they jostled against each other, fell down, and they could hardly see in the unaccustomed light, and did not recognize each other. It was terrible. What seemed particularly dreadful was that doves were flying over the fire in the smoke; and in the tavern, where they did not yet know of the fire, they were still singing and playing the concertina as though there were nothing the matter.

" Uncle Semyon's on fire," shouted a loud, coarse voice.

Marya was fussing about round her hut, weeping and wringing her hands, while her teeth chattered, though the fire was a long way off at the other end of the village. Nikolay came out in high felt boots, the children ran out in their little smocks. Near the village constable's hut an iron sheet was struck. Boom, boom, boom ! . . . floated through the air, and this repeated, persistent sound sent a pang to the heart and turned one cold. The old women stood with the holy ikons. Sheep, calves, cows were driven out of the back-yards into the street; boxes, sheep-skins, tubs were carried out. A black stallion, who was kept apart from the drove of horses because he kicked and injured them, on being set free ran once or twice up and down the village, neighing and paw-ing the ground; then suddenly stopped short near a cart and began kicking it with his hind-legs.

Peasants

They began ringing the bells in the church on the other side of the river.

Near the burning hut it was hot and so light that one could distinctly see every blade of grass. Semyon, a red-haired peasant with a long nose, wearing a reefer-jacket and a cap pulled down right over his ears, sat on one of the boxes which they had succeeded in bringing out: his wife was lying on her face, moaning and unconscious. A little old man of eighty, with a big beard, who looked like a gnome — not one of the villagers, though obviously connected in some way with the fire — walked about bareheaded, with a white bundle in his arms. The glare was reflected on his bald head. The village elder, Antip Syedelnikov, as swarthy and black-haired as a gypsy, went up to the hut with an axe, and hacked out the windows one after another — no one knew why — then began chopping up the roof.

" Women, water! " he shouted. " Bring the engine! Look sharp! "

The peasants, who had been drinking in the tavern just before, dragged the engine up. They were all drunk; they kept stumbling and falling down, and all had a helpless expression and tears in their eyes.

" Wenches, water! " shouted the elder, who was drunk, too. " Look sharp, wenches! "

The women and the girls ran downhill to where there was a spring, and kept hauling pails and buckets of water up the hill, and, pouring it into the engine, ran down again. Olga and Marya and Sasha and Motka all brought water. The women and the boys pumped the water; the pipe hissed, and the elder, directing it now at the door, now at the windows, held back the stream with his finger, which made it hiss more sharply still.

" Bravo, Antip! " voices shouted approvingly. " Do your best."

Antip went inside the hut into the fire and shouted from within.

" Pump! Bestir yourselves, good Christian folk, in such a terrible mischance! "

The peasants stood round in a crowd, doing nothing but staring at the fire. No one knew what to do, no one had the sense to do anything, though there were stacks of wheat, hay, barns, and piles of faggots standing all round. Kiryak and old Osip, his father, both tipsy, were standing there, too. And as though to justify his doing nothing, old Osip said, addressing the woman who lay on the ground:

" What is there to trouble about, old girl! The hut is insured — why are you taking on? "

Semyon, addressing himself first to one person and then to another, kept describing how the fire had started.

" That old man, the one with the bundle, a house-serf of General Zhukov's. . . . He was cook at our general's, God rest his soul! He came over this evening: ' Let me stay the night,' says he. . . . Well, we had a glass, to be sure. . . . The wife got the samovar — she was going to give the old fellow a cup of tea, and in an unlucky hour she set the samovar in the entrance. The sparks from the chimney must have blown straight up to the thatch; that's how it was. We were almost burnt ourselves.

And the old fellow's cap has been burnt; what a shame!"

And the sheet of iron was struck indefatigably, and the bells kept ringing in the church the other side of the river. In the glow of the fire Olga, breathless, looking with horror at the red sheep and the pink doves flying in the smoke, kept running down the hill and up again. It seemed to her that the ringing went to her heart with a sharp stab, that the fire would never be over, that Sasha was lost. . . . And when the ceiling of the hut fell in with a crash, the thought that now the whole village would be burnt made her weak and faint, and she could not go on fetching water, but sat down on the ravine, setting the pail down near her; beside her and below her, the peasant women sat wailing as though at a funeral.

Then the stewards and watchmen from the estate the other side of the river arrived in two carts, bringing with them a fire-engine. A very young student in an unbuttoned white tunic rode up on horseback. There was the thud of axes. They put a ladder to the burning framework of the house, and five men ran up it at once. Foremost of them all was the student, who was red in the face and shouting in a harsh hoarse voice, and in a tone as though putting out fires was a thing he was used to. They pulled the house to pieces, a beam at a time; they dragged away the corn, the hurdles, and the stacks that were near.

"Don't let them break it up!" cried stern voices in the crowd. "Don't let them."

Kiryak made his way up to the hut with a resolute air, as though he meant to prevent the newcomers from breaking up the hut, but one of the workmen turned him back with a blow in his neck. There was the sound of laughter, the workman dealt him another blow, Kiryak fell down, and crawled back into the crowd on his hands and knees.

Two handsome girls in hats, probably the student's sisters, came from the other side of the river. They stood a little way off, looking at the fire. The beams that had been dragged apart were no longer burning, but were smoking vigorously; the student, who was working the hose, turned the water, first on the beams, then on the peasants, then on the women who were bringing the water.

" George! " the girls called to him reproachfully in anxiety, " George! "

The fire was over. And only when they began to disperse they noticed that the day was breaking, that everyone was pale and rather dark in the face, as it always seems in the early morning when the last stars are going out. As they separated, the peasants laughed and made jokes about General Zhukov's cook and his cap which had been burnt; they already wanted to turn the fire into a joke, and even seemed sorry that it had so soon been put out.

" How well you extinguished the fire, sir! " said Olga to the student. " You ought to come to us in Moscow: there we have a fire every day."

" Why, do you come from Moscow? " asked one of the young ladies.

" Yes, miss. My husband was a waiter at the

Slavyansky Bazaar. And this is my daughter," she said, indicating Sasha, who was cold and huddling up to her. " She is a Moscow girl, too."

The two young ladies said something in French to the student, and he gave Sasha a twenty-kopeck piece.

Old Father Osip saw this, and there was a gleam of hope in his face.

" We must thank God, your honour, there was no wind," he said, addressing the student, " or else we should have been all burnt up together. Your honour, kind gentlefolks," he added in embarrassment in a lower tone, " the morning's chilly . . . something to warm one . . . half a bottle to your honour's health."

Nothing was given him, and clearing his throat he slouched home. Olga stood afterwards at the end of the street and watched the two carts crossing the river by the ford and the gentlefolks walking across the meadow; a carriage was waiting for them the other side of the river. Going into the hut, she described to her husband with enthusiasm:

" Such good people! And so beautiful! The young ladies were like cherubim."

" Plague take them! " Fyokla, sleepy, said spitefully.

VI

Marya thought herself unhappy, and said that she would be very glad to die; Fyokla, on the other hand, found all this life to her taste: the poverty, the uncleanliness, and the incessant quarrelling.

She ate what was given her without discrimination; slept anywhere, on whatever came to hand. She would empty the slops just at the porch, would splash them out from the doorway, and then walk barefoot through the puddle. And from the very first day she took a dislike to Olga and Nikolay just because they did not like this life.

"We shall see what you'll find to eat here, you Moscow gentry!" she said malignantly. "We shall see!"

One morning, it was at the beginning of September, Fyokla, vigorous, good-looking, and rosy from the cold, brought up two pails of water; Marya and Olga were sitting meanwhile at the table drinking tea.

"Tea and sugar," said Fyokla sarcastically. "The fine ladies!" she added, setting down the pails. "You have taken to the fashion of tea every day. You better look out that you don't burst with your tea-drinking," she went on, looking with hatred at Olga. "That's how you have come by your fat mug, having a good time in Moscow, you lump of flesh!" She swung the yoke and hit Olga such a blow on the shoulder that the two sisters-in-law could only clasp their hands and say:

"Oh, holy Saints!"

Then Fyokla went down to the river to wash the clothes, swearing all the time so loudly that she could be heard in the hut.

The day passed and was followed by the long autumn evening. They wound silk in the hut; everyone did it except Fyokla; she had gone over the river. They got the silk from a factory close by, and the whole family working together earned next to nothing, twenty kopecks a week.

" Things were better in the old days under the gentry," said the old father as he wound silk. " You worked and ate and slept, everything in its turn. At dinner you had cabbage-soup and boiled grain, and at supper the same again. Cucumbers and cabbage in plenty: you could eat to your heart's content, as much as you wanted. And there was more strictness. Everyone minded what he was about."

The hut was lighted by a single little lamp, which burned dimly and smoked. When someone screened the lamp and a big shadow fell across the window, the bright moonlight could be seen. Old Osip, speaking slowly, told them how they used to live before the emancipation; how in those very parts, where life was now so poor and so dreary, they used to hunt with harriers, greyhounds,. retrievers, and when they went out as beaters the peasants were given vodka; how whole waggonloads of game used to be sent to Moscow for the young masters; how the bad were beaten with rods or sent away to the Tver estate, while the good were rewarded. And Granny told them something, too. She remembered everything, positively everything. She described her mistress, a kind, God-fearing woman, whose husband was a profligate and a rake, and all of whose daughters made unlucky marriages: one married a drunkard, another married a workman, the other eloped secretly (Granny herself, at that time a young girl, helped in the elopement), and they had all three as well as their mother died early from grief. And remembering all this, Granny positively began to shed tears.

All at once someone knocked at the door, and they all started.

"Uncle Osip, give me a night's lodging."

The little bald old man, General Zhukov's cook, the one whose cap had been burnt, walked in. He sat down and listened, then he, too, began telling stories of all sorts. Nikolay, sitting on the stove with his legs hanging down, listened and asked questions about the dishes that were prepared in the old days for the gentry. They talked of rissoles, cutlets, various soups and sauces, and the cook, who remembered everything very well, mentioned dishes that are no longer served. There was one, for instance — a dish made of bulls' eyes, which was called "waking up in the morning."

"And used you to do cutlets *à la maréchal?*" asked Nikolay.

"No."

Nikolay shook his head reproachfully and said: "Tut, tut! You were not much of a cook!"

The little girls sitting and lying on the stove stared down without blinking; it seemed as though there were a great many of them, like cherubim in the clouds. They liked the stories: they were breathless; they shuddered and turned pale with alternate rapture and terror, and they listened breathlessly, afraid to stir, to Granny, whose stories were the most interesting of all.

Peasants

They lay down to sleep in silence; and the old people, troubled and excited by their reminiscences, thought how precious was youth, of which, whatever it might have been like, nothing was left in the memory but what was living, joyful, touching, and how terribly cold was death, which was not far off, better not think of it! The lamp died down. And the dusk, and the two little windows sharply defined by the moonlight, and the stillness and the creak of the cradle, reminded them for some reason that life was over, that nothing one could do would bring it back. . . . You doze off, you forget yourself, and suddenly someone touches your shoulder or breathes on your cheek — and sleep is gone; your body feels cramped, and thoughts of death keep creeping into your mind. You turn on the other side: death is forgotten, but old dreary, sickening thoughts of poverty, of food, of how dear flour is getting, stray through the mind, and a little later again you remember that life is over and you cannot bring it back. . . .

" Oh, Lord! " sighed the cook.

Someone gave a soft, soft tap at the window. It must be Fyokla come back. Olga got up, and yawning and whispering a prayer, opened the door, then drew the bolt in the outer room, but no one came in; only from the street came a cold draught and a sudden brightness from the moonlight. The street, still and deserted, and the moon itself floating across the sky, could be seen at the open door.

" Who is there? " called Olga.

" I," she heard the answer —" it is I."

Near the door, crouching against the wall, stood Fyokla, absolutely naked. She was shivering with cold, her teeth were chattering, and in the bright moonlight she looked very pale, strange, and beautiful. The shadows on her, and the bright moonlight on her skin, stood out vividly, and her dark eyebrows and firm, youthful bosom were defined with peculiar distinctness.

" The ruffians over there undressed me and turned me out like this," she said. " I've come home without my clothes . . . naked as my mother bore me. Bring me something to put on."

" But go inside! " Olga said softly, beginning to shiver, too.

" I don't want the old folks to see." Granny was, in fact, already stirring and muttering, and the old father asked: " Who is there? " Olga brought her own smock and skirt, dressed Fyokla, and then both went softly into the inner room, trying not to make a noise with the door.

" Is that you, you sleek one? " Granny grumbled angrily, guessing who it was. " Fie upon you, nightwalker! . . . Bad luck to you! "

" It's all right, it's all right," whispered Olga, wrapping Fyokla up; " it's all right, dearie."

All was stillness again. They always slept badly; everyone was kept awake by something worrying and persistent: the old man by the pain in his back, Granny by anxiety and anger, Marya by terror, the children by itch and hunger. Now, too, their sleep was troubled; they kept turning over from one side to the other, talking in their sleep, getting up for a drink.

Fyokla suddenly broke into a loud, coarse howl, but immediately checked herself, and only uttered sobs from time to time, growing softer and on a lower note, until she relapsed into silence. From time to time from the other side of the river there floated the sound of the beating of the hours; but the time seemed somehow strange — five was struck and then three.

" Oh Lord! " sighed the cook.

Looking at the windows, it was difficult to tell whether it was still moonlight or whether the dawn had begun. Marya got up and went out, and she could be heard milking the cows and saying, " Stea-dy! " Granny went out, too. It was still dark in the hut, but all the objects in it could be discerned.

Nikolay, who had not slept all night, got down from the stove. He took his dress-coat out of a green box, put it on, and going to the window, stroked the sleeves and took hold of the coat-tails — and smiled. Then he carefully took off the coat, put it away in his box, and lay down again.

Marya came in again and began lighting the stove. She was evidently hardly awake, and seemed dropping asleep as she walked. Probably she had had some dream, or the stories of the night before came into her mind as, stretching luxuriously before the stove, she said:

" No, freedom is better."

VII

The master arrived — that was what they called the police inspector. When he would come and what he was coming for had been known for the last week. There were only forty households in Zhukovo, but more than two thousand roubles of arrears of rates and taxes had accumulated.

The police inspector stopped at the tavern. He drank there two glasses of tea, and then went on foot to the village elder's hut, near which a crowd of those who were in debt stood waiting. The elder, Antip Syedelnikov, was, in spite of his youth — he was only a little over thirty — strict and always on the side of the authorities, though he himself was poor and did not pay his taxes regularly. Evidently he enjoyed being elder, and liked the sense of authority, which he could only display by strictness. In the village council the peasants were afraid of him and obeyed him. It would sometimes happen that he would pounce on a drunken man in the street or near the tavern, tie his hands behind him, and put him in the lock-up. On one occasion he even put Granny in the lock-up because she went to the village council instead of Osip, and began swearing, and he kept her there for a whole day and night. He had never lived in a town or read a book, but somewhere or other had picked up various learned expressions, and loved to make use of them in conversation, and he was respected for this though he was not always understood.

Peasants

When Osip came into the village elder's hut with his tax book, the police inspector, a lean old man with a long grey beard, in a grey tunic, was sitting at a table in the passage, writing something. It was clean in the hut; all the walls were dotted with pictures cut out of the illustrated papers, and in the most conspicuous place near the ikon there was a portrait of the Battenburg who was the Prince of Bulgaria. By the table stood Antip Syedelnikov with his arms folded.

"There is one hundred and nineteen roubles standing against him," he said when it came to Osip's turn. "Before Easter he paid a rouble, and he has not paid a kopeck since."

The police inspector raised his eyes to Osip and asked:

"Why is this, brother?"

"Show Divine mercy, your honour," Osip began, growing agitated. "Allow me to say last year the gentleman at Lutorydsky said to me, 'Osip,' he said, 'sell your hay . . . you sell it,' he said. Well, I had a hundred poods for sale; the women mowed it on the water-meadow. Well, we struck a bargain all right, willingly. . . ."

He complained of the elder, and kept turning round to the peasants as though inviting them to bear witness; his face flushed red and perspired, and his eyes grew sharp and angry.

"I don't know why you are saying all this," said the police inspector. "I am asking you . . . I am asking you why you don't pay your arrears. You don't pay, any of you, and am I to be responsible for you?"

"I can't do it."

"His words have no sequel, your honour," said the elder. "The Tchikildyeevs certainly are of a defective class, but if you will just ask the others, the root of it all is vodka, and they are a very bad lot. With no sort of understanding."

The police inspector wrote something down, and said to Osip quietly, in an even tone, as though he were asking him for water:

"Be off."

Soon he went away; and when he got into his cheap chaise and cleared his throat, it could be seen from the very expression of his long thin back that he was no longer thinking of Osip or of the village elder, nor of the Zhukovo arrears, but was thinking of his own affairs. Before he had gone three-quarters of a mile Antip was already carrying off the samovar from the Tchikildyeevs' cottage, followed by Granny, screaming shrilly and straining her throat:

"I won't let you have it, I won't let you have it, damn you!"

He walked rapidly with long steps, and she pursued him panting, almost falling over, a bent, ferocious figure; her kerchief slipped on to her shoulders, her grey hair with greenish lights on it was blown about in the wind. She suddenly stopped short, and like a genuine rebel, fell to beating her breast with her fists and shouting louder than ever in a sing-song voice, as though she were sobbing:

" Good Christians and believers in God! Neighbours, they have ill-treated me! Kind friends, they have oppressed me! Oh, oh! dear people, take my part."

" Granny, Granny! " said the village elder sternly, " have some sense in your head! "

It was hopelessly dreary in the Tchikildyeevs' hut without the samovar; there was something humiliating in this loss, insulting, as though the honour of the hut had been outraged. Better if the elder had carried off the table, all the benches, all the pots — it would not have seemed so empty. Granny screamed, Marya cried, and the little girls, looking at her, cried, too. The old father, feeling guilty, sat in the corner with bowed head and said nothing. And Nikolay, too, was silent. Granny loved him and was sorry for him, but now, forgetting her pity, she fell upon him with abuse, with reproaches, shaking her fist right in his face. She shouted that it was all his fault; why had he sent them so little when he boasted in his letters that he was getting fifty roubles a month at the Slavyansky Bazaar? Why had he come, and with his family, too? If he died, where was the money to come from for his funeral . . . ? And it was pitiful to look at Nikolay, Olga, and Sasha.

The old father cleared his throat, took his cap, and went off to the village elder. Antip was soldering something by the stove, puffing out his cheeks; there was a smell of burning. His children, emaciated and unwashed, no better than the Tchikildyeevs, were scrambling about the floor; his wife, an ugly, freckled woman with a prominent stomach, was winding silk. They were a poor, unlucky family, and Antip was the only one who looked vigorous and handsome. On a bench there were five samovars standing in a row. The old man said his prayer to Battenburg and said:

"Antip, show the Divine mercy. Give me back the samovar, for Christ's sake!"

"Bring three roubles, then you shall have it."

"I can't do it!"

Antip puffed out his cheeks, the fire roared and hissed, and the glow was reflected in the samovar. The old man crumpled up his cap and said after a moment's thought:

"You give it me back."

The swarthy elder looked quite black, and was like a magician; he turned round to Osip and said sternly and rapidly:

"It all depends on the rural captain. On the twenty-sixth instant you can state the grounds for your dissatisfaction before the administrative session, verbally or in writing."

Osip did not understand a word, but he was satisfied with that and went home.

Ten days later the police inspector came again, stayed an hour and went away. During those days the weather had changed to cold and windy; the river had been frozen for some time past, but still there was no snow, and people found it difficult to get about. On the eve of a holiday some of the neighbours came in to Osip's to sit and have a talk. They did not light the lamp, as it would have been a sin to work, but talked in the darkness. There were some items of news, all rather unpleasant. In two or three households hens had been taken for the arrears, and had been sent to the district police station, and there they had died because no one had fed them; they had taken sheep, and while they were being driven away tied to one another, shifted into another cart at each village, one of them had died. And now they were discussing the question, who was to blame?

"The Zemstvo," said Osip. "Who else?"

"Of course it is the Zemstvo."

The Zemstvo was blamed for everything — for the arrears, and for the oppressions, and for the failure of the crops, though no one of them knew what was meant by the Zemstvo. And this dated from the time when well-to-do peasants who had factories, shops, and inns of their own were members of the Zemstvos, were dissatisfied with them, and took to swearing at the Zemstvos in their factories and inns.

They talked of God's not sending the snow; they had to bring in wood for fuel, and there was no driving nor walking in the frozen ruts. In old days fifteen to twenty years ago conversation was much more interesting in Zhukovo. In those days every old man looked as though he were treasuring some secret; as though he knew something and was expecting something. They used to talk about an edict in golden letters, about the division of lands, about new land, about treasures; they hinted at something. Now the people of Zhukovo had no mystery at all; their whole life was bare and open in the sight of all, and they could talk of nothing but poverty, food, there being no snow yet. . . .

There was a pause. Then they thought again of the hens, of the sheep, and began discussing whose fault it was.

"The Zemstvo," said Osip wearily. "Who else?"

VIII

The parish church was nearly five miles away at Kosogorovo, and the peasants only attended it when they had to do so for baptisms, weddings, or funerals; they went to the services at the church across the river. On holidays in fine weather the girls dressed up in their best and went in a crowd together to church, and it was a cheering sight to see them in their red, yellow, and green dresses cross the meadow; in bad weather they all stayed at home. They went for the sacrament to the parish church. From each of those who did not manage in Lent to go to confession in readiness for the sacrament the parish priest, going the round of the huts with the cross at Easter, took fifteen kopecks.

The old father did not believe in God, for he hardly ever thought about Him; he recognized the supernatural, but considered it was entirely the women's concern, and when religion or miracles were discussed before him, or a question were put to him, he would say reluctantly, scratching himself:

"Who can tell!"

Granny believed, but her faith was somewhat

hazy; everything was mixed up in her memory, and she could scarcely begin to think of sins, of death, of the salvation of the soul, before poverty and her daily cares took possession of her mind, and she instantly forgot what she was thinking about. She did not remember the prayers, and usually in the evenings, before lying down to sleep, she would stand before the ikons and whisper:

"Holy Mother of Kazan, Holy Mother of Smolensk, Holy Mother of Troerutchitsy. . . ."

Marya and Fyokla crossed themselves, fasted, and took the sacrament every year, but understood nothing. The children were not taught their prayers, nothing was told them about God, and no moral principles were instilled into them; they were only forbidden to eat meat or milk in Lent. In the other families it was much the same: there were few who believed, few who understood. At the same time everyone loved the Holy Scripture, loved it with a tender, reverent love; but they had no Bible, there was no one to read it and explain it, and because Olga sometimes read them the gospel, they respected her, and they all addressed her and Sasha as though they were superior to themselves.

For church holidays and services Olga often went to neighbouring villages, and to the district town, in which there were two monasteries and twenty-seven churches. She was dreamy, and when she was on these pilgrimages she quite forgot her family, and only when she got home again suddenly made the joyful discovery that she had a husband and daughter, and then would say, smiling and radiant:

" God has sent me blessings ! "

What went on in the village worried her and seemed to her revolting. On Elijah's Day they drank, at the Assumption they drank, at the Ascension they drank. The Feast of the Intercession was the parish holiday for Zhukovo, and the peasants used to drink then for three days; they squandered on drink fifty roubles of money belonging to the Mir, and then collected more for vodka from all the households. On the first day of the feast the Tchikildyeevs killed a sheep and ate of it in the morning, at dinner-time, and in the evening; they ate it ravenously, and the children got up at night to eat more. Kiryak was fearfully drunk for three whole days; he drank up everything, even his boots and cap, and beat Marya so terribly that they had to pour water over her. And then they were all ashamed and sick.

However, even in Zhukovo, in this " Slaveytown," there was once an outburst of genuine religious enthusiasm. It was in August, when throughout the district they carried from village to village the Holy Mother, the giver of life. It was still and overcast on the day when they expected *Her* at Zhukovo. The girls set off in the morning to meet the ikon, in their bright holiday dresses, and brought Her towards the evening, in procession with the cross and with singing, while the bells pealed in the church across the river. An immense crowd of villagers and strangers flooded the street; there was noise, dust, a great crush. . . . And the old father and Granny and Kiryak — all stretched out their hands to the ikon, looked eagerly at it and said, weeping:

"Defender! Mother! Defender!"

All seemed suddenly to realize that there was not an empty void between earth and heaven, that the rich and the powerful had not taken possession of everything, that there was still a refuge from injury, from slavish bondage, from crushing, unendurable poverty, from the terrible vodka.

"Defender! Mother!" sobbed Marya. "Mother!"

But the thanksgiving service ended and the ikon was carried away, and everything went on as before; and again there was a sound of coarse drunken oaths from the tavern.

Only the well-to-do peasants were afraid of death; the richer they were the less they believed in God, and in the salvation of souls, and only through fear of the end of the world put up candles and had services said for them, to be on the safe side. The peasants who were rather poorer were not afraid of death. The old father and Granny were told to their faces that they had lived too long, that it was time they were dead, and they did not mind. They did not hinder Fyokla from saying in Nikolay's presence that when Nikolay died her husband Denis would get exemption — to return home from the army. And Marya, far from fearing death, regretted that it was so slow in coming, and was glad when her children died.

Death they did not fear, but of every disease they had an exaggerated terror. The merest trifle was

enough — a stomach upset, a slight chill, and Granny
would be wrapped up on the stove, and would begin
moaning loudly and incessantly:

" I am dy-ing! "

The old father hurried off for the priest, and
Granny received the sacrament and extreme unction. They often talked of colds, of worms, of
tumours which move in the stomach and coil round
to the heart. Above all, they were afraid of catching cold, and so put on thick clothes even in the summer and warmed themselves at the stove. Granny
was fond of being doctored, and often went to the
hospital, where she used to say she was not seventy,
but fifty-eight; she supposed that if the doctor knew
her real age he would not treat her, but would say
it was time she died instead of taking medicine.
She usually went to the hospital early in the morning, taking with her two or three of the little girls,
and came back in the evening, hungry and ill-tempered — with drops for herself and ointments for
the little girls. Once she took Nikolay, who swal-
lowed drops for a fortnight afterwards, and said he
felt better.

Granny knew all the doctors and their assistants
and the wise men for twenty miles round, and not
one of them she liked. At the Intercession, when
the priest made the round of the huts with the
cross, the deacon told her that in the town near
the prison lived an old man who had been a medical orderly in the army, and who made wonderful
cures, and advised her to try him. Granny took
his advice. When the first snow fell she drove to

the town and fetched an old man with a big beard, a converted Jew, in a long gown, whose face was covered with blue veins. There were outsiders at work in the hut at the time: an old tailor, in terrible spectacles, was cutting a waistcoat out of some rags, and two young men were making felt boots out of wool; Kiryak, who had been dismissed from his place for drunkenness, and now lived at home, was sitting beside the tailor mending a bridle. And it was crowded, stifling, and noisome in the hut. The converted Jew examined Nikolay and said that it was necessary to try cupping.

He put on the cups, and the old tailor, Kiryak, and the little girls stood round and looked on, and it seemed to them that they saw the disease being drawn out of Nikolay; and Nikolay, too, watched how the cups suckling at his breast gradually filled with dark blood, and felt as though there really were something coming out of him, and smiled with pleasure.

"It's a good thing," said the tailor. "Please God, it will do you good."

The Jew put on twelve cups and then another twelve, drank some tea, and went away. Nikolay began shivering; his face looked drawn, and, as the women expressed it, shrank up like a fist; his fingers turned blue. He wrapped himself up in a quilt and in a sheepskin, but got colder and colder. Towards the evening he began to be in great distress; asked to be laid on the ground, asked the tailor not to smoke; then he subsided under the sheepskin and towards morning he died.

IX

Oh, what a grim, what a long winter!

Their own grain did not last beyond Christmas, and they had to buy flour. Kiryak, who lived at home now, was noisy in the evenings, inspiring terror in everyone, and in the mornings he suffered from headache and was ashamed; and he was a pitiful sight. In the stall the starved cows bellowed day and night — a heart-rending sound to Granny and Marya. And as ill-luck would have it, there was a sharp frost all the winter, the snow drifted in high heaps, and the winter dragged on. At Annunciation there was a regular blizzard, and there was a fall of snow at Easter.

But in spite of it all the winter did end. At the beginning of April there came warm days and frosty nights. Winter would not give way, but one warm day overpowered it at last, and the streams began to flow and the birds began to sing. The whole meadow and the bushes near the river were drowned in the spring floods, and all the space between Zhukovo and the further side was filled up with a vast sheet of water, from which wild ducks rose up in flocks here and there. The spring sunset, flaming among gorgeous clouds, gave every evening something new, extraordinary, incredible — just what one does not believe in afterwards, when one sees those very colours and those very clouds in a picture.

The cranes flew swiftly, swiftly, with mournful

cries, as though they were calling themselves. Standing on the edge of the ravine, Olga looked a long time at the flooded meadow, at the sunshine, at the bright church, that looked as though it had grown younger; and her tears flowed and her breath came in gasps from her passionate longing to go away, to go far away to the end of the world. It was already settled that she should go back to Moscow to be a servant, and that Kiryak should set off with her to get a job as a porter or something. Oh, to get away quickly!

As soon as it dried up and grew warm they got ready to set off. Olga and Sasha, with wallets on their backs and shoes of plaited bark on their feet, came out before daybreak: Marya came out, too, to see them on their way. Kiryak was not well, and was kept at home for another week. For the last time Olga prayed at the church and thought of her husband, and though she did not shed tears, her face puckered up and looked ugly like an old woman's. During the winter she had grown thinner and plainer, and her hair had gone a little grey, and instead of the old look of sweetness and the pleasant smile on her face, she had the resigned, mournful expression left by the sorrows she had been through, and there was something blank and irresponsive in her eyes, as though she did not hear what was said. She was sorry to part from the village and the peasants. She remembered how they had carried out Nikolay, and how a requiem had been ordered for him at almost every hut, and all had shed tears in sympathy with her grief. In the course of the summer and the winter there had been hours and days when it seemed as though these people lived worse than the beasts, and to live with them was terrible; they were coarse, dishonest, filthy, and drunken; they did not live in harmony, but quarrelled continually, because they distrusted and feared and did not respect one another. Who keeps the tavern and makes the people drunken? A peasant. Who wastes and spends on drink the funds of the commune, of the schools, of the church? A peasant. Who stole from his neighbours, set fire to their property, gave false witness at the court for a bottle of vodka? At the meetings of the Zemstvo and other local bodies, who was the first to fall foul of the peasants? A peasant. Yes, to live with them was terrible; but yet, they were human beings, they suffered and wept like human beings, and there was nothing in their lives for which one could not find excuse. Hard labour that made the whole body ache at night, the cruel winters, the scanty harvests, the overcrowding; and they had no help and none to whom they could look for help. Those of them who were a little stronger and better off could be no help, as they were themselves coarse, dishonest, drunken, and abused one another just as revoltingly; the paltriest little clerk or official treated the peasants as though they were tramps, and addressed even the village elders and church wardens as inferiors, and considered they had a right to do so. And, indeed, can any sort of help or good example be given by mercenary, greedy, depraved, and idle persons who only visit the village in order to insult, to despoil, and to terrorize? Olga remembered the pitiful, humiliated look of the old people when in the winter Kiryak had been taken to be flogged. . . . And now she felt sorry for all these people, painfully so, and as she walked on she kept looking back at the huts.

After walking two miles with them Marya said good-bye, then kneeling, and falling forward with her face on the earth, she began wailing:

"Again I am left alone. Alas, for poor me! poor, unhappy! . . ."

And she wailed like this for a long time, and for a long way Olga and Sasha could still see her on her knees, bowing down to someone at the side and clutching her head in her hands, while the rooks flew over her head.

The sun rose high; it began to get hot. Zhukovo was left far behind. Walking was pleasant. Olga and Sasha soon forgot both the village and Marya; they were gay and everything entertained them. Now they came upon an ancient barrow, now upon a row of telegraph posts running one after another into the distance and disappearing into the horizon, and the wires hummed mysteriously. Then they saw a homestead, all wreathed in green foliage; there came a scent from it of dampness, of hemp, and it seemed for some reason that happy people lived there. Then they came upon a horse's skeleton whitening in solitude in the open fields. And the larks trilled unceasingly, the corncrakes called to one another, and the landrail cried as though someone were really scraping at an old iron rail.

At midday Olga and Sasha reached a big village. There in the broad street they met the little old man who was General Zhukov's cook. He was hot, and his red, perspiring bald head shone in the sunshine. Olga and he did not recognize each other, then looked round at the same moment, recognized each other, and went their separate ways without saying a word. Stopping near the hut which looked newest and most prosperous, Olga bowed down before the open windows, and said in a loud, thin, chanting voice:

" Good Christian folk, give alms, for Christ's sake, that God's blessing may be upon you, and that your parents may be in the Kingdom of Heaven in peace eternal."

" Good Christian folk," Sasha began chanting, " give, for Christ's sake, that God's blessing, the Heavenly Kingdom . . ."

1897

THE MAN IN A CASE

At the furthest end of the village of Mironositskoe some belated sportsmen lodged for the night in the elder Prokofy's barn. There were two of them, the veterinary surgeon Ivan Ivanovitch and the schoolmaster Burkin. Ivan Ivanovitch had a rather strange double-barrelled surname — Tchimsha-Himalaisky — which did not suit him at all, and he was called simply Ivan Ivanovitch all over the province. He lived at a stud-farm near the town, and had come out shooting now to get a breath of fresh air. Burkin, the high-school teacher, stayed every summer at Count P——'s, and had been thoroughly at home in this district for years.

They did not sleep. Ivan Ivanovitch, a tall, lean old fellow with long moustaches, was sitting outside the door, smoking a pipe in the moonlight. Burkin was lying within on the hay, and could not be seen in the darkness.

They were telling each other all sorts of stories. Among other things, they spoke of the fact that the elder's wife, Mavra, a healthy and by no means stupid woman, had never been beyond her native village, had never seen a town nor a railway in her life, and had spent the last ten years sitting behind the stove, and only at night going out into the street.

"What is there wonderful in that!" said Burkin.

" There are plenty of people in the world, solitary by temperament, who try to retreat into their shell like a hermit crab or a snail. Perhaps it is an instance of atavism, a return to the period when the ancestor of man was not yet a social animal and lived alone in his den, or perhaps it is only one of the diversities of human character — who knows? I am not a natural science man, and it is not my business to settle such questions; I only mean to say that people like Mavra are not uncommon. There is no need to look far; two months ago a man called Byelikov, a colleague of mine, the Greek master, died in our town. You have heard of him, no doubt. He was remarkable for always wearing goloshes and a warm wadded coat, and carrying an umbrella even in the very finest weather. And his umbrella was in a case, and his watch was in a case made of grey chamois leather, and when he took out his penknife to sharpen his pencil, his penknife, too, was in a little case; and his face seemed to be in a case too, because he always hid it in his turned-up collar. He wore dark spectacles and flannel vests, stuffed up his ears with cotton-wool, and when he got into a cab always told the driver to put up the hood. In short, the man displayed a constant and insurmountable impulse to wrap himself in a covering, to make himself, so to speak, a case which would isolate him and protect him from external influences. Reality irritated him, frightened him, kept him in continual agitation, and, perhaps to justify his timidity, his aversion for the actual, he always praised the past and what had never existed; and even the classical languages which he taught were in reality for him goloshes and umbrellas in which he sheltered himself from real life.

"'Oh, how sonorous, how beautiful is the Greek language!' he would say, with a sugary expression; and as though to prove his words he would screw up his eyes and, raising his finger, would pronounce 'Anthropos!'

"And Byelikov tried to hide his thoughts also in a case. The only things that were clear to his mind were government circulars and newspaper articles in which something was forbidden. When some proclamation prohibited the boys from going out in the streets after nine o'clock in the evening, or some article declared carnal love unlawful, it was to his mind clear and definite; it was forbidden, and that was enough. For him there was always a doubtful element, something vague and not fully expressed, in any sanction or permission. When a dramatic club or a reading-room or a tea-shop was licensed in the town, he would shake his head and say softly:

"'It is all right, of course; it is all very nice, but I hope it won't lead to anything!'

"Every sort of breach of order, deviation or departure from rule, depressed him, though one would have thought it was no business of his. If one of his colleagues was late for church or if rumours reached him of some prank of the high-school boys, or one of the mistresses was seen late in the evening in the company of an officer, he was much disturbed, and said he hoped that nothing would come of it. At the teachers' meetings he simply oppressed us with his caution, his circumspection, and his characteristic reflection on the ill-behaviour of the young people in both male and female high-schools, the uproar in the classes. . . .

"Oh, he hoped it would not reach the ears of the authorities; oh, he hoped nothing would come of it; and he thought it would be a very good thing if Petrov were expelled from the second class and Yegorov from the fourth. And, do you know, by his sighs, his despondency, his black spectacles on his pale little face, a little face like a pole-cat's, you know, he crushed us all, and we gave way, reduced Petrov's and Yegorov's marks for conduct, kept them in, and in the end expelled them both. He had a strange habit of visiting our lodgings. He would come to a teacher's, would sit down, and remain silent, as though he were carefully inspecting something. He would sit like this in silence for an hour or two and then go away. This he called 'maintaining good relations with his colleagues'; and it was obvious that coming to see us and sitting there was tiresome to him, and that he came to see us simply because he considered it his duty as our colleague. We teachers were afraid of him. And even the headmaster was afraid of him. Would you believe it, our teachers were all intellectual, right-minded people, brought up on Turgenev and Shtchedrin, yet this little chap, who always went about with goloshes and an umbrella, had the whole high-school under his thumb for fifteen long years! High-school, indeed — he had the whole town under his thumb! Our ladies did not get up private theatricals on Saturdays for fear he should hear of it, and the clergy dared not eat meat or play cards in his presence. Under the influence of people like Byelikov we have got into the way of being afraid of everything in our town for the last ten or fifteen years. They are afraid to speak aloud, afraid to send letters, afraid to make acquaintances, afraid to read books, afraid to help the poor, to teach people to read and write. . . ."

Ivan Ivanovitch cleared his throat, meaning to say something, but first lighted his pipe, gazed at the moon, and then said, with pauses:

"Yes, intellectual, right minded people read Shtchedrin and Turgenev, Buckle, and all the rest of them, yet they knocked under and put up with it . . . that's just how it is."

"Byelikov lived in the same house as I did," Burkin went on, "on the same storey, his door facing mine; we often saw each other, and I knew how he lived when he was at home. And at home it was the same story: dressing-gown, nightcap, blinds, bolts, a perfect succession of prohibitions and restrictions of all sorts, and —'Oh, I hope nothing will come of it!' Lenten fare was bad for him, yet he could not eat meat, as people might perhaps say Byelikov did not keep the fasts, and he ate fresh-water fish with butter — not a Lenten dish, yet one could not say that it was meat. He did not keep a female servant for fear people might think evil of him, but had as cook an old man of sixty, called Afanasy, half-witted and given to tippling, who had once been an officer's servant and could cook after a fashion. This Afanasy was usually standing at the door with his arms folded; with a deep sigh, he would mutter always the same thing:

" ' There are plenty of *them* about nowadays! '

" Byelikov had a little bedroom like a box; his bed had curtains. When he went to bed he covered his head over; it was hot and stuffy; the wind battered on the closed doors; there was a droning noise in the stove and a sound of sighs from the kitchen — ominous sighs. . . . And he felt frightened under the bed-clothes. He was afraid that something might happen, that Afanasy might murder him, that thieves might break in, and so he had troubled dreams all night, and in the morning, when we went together to the high-school, he was depressed and pale, and it was evident that the high-school full of people excited dread and aversion in his whole being, and that to walk beside me was irksome to a man of his solitary temperament.

" ' They make a great noise in our classes,' he used to say, as though trying to find an explanation for his depression. ' It's beyond anything.'

" And the Greek master, this man in a case — would you believe it? — almost got married."

Ivan Ivanovitch glanced quickly into the barn, and said:

" You are joking! "

" Yes, strange as it seems, he almost got married. A new teacher of history and geography, Milhail Savvitch Kovalenko, a Little Russian, was appointed. He came, not alone, but with his sister Varinka. He was a tall, dark young man with huge hands, and one

The Man in a Case

could see from his face that he had a bass voice, and, in fact, he had a voice that seemed to come out of a barrel —' boom, boom, boom!' And she was not so young, about thirty, but she, too, was tall, well-made, with black eyebrows and red cheeks — in fact, she was a regular sugar-plum, and so sprightly, so noisy; she was always singing Little Russian songs and laughing. For the least thing she would go off into a ringing laugh —' Ha-ha-ha!' We made our first thorough acquaintance with the Kovalenkos at the headmaster's name-day party. Among the glum and intensely bored teachers who came even to the name-day party as a duty we suddenly saw a new Aphrodite risen from the waves; she walked with her arms akimbo, laughed, sang, danced. . . . She sang with feeling ' The Winds do Blow,' then another song, and another, and she fascinated us all — all, even Byelikov He sat down by her and said with a honeyed smile:

" ' The Little Russian reminds one of the ancient Greek in its softness and agreeable resonance.'

" That flattered her, and she began telling him with feeling and earnestness that they had a farm in the Gadyatchsky district, and that her mamma lived at the farm, and that they had such pears, such melons, such *kabaks!* The Little Russians call pumpkins *kabaks* (*i.e.,* pothouses), while their pothouses they call *shinki,* and they make a beetroot soup with tomatoes and aubergines in it, ' which was so nice — awfully nice!'

" We listened and listened, and suddenly the same idea dawned upon us all:

" ' It would be a good thing to make a match of it,' the headmaster's wife said to me softly.

" We all for some reason recalled the fact that our friend Byelikov was not married, and it now seemed to us strange that we had hitherto failed to observe, and had in fact completely lost sight of, a detail so important in his life. What was his attitude to woman? How had he settled this vital question for himself? This had not interested us in the least till then; perhaps we had not even admitted the idea that a man who went out in all weathers in goloshes and slept under curtains could be in love.

" ' He is a good deal over forty and she is thirty,' the headmaster's wife went on, developing her idea. ' I believe she would marry him.'

" All sorts of things are done in the provinces through boredom, all sorts of unnecessary and non-sensical things! And that is because what is necessary is not done at all. What need was there, for instance, for us to make a match for this Byelikov, whom one could not even imagine married? The headmaster's wife, the inspector's wife, and all our high-school ladies, grew livelier and even better-looking, as though they had suddenly found a new object in life. The headmaster's wife would take a box at the theatre, and we beheld sitting in her box Varinka, with such a fan, beaming and happy, and beside her Byelikov, a little bent figure, looking as though he had been extracted from his house by pincers. I would give an evening party, and the ladies would insist on my inviting Byelikov and Varinka. In short, the machine was set in motion. It appeared that Varinka was not averse to matrimony. She had not a very cheerful life with her brother; they could do nothing but quarrel and scold one another from morning till night. Here is a scene, for instance. Kovalenko would be coming along the street, a tall, sturdy young ruffian, in an embroidered shirt, his love-locks falling on his forehead under his cap, in one hand a bundle of books, in the other a thick knotted stick, followed by his sister, also with books in her hand.

" ' But you haven't read it, Mihalik! ' she would be arguing loudly. ' I tell you, I swear you have not read it at all! '

" ' And I tell you I have read it,' cries Kovalenko, thumping his stick on the pavement.

" ' Oh, my goodness, Mihalik! why are you so cross? We are arguing about principles.'

" ' I tell you that I have read it!' Kovalenko would shout, more loudly than ever.

" And at home, if there was an outsider present, there was sure to be a skirmish. Such a life must have been wearisome, and of course she must have longed for a home of her own. Besides, there was her age to be considered; there was no time left to pick and choose; it was a case of marrying anybody, even a Greek master. And, indeed, most of our young ladies don't mind whom they marry so long as they do get married. However that may be, Varinka began to show an unmistakable partiality for Byelikov.

" And Byelikov? He used to visit Kovalenko just

as he did us. He would arrive, sit down, and remain silent. He would sit quiet, and Varinka would sing to him ' The Winds do Blow,' or would look pensively at him with her dark eyes, or would suddenly go off into a peal —' Ha-ha-ha!'

" Suggestion plays a great part in love affairs, and still more in getting married. Everybody — both his colleagues and the ladies — began assuring Byelikov that he ought to get married, that there was nothing left for him in life but to get married; we all congratulated him, with solemn countenances delivered ourselves of various platitudes, such as ' Marriage is a serious step.' Besides, Varinka was good-looking and interesting; she was the daughter of a civil councillor, and had a farm; and what was more, she was the first woman who had been warm and friendly in her manner to him. His head was turned, and he decided that he really ought to get married."

" Well, at that point you ought to have taken away his goloshes and umbrella," said Ivan Ivanovitch.

" Only fancy! that turned out to be impossible. He put Varinka's portrait on his table, kept coming to see me and talking about Varinka, and home life, saying marriage was a serious step. He was frequently at Kovalenko's, but he did not alter his manner of life in the least; on the contrary, indeed, his determination to get married seemed to have a depressing effect on him. He grew thinner and paler, and seemed to retreat further and further into his case.

The Man in a Case

" ' I like Varvara Savvishna,' he used to say to me, with a faint and wry smile, ' and I know that every one ought to get married, but . . . you know all this has happened so suddenly. . . . One must think a little.'

" ' What is there to think over? ' I used to say to him. ' Get married — that is all.'

" ' No; marriage is a serious step. One must first weigh the duties before one, the responsibilities . . . that nothing may go wrong afterwards. It worries me so much that I don't sleep at night. And I must confess I am afraid: her brother and she have a strange way of thinking; they look at things strangely, you know, and her disposition is very impetuous. One may get married, and then, there is no knowing, one may find oneself in an unpleasant position.'

" And he did not make an offer; he kept putting it off, to the great vexation of the headmaster's wife and all our ladies; he went on weighing his future duties and responsibilities, and meanwhile he went for a walk with Varinka almost every day — possibly he thought that this was necessary in his position — and came to see me to talk about family life. And in all probability in the end he would have proposed to her, and would have made one of those unnecessary, stupid marriages such as are made by thousands among us from being bored and having nothing to do, if it had not been for a *kolossalische scandal.* I must mention that Varinka's brother, Kovalenko, detested Byelikov from the first day of their acquaintance, and could not endure him.

303

" ' I don't understand,' he used to say to us, shrugging his shoulders —' I don't understand how you can put up with that sneak, that nasty phiz. Ugh! how can you live here! The atmosphere is stifling and unclean! Do you call yourselves schoolmasters, teachers? You are paltry government clerks. You keep, not a temple of science, but a department for red tape and loyal behaviour, and it smells as sour as a police-station. No, my friends; I will stay with you for a while, and then I will go to my farm and there catch crabs and teach the Little Russians. I shall go, and you can stay here with your Judas — damn his soul! '

" Or he would laugh till he cried, first in a loud bass, then in a shrill, thin laugh, and ask me, waving his hands:

" ' What does he sit here for? What does he want? He sits and stares.'

" He even gave Byelikov a nickname, ' The Spider.' And it will readily be understood that we avoided talking to him of his sister's being about to marry ' The Spider.'

" And on one occasion, when the headmaster's wife hinted to him what a good thing it would be to secure his sister's future with such a reliable, universally respected man as Byelikov, he frowned and muttered:

" ' It's not my business; let her marry a reptile if she likes. I don't like meddling in other people's affairs.'

" Now hear what happened next. Some mischievous person drew a caricature of Byelikov walking along in his goloshes with his trousers tucked up, under his umbrella, with Varinka on his arm; below, the inscription ' Anthropos in love.' The expression was caught to a marvel, you know. The artist must have worked for more than one night, for the teachers of both the boys' and girls' high-schools, the teachers of the seminary, the government officials, all received a copy. Byelikov received one, too. The caricature made a very painful impression on him.

" We went out together; it was the first of May, a Sunday, and all of us, the boys and the teachers, had agreed to meet at the high-school and then to go for a walk together to a wood beyond the town. We set off, and he was green in the face and gloomier than a storm-cloud.

" ' What wicked, ill-natured people there are ! ' he said, and his lips quivered.

" I felt really sorry for him. We were walking along, and all of a sudden — would you believe it? — Kovalenko came bowling along on a bicycle, and after him, also on a bicycle, Varinka, flushed and exhausted, but good-humoured and gay.

" ' We are going on ahead,' she called. ' What lovely weather ! Awfully lovely ! '

" And they both disappeared from our sight. Byelikov turned white instead of green, and seemed petrified. He stopped short and stared at me. . . .

" ' What is the meaning of it? Tell me, please ! ' he asked. ' Can my eyes have deceived me? Is it the proper thing for high-school masters and ladies to ride bicycles ? '

" 'What is there improper about it?' I said. 'Let them ride and enjoy themselves.'

" 'But how can that be?' he cried, amazed at my calm. 'What are you saying?'

" And he was so shocked that he was unwilling to go on, and returned home.

" Next day he was continually twitching and nervously rubbing his hands, and it was evident from his face that he was unwell. And he left before his work was over, for the first time in his life. And he ate no dinner. Towards evening he wrapped himself up warmly, though it was quite warm weather, and sallied out to the Kovalenkos'. Varinka was out; he found her brother, however.

" 'Pray sit down,' Kovalenko said coldly, with a frown. His face looked sleepy; he had just had a nap after dinner, and was in a very bad humour.

" Byelikov sat in silence for ten minutes, and then began:

" 'I have come to see you to relieve my mind. I am very, very much troubled. Some scurrilous fellow has drawn an absurd caricature of me and another person, in whom we are both deeply interested. I regard it as a duty to assure you that I have had no hand in it. . . . I have given no sort of ground for such ridicule — on the contrary, I have always behaved in every way like a gentleman.'

" Kovalenko sat sulky and silent. Byelikov waited a little, and went on slowly in a mournful voice:

" 'And I have something else to say to you. I have been in the service for years, while you have only lately entered it, and I consider it my duty as an older colleague to give you a warning. You ride on a bicycle, and that pastime is utterly unsuitable for an educator of youth.'

" ' Why so? ' asked Kovalenko in his bass.

" ' Surely that needs no explanation, Mihail Savvitch — surely you can understand that? If the teacher rides a bicycle, what can you expect the pupils to do? You will have them walking on their heads next! And so long as there is no formal permission to do so, it is out of the question. I was horrified yesterday! When I saw your sister everything seemed dancing before my eyes. A lady or a young girl on a bicycle — it's awful! '

" ' What is it you want exactly? '

" ' All I want is to warn you, Mihail Savvitch. You are a young man, you have a future before you, you must be very, very careful in your behaviour, and you are so careless — oh, so careless! You go about in an embroidered shirt, are constantly seen in the street carrying books, and now the bicycle, too. The headmaster will learn that you and your sister ride the bicycle, and then it will reach the higher authorities. . . . Will that be a good thing? '

" ' It's no business of anybody else if my sister and I do bicycle! ' said Kovalenko, and he turned crimson. ' And damnation take any one who meddles in my private affairs! '

" Byelikov turned pale and got up.

" ' If you speak to me in that tone I cannot continue,' he said. ' And I beg you never to express yourself like that about our superiors in my presence; you ought to be respectful to the authorities.'

" ' Why, have I said any harm of the authorities? '
asked Kóvalenko, looking at him wrathfully.
' Please leave me alone. I am an honest man, and
do not care to talk to a gentleman like you. I
don't like sneaks! '

" Byelikov flew into a nervous flutter, and began
hurriedly putting on his coat, with an expression of
horror on his face. It was the first time in his life
he had been spoken to so rudely.

" ' You can say what you please,' he said, as he
went out from the entry to the landing on the staircase. ' I ought only to warn you: possibly some one
may have overheard us, and that our conversation
may not be misunderstood and harm come of it, I
shall be compelled to inform our headmaster of our
conversation . . . in its main features. I am bound
to do so.'

" ' Inform him? You can go and make your report! '

" Kovalenko seized him from behind by the collar
and gave him a push, and Byelikov rolled downstairs, thudding with his goloshes. The staircase
was high and steep, but he rolled to the bottom unhurt, got up, and touched his nose to see whether
his spectacles were all right. But just as he was
falling down the stairs Varinka came in, and with
her two ladies; they stood below staring, and to
Byelikov this was more terrible than anything. I believe he would rather have broken his neck or both
legs than have been an object of ridicule. Why,
now the whole town would hear of it; it would come
to the headmaster's ears, would reach the higher

authorities — oh, it might lead to something! There would be another caricature, and it would all end in his being asked to resign his post. . . .

" When he got up, Varinka recognized him, and, looking at his ridiculous face, his crumpled overcoat, and his goloshes, not understanding what had happened and supposing that he had slipped down by accident, could not restrain herself, and laughed loud enough to be heard by all the flats:

" ' Ha-ha-ha! '

" And this pealing, ringing ' Ha-ha-ha! ' was the last straw that put an end to everything: to the proposed match and to Byelikov's earthly existence. He did not hear what Varinka said to him; he saw nothing. On reaching home, the first thing he did was to remove her portrait from the table; then he went to bed, and he never got up again.

" Three days later Afanasy came to me and asked whether we should not send for the doctor, as there was something wrong with his master. I went in to Byelikov. He lay silent behind the curtain, covered with a quilt; if one asked him a question, he said ' Yes ' or ' No ' and not another sound. He lay there while Afanasy, gloomy and scowling, hovered about him, sighing heavily, and smelling like a pothouse.

" A month later Byelikov died. We all went to his funeral — that is, both the high-schools and the seminary. Now when he was lying in his coffin his expression was mild, agreeable, even cheerful, as though he were glad that he had at last been put into a case which he would never leave again. Yes, he had attained his ideal! And, as though in his honour, it was dull, rainy weather on the day of his funeral, and we all wore goloshes and took our umbrellas. Varinka, too, was at the funeral, and when the coffin was lowered into the grave she burst into tears. I have noticed that Little Russian women are always laughing or crying — no intermediate mood.

" One must confess that to bury people like Byelikov is a great pleasure. As we were returning from the cemetery we wore discreet Lenten faces; no one wanted to display this feeling of pleasure — a feeling like that we had experienced long, long ago as children when our elders had gone out and we ran about the garden for an hour or two, enjoying complete freedom. Ah, freedom, freedom! The merest hint, the faintest hope of its possibility gives wings to the soul, does it not?

" We returned from the cemetery in a good humour. But not more than a week had passed before life went on as in the past, as gloomy, oppressive, and senseless — a life not forbidden by government prohibition, but not fully permitted, either: it was no better. And, indeed, though we had buried Byelikov, how many such men in cases were left, how many more of them there will be! "

" That's just how it is," said Ivan Ivanovitch and he lighted his pipe.

" How many more of them there will be! " repeated Burkin.

The schoolmaster came out of the barn. He was a short, stout man, completely bald, with a black beard down to his waist. The two dogs came out with him.

"What a moon!" he said, looking upwards.

It was midnight. On the right could be seen the whole village, a long street stretching far away for four miles. All was buried in deep silent slumber; not a movement, not a sound; one could hardly believe that nature could be so still. When on a moonlight night you see a broad village street, with its cottages, haystacks, and slumbering willows, a feeling of calm comes over the soul; in this peace, wrapped away from care, toil, and sorrow in the darkness of night, it is mild, melancholy, beautiful, and it seems as though the stars look down upon it kindly and with tenderness, and as though there were no evil on earth and all were well. On the left the open country began from the end of the village; it could be seen stretching far away to the horizon, and there was no movement, no sound in that whole expanse bathed in moonlight.

"Yes, that is just how it is," repeated Ivan Ivanovitch; "and isn't our living in town, airless and crowded, our writing useless papers, our playing *vint* — isn't that all a sort of case for us? And our spending our whole lives among trivial, fussy men and silly, idle women, our talking and our listening to all sorts of nonsense — isn't that a case for us, too? If you like, I will tell you a very edifying story."

"No; it's time we were asleep," said Burkin. "Tell it tomorrow."

They went into the barn and lay down on the hay. And they were both covered up and beginning to doze when they suddenly heard light footsteps — patter, patter. . . . Some one was walking not far from the barn, walking a little and stopping, and a minute later, patter, patter again. . . . The dogs began growling.

"That's Mavra," said Burkin.

The footsteps died away.

"You see and hear that they lie," said Ivan Ivanovitch, turning over on the other side, "and they call you a fool for putting up with their lying. You endure insult and humiliation, and dare not openly say that you are on the side of the honest and the free, and you lie and smile yourself; and all that for the sake of a crust of bread, for the sake of a warm corner, for the sake of a wretched little worthless rank in the service. No, one can't go on living like this."

"Well, you are off on another tack now, Ivan Ivanovitch," said the schoolmaster. "Let us go to sleep!"

And ten minutes later Burkin was asleep. But Ivan Ivanovitch kept sighing and turning over from side to side; then he got up, went outside again, and, sitting in the doorway, lighted his pipe.

1898

312

GOOSEBERRIES

THE whole sky had been overcast with rain-clouds from early morning; it was a still day, not hot, but heavy, as it is in grey dull weather when the clouds have been hanging over the country for a long while, when one expects rain and it does not come. Ivan Ivanovitch, the veterinary surgeon, and Burkin, the high-school teacher, were already tired from walking, and the fields seemed to them endless. Far ahead of them they could just see the windmills of the village of Mironositskoe; on the right stretched a row of hillocks which disappeared in the distance behind the village, and they both knew that this was the bank of the river, that there were meadows, green willows, homesteads there, and that if one stood on one of the hillocks one could see from it the same vast plain, telegraph-wires, and a train which in the distance looked like a crawling cater-pillar, and that in clear weather one could even see the town. Now, in still weather, when all nature seemed mild and dreamy, Ivan Ivanovitch and Bur-kin were filled with love of that countryside, and both thought how great, how beautiful a land it was.

"Last time we were in Prokofy's barn," said Burkin, "you were about to tell me a story."

"Yes; I meant to tell you about my brother."

Ivan Ivanovitch heaved a deep sigh and lighted a pipe to begin to tell his story, but just at that moment the rain began. And five minutes later heavy rain came down, covering the sky, and it was hard to tell when it would be over. Ivan Ivanovitch and Burkin stopped in hesitation; the dogs, already drenched, stood with their tails between their legs gazing at them feelingly.

"We must take shelter somewhere," said Burkin. "Let us go to Alehin's; it's close by."

"Come along."

They turned aside and walked through mown fields, sometimes going straight forward, sometimes turning to the right, till they came out on the road. Soon they saw poplars, a garden, then the red roofs of barns; there was a gleam of the river, and the view opened on to a broad expanse of water with a windmill and a white bath-house: this was Sofino, where Alehin lived.

The watermill was at work, drowning the sound of the rain; the dam was shaking. Here wet horses with drooping heads were standing near their carts, and men were walking about covered with sacks. It was damp, muddy, and desolate; the water looked cold and malignant. Ivan Ivanovitch and Burkin were already conscious of a feeling of wetness, messiness, and discomfort all over; their feet were heavy with mud, and when, crossing the dam, they went up to the barns, they were silent, as though they were angry with one another.

In one of the barns there was the sound of a winnowing machine, the door was open, and clouds of dust were coming from it. In the doorway was standing Alehin himself, a man of forty, tall and stout, with long hair, more like a professor or an artist than a landowner. He had on a white shirt that badly needed washing, a rope for a belt, drawers instead of trousers, and his boots, too, were plastered up with mud and straw. His eyes and nose were black with dust. He recognized Ivan Ivanovitch and Burkin, and was apparently much delighted to see them.

"Go into the house, gentlemen," he said, smiling; "I'll come directly, this minute."

It was a big two-storeyed house. Alehin lived in the lower storey, with arched ceilings and little windows, where the bailiffs had once lived; here everything was plain, and there was a smell of rye bread, cheap vodka, and harness. He went upstairs into the best rooms only on rare occasions, when visitors came. Ivan Ivanovitch and Burkin were met in the house by a maid-servant, a young woman so beautiful that they both stood still and looked at one another.

"You can't imagine how delighted I am to see you, my friends," said Alehin, going into the hall with them. "It is a surprise! Pelagea," he said, addressing the girl, "give our visitors something to change into. And, by the way, I will change too. Only I must first go and wash, for I almost think I have not washed since spring. Wouldn't you like to come into the bath-house? and meanwhile they will get things ready here."

Beautiful Pelagea, looking so refined and soft,

brought them towels and soap, and Alehin went to the bath-house with his guests.

"It's a long time since I had a wash," he said, undressing. "I have got a nice bath-house, as you see — my father built it — but I somehow never have time to wash."

He sat down on the steps and soaped his long hair and his neck, and the water round him turned brown.

"Yes, I must say," said Ivan Ivanovitch meaningly, looking at his head.

"It's a long time since I washed . . ." said Alehin with embarrassment, giving himself a second soaping, and the water near him turned dark blue, like ink.

Ivan Ivanovitch went outside, plunged into the water with a loud splash, and swam in the rain, flinging his arms out wide. He stirred the water into waves which set the white lilies bobbing up and down; he swam to the very middle of the millpond and dived, and came up a minute later in another place, and swam on, and kept on diving, trying to touch the bottom.

"Oh, my goodness!" he repeated continually, enjoying himself thoroughly. "Oh, my goodness!" He swam to the mill, talked to the peasants there, then returned and lay on his back in the middle of the pond, turning his face to the rain. Burkin and Alehin were dressed and ready to go, but he still went on swimming and diving. "Oh, my goodness! . . ." he said. "Oh, Lord, have mercy on me! . . ."

"That's enough!" Burkin shouted to him.

Gooseberries

They went back to the house. And only when the lamp was lighted in the big drawing-room upstairs, and Burkin and Ivan Ivanovitch, attired in silk dressing-gowns and warm slippers, were sitting in arm-chairs; and Alehin, washed and combed, in a new coat, was walking about the drawing-room, evidently enjoying the feeling of warmth, cleanliness, dry clothes, and light shoes; and when lovely Pelagea, stepping noiselessly on the carpet and smiling softly, handed tea and jam on a tray — only then Ivan Ivanovitch began on his story, and it seemed as though not only Burkin and Alehin were listening, but also the ladies, young and old, and the officers who looked down upon them sternly and calmly from their gold frames.

"There are two of us brothers," he began —" I, Ivan Ivanovitch, and my brother, Nikolay Ivanovitch, two years younger. I went in for a learned profession and became a veterinary surgeon, while Nikolay sat in a government office from the time he was nineteen. Our father, Tchimsha-Himalaisky, was a kantonist, but he rose to be an officer and left us a little estate and the rank of nobility. After his death the little estate went in debts and legal expenses; but, anyway, we had spent our childhood running wild in the country. Like peasant children, we passed our days and nights in the fields and the woods, looked after horses, stripped the bark off the trees, fished, and so on. . . . And, you know, whoever has once in his life caught perch or has seen the migrating of the thrushes in autumn, watched how they float in flocks over the village on bright, cool days, he will never be a real townsman, and will have a yearning for freedom to the day of his death. My brother was miserable in the government office. Years passed by, and he went on sitting in the same place, went on writing the same papers and thinking of one and the same thing — how to get into the country. And this yearning by degrees passed into a definite desire, into a dream of buying himself a little farm somewhere on the banks of a river or a lake.

" He was a gentle, good-natured fellow, and I was fond of him, but I never sympathized with this desire to shut himself up for the rest of his life in a little farm of his own. It's the correct thing to say that a man needs no more than six feet of earth. But six feet is what a corpse needs, not a man. And they say, too, now, that if our intellectual classes are attracted to the land and yearn for a farm, it's a good thing. But these farms are just the same as six feet of earth. To retreat from town, from the struggle, from the bustle of life, to retreat and bury oneself in one's farm — it's not life, it's egoism, laziness, it's monasticism of a sort, but monasticism without good works. A man does not need six feet of earth or a farm, but the whole globe, all nature, where he can have room to display all the qualities and peculiarities of his free spirit.

" My brother Nikolay, sitting in his government office, dreamed of how he would eat his own cabbages, which would fill the whole yard with such a savoury smell, take his meals on the green grass, sleep in the sun, sit for whole hours on the seat by the gate gazing at the fields and the forest. Gardening books and the agricultural hints in calendars were his delight, his favourite spiritual sustenance; he enjoyed reading newspapers, too, but the only things he read in them were the advertisements of so many acres of arable land and a grass meadow with farm-houses and buildings, a river, a garden, a mill and millponds, for sale. And his imagination pictured the garden-paths, flowers and fruit, starling cotes, the carp in the pond, and all that sort of thing, you know. These imaginary pictures were of different kinds according to the advertisements which he came across, but for some reason in every one of them he had always to have gooseberries. He could not imagine a homestead, he could not picture an idyllic nook, without gooseberries.

"'Country life has its conveniences,' he would sometimes say. 'You sit on the verandah and you drink tea, while your ducks swim on the pond, there is a delicious smell everywhere, and . . . and the gooseberries are growing.'

"He used to draw a map of his property, and in every map there were the same things — (*a*) house for the family, (*b*) servants' quarters, (*c*) kitchen-garden, (*d*) gooseberry-bushes. He lived parsimoniously, was frugal in food and drink, his clothes were beyond description; he looked like a beggar, but kept on saving and putting money in the bank. He grew fearfully avaricious. I did not like to look at him, and I used to give him something and send him presents for Christmas and Easter, but he used to save that too. Once a man is absorbed by an idea there is no doing anything with him.

"Years passed: he was transferred to another province. He was over forty, and he was still reading the advertisements in the papers and saving up. Then I heard he was married. Still with the same object of buying a farm and having gooseberries, he married an elderly and ugly widow without a trace of feeling for her, simply because she had filthy lucre. He went on living frugally after marrying her, and kept her short of food, while he put her money in the bank in his name.

"Her first husband had been a postmaster, and with him she was accustomed to pies and home-made wines, while with her second husband she did not get enough black bread; she began to pine away with this sort of life, and three years later she gave up her soul to God. And I need hardly say that my brother never for one moment imagined that he was responsible for her death. Money, like vodka, makes a man queer. In our town there was a merchant who, before he died, ordered a plateful of honey and ate up all his money and lottery tickets with the honey, so that no one might get the benefit of it. While I was inspecting cattle at a railway-station, a cattle-dealer fell under an engine and had his leg cut off. We carried him into the waiting-room, the blood was flowing — it was a horrible thing — and he kept asking them to look for his leg and was very much worried about it; there were twenty roubles in the boot on the leg that had been cut off, and he was afraid they would be lost."

"That's a story from a different opera," said Burkin.

"After his wife's death," Ivan Ivanovitch went on, after thinking for half a minute, "my brother began looking out for an estate for himself. Of course, you may look about for five years and yet end by making a mistake, and buying something quite different from what you have dreamed of. My brother Nikolay bought through an agent a mortgaged estate of three hundred and thirty acres, with a house for the family, with servants' quarters, with a park, but with no orchard, no gooseberry-bushes, and no duck-pond; there was a river, but the water in it was the colour of coffee, because on one side of the estate there was a brickyard and on the other a factory for burning bones. But Nikolay Ivanovitch did not grieve much; he ordered twenty gooseberry-bushes, planted them, and began living as a country gentleman.

"Last year I went to pay him a visit. I thought I would go and see what it was like. In his letters my brother called his estate 'Tchumbaroklov Waste, alias Himalaiskoe.' I reached 'alias Himalaiskoe' in the afternoon. It was hot. Everywhere there were ditches, fences, hedges, fir-trees planted in rows, and there was no knowing how to get to the yard, where to put one's horse. I went up to the house, and was met by a fat red dog that looked like a pig. It wanted to bark, but it was too lazy. The cook, a fat, barefooted woman, came out of the kitchen, and she, too, looked like a pig, and said that her master was resting after dinner. I went in to see my brother. He was sitting up in bed with a quilt over his legs; he had grown older, fatter, wrinkled; his cheeks, his nose, and his mouth all stuck out — he looked as though he might begin grunting into the quilt at any moment.

" We embraced each other, and shed tears of joy and of sadness at the thought that we had once been young and now were both grey-headed and near the grave. He dressed, and led me out to show me the estate.

" ' Well, how are you getting on here?' I asked.

" ' Oh, all right, thank God; I am getting on very well.'

" He was no more a poor timid clerk, but a real landowner, a gentleman. He was already accustomed to it, had grown used to it, and liked it. He ate a great deal, went to the bath-house, was growing stout, was already at law with the village commune and both factories, and was very much offended when the peasants did not call him ' Your Honour.' And he concerned himself with the salvation of his soul in a substantial, gentlemanly manner, and performed deeds of charity, not simply, but with an air of consequence. And what deeds of charity! He treated the peasants for every sort of disease with soda and castor oil, and on his name-day had a thanksgiving service in the middle of the village, and then treated the peasants to a gallon of vodka — he thought that was the thing to do. Oh, those horrible

Gooseberries

gallons of vodka! One day the fat landowner hauls the peasants up before the district captain for trespass, and next day, in honour of a holiday, treats them to a gallon of vodka, and they drink and shout 'Hurrah!' and when they are drunk bow down to his feet. A change of life for the better, and being well-fed and idle develop in a Russian the most insolent self-conceit. Nikolay Ivanovitch, who at one time in the government office was afraid to have any views of his own, now could say nothing that was not gospel truth, and uttered such truths in the tone of a prime minister. 'Education is essential, but for the peasants it is premature.' 'Corporal punishment is harmful as a rule, but in some cases it is necessary and there is nothing to take its place.'

"'I know the peasants and understand how to treat them,' he would say. 'The peasants like me. I need only to hold up my little finger and the peasants will do anything I like.'

"And all this, observe, was uttered with a wise, benevolent smile. He repeated twenty times over 'We noblemen,' 'I as a noble'; obviously he did not remember that our grandfather was a peasant, and our father a soldier. Even our surname Tchimsha-Himaláisky, in reality so incongruous, seemed to him now melodious, distinguished, and very agreeable.

"But the point just now is not he, but myself. I want to tell you about the change that took place in me during the brief hours I spent at his country place. In the evening, when we were drinking tea, the cook put on the table a plateful of gooseberries. They were not bought, but his own goosberries, gath-

ered for the first time since the bushes were planted.
Nikolay Ivanovitch laughed and looked for a minute
in silence at the gooseberries, with tears in his eyes;
he could not speak for excitement. Then he put
one gooseberry in his mouth, looked at me with the
triumph of a child who has at last received his favourite toy, and said:

" ' How delicious! '

" And he ate them greedily, continually repeating,
' Ah, how delicious! Do taste them! '

" They were sour and unripe, but, as Pushkin says:

> " ' Dearer to us the falsehood that exalts
> Than hosts of baser truths.'

" I saw a happy man whose cherished dream was
so obviously fulfilled, who had attained his object
in life, who had gained what he wanted, who was
satisfied with his fate and himself. There is always,
for some reason, an element of sadness mingled with
my thoughts of human happiness, and, on this occasion, at the sight of a happy man I was overcome
by an oppressive feeling that was close upon despair.
It was particularly oppressive at night. A bed was
made up for me in the room next to my brother's
bedroom, and I could hear that he was awake, and
that he kept getting up and going to the plate of
gooseberries and taking one. I reflected how many
satisfied, happy people there really are! What a
suffocating force it is! You look at life: the insolence and idleness of the strong, the ignorance and
brutishness of the weak, incredible poverty all about
us, overcrowding, degeneration, drunkenness, hy-

pocrisy, lying. . . . Yet all is calm and stillness in the houses and in the streets; of the fifty thousand living in a town, there is not one who would cry out, who would give vent to his indignation aloud. We see the people going to market for provisions, eating by day, sleeping by night, talking their silly nonsense, getting married, growing old, serenely escorting their dead to the cemetery; but we do not see and we do not hear those who suffer, and what is terrible in life goes on somewhere behind the scenes. . . . Everything is quiet and peaceful, and nothing protests but mute statistics: so many people gone out of their minds, so many gallons of vodka drunk, so many children dead from malnutrition. . . . And this order of things is evidently necessary; evidently the happy man only feels at ease because the unhappy bear their burdens in silence, and without that silence happiness would be impossible. It's a case of general hypnotism. There ought to be behind the door of every happy, contented man some one standing with a hammer continually reminding him with a tap that there are unhappy people; that however happy he may be, life will show him her laws sooner or later, trouble will come for him — disease, poverty, losses, and no one will see or hear, just as now he neither sees nor hears others. But there is no man with a hammer; the happy man lives at his ease, and trivial daily cares faintly agitate him like the wind in the aspen-tree — and all goes well.

"That night I realized that I, too, was happy and contented," Ivan Ivanovitch went on, getting up. "I, too, at dinner and at the hunt liked to lay down the law on life and religion, and the way to manage the peasantry. I, too, used to say that science was light, that culture was essential, but for the simple people reading and writing was enough for the time. Freedom is a blessing, I used to say; we can no more do without it than without air, but we must wait a little. Yes, I used to talk like that, and now I ask, 'For what reason are we to wait?'" asked Ivan Ivanovitch, looking angrily at Burkin. "Why wait, I ask you? What grounds have we for waiting? I shall be told, it can't be done all at once; every idea takes shape in life gradually, in its due time. But who is it says that? Where is the proof that it's right? You will fall back upon the natural order of things, the uniformity of phenomena; but is there order and uniformity in the fact that I, a living, thinking man, stand over a chasm and wait for it to close of itself, or to fill up with mud at the very time when perhaps I might leap over it or build a bridge across it? And again, wait for the sake of what? Wait till there's no strength to live? And meanwhile one must live, and one wants to live!

"I went away from my brother's early in the morning, and ever since then it has been unbearable for me to be in town. I am oppressed by its peace and quiet; I am afraid to look at the windows, for there is no spectacle more painful to me now than the sight of a happy family sitting round the table drinking tea. I am old and am not fit for the struggle; I am not even capable of hatred; I can only grieve inwardly, feel irritated and vexed; but at night

Gooseberries

my head is hot from the rush of ideas, and I cannot sleep. . . . Ah, if I were young!"

Ivan Ivanovitch walked backwards and forwards in excitement, and repeated: "If I were young!"

He suddenly went up to Alehin and began pressing first one of his hands and then the other.

"Pavel Konstantinovitch," he said in an imploring voice, "don't be calm and contented, don't let yourself be put to sleep! While you are young, strong, confident, be not weary in well-doing! There is no happiness, and there ought not to be; but if there is a meaning and an object in life, that meaning and object is not our happiness, but something greater and more rational. Do good!"

And all this Ivan Ivanovitch said with a pitiful, imploring smile, as though he were asking him a personal favour.

Then all three sat in arm-chairs at different ends of the drawing-room and were silent. Ivan Ivanovitch's story had not satisfied either Burkin or Alehin. When the generals and ladies gazed down from their gilt frames, looking in the dusk as though they were alive, it was dreary to listen to the story of the poor clerk who ate gooseberries. They felt inclined, for some reason, to talk about elegant people, about women. And their sitting in the drawing-room where everything — the chandeliers in their covers, the arm-chairs, and the carpet under their feet — reminded them that those very people who were now looking down from their frames had once moved about, sat, drunk tea in this room, and the fact that lovely Pelagea was moving noiselessly about was better than any story.

Alehin was fearfully sleepy; he had got up early, before three o'clock in the morning, to look after his work, and now his eyes were closing; but he was afraid his visitors might tell some interesting story after he had gone, and he lingered on. He did not go into the question whether what Ivan Ivanovitch had just said was right and true. His visitors did not talk of groats, nor of hay, nor of tar, but of something that had no direct bearing on his life, and he was glad and wanted them to go on.

" It's bed-time, though," said Burkin, getting up. " Allow me to wish you good-night."

Alehin said good-night and went downstairs to his own domain, while the visitors remained upstairs. They were both taken for the night to a big room where there stood two old wooden beds decorated with carvings, and in the corner was an ivory crucifix. The big cool beds, which had been made by the lovely Pelagea, smelt agreeably of clean linen.

Ivan Ivanovitch undressed in silence and got into bed.

" Lord forgive us sinners! " he said, and put his head under the quilt.

His pipe lying on the table smelt strongly of stale tobacco, and Burkin could not sleep for a long while, and kept wondering where the oppressive smell came from.

The rain was pattering on the window-panes all night.

1898

ABOUT LOVE

AT lunch next day there were very nice pies, crayfish, and mutton cutlets; and while we were eating, Nikanor, the cook, came up to ask what the visitors would like for dinner. He was a man of medium height, with a puffy face and little eyes; he was close-shaven, and it looked as though his moustaches had not been shaved, but had been pulled out by the roots. Alehin told us that the beautiful Pelagea was in love with this cook. As he drank and was of a violent character, she did not want to marry him, but was willing to live with him without. He was very devout, and his religious convictions would not allow him to " live in sin "; he insisted on her marrying him, and would consent to nothing else, and when he was drunk he used to abuse her and even beat her. Whenever he got drunk she used to hide upstairs and sob, and on such occasions Alehin and the servants stayed in the house to be ready to defend her in case of necessity.

We began talking about love.

" How love is born," said Alehin, " why Pelagea does not love somebody more like herself in her spiritual and external qualities, and why she fell in love with Nikanor, that ugly snout — we all call him ' The Snout '— how far questions of personal happiness are of consequence in love — all that is unknown; one can take what view one likes of it. So far only one incontestable truth has been. uttered about love: 'This is a great mystery.' Everything else that has been written or said about love is not a conclusion, but only a statement of questions which have remained unanswered. The explanation which would seem to fit one case does not apply in a dozen others, and the very best thing, to my mind, would be to explain every case individually without attempting to generalize. We ought, as the doctors say, to individualize each case."

"Perfectly true," Burkin assented.

"We Russians of the educated class have a partiality for these questions that remain unanswered. Love is usually poeticized, decorated with roses, nightingales; we Russians decorate our loves with these momentous questions, and select the most uninteresting of them, too. In Moscow, when I was a student, I had a friend who shared my life, a charming lady, and every time I took her in my arms she was thinking what I would allow her a month for housekeeping and what was the price of beef a pound. In the same way, when we are in love we are never tired of asking ourselves questions: whether it is honourable or dishonourable, sensible or stupid, what this love is leading up to, and so on. Whether it is a good thing or not I don't know, but that it is in the way, unsatisfactory, and irritating, I do know."

It looked as though he wanted to tell some story. People who lead a solitary existence always have something in their hearts which they are eager to talk about. In town bachelors visit the baths and the restaurants on purpose to talk, and sometimes tell the most interesting things to bath attendants and waiters; in the country, as a rule, they unbosom themselves to their guests. Now from the window we could see a grey sky, trees drenched in the rain; in such weather we could go nowhere, and there was nothing for us to do but to tell stories and to listen.

" I have lived at Sofino and been farming for a long time," Alehin began, " ever since I left the University. I am an idle gentleman by education, a studious person by disposition; but there was a big debt owing on the estate when I came here, and as my father was in debt partly because he had spent so much on my education, I resolved not to go away, but to work till I paid off the debt. I made up my mind to this and set to work, not, I must confess, without some repugnance. The land here does not yield much, and if one is not to farm at a loss one must employ serf labour or hired labourers, which is almost the same thing, or put it on a peasant footing — that is, work the fields oneself and with one's family. There is no middle path. But in those days I did not go into such subtleties. I did not leave a clod of earth unturned; I gathered together all the peasants, men and women, from the neighbouring villages; the work went on at a tremendous pace. I myself ploughed and sowed and reaped, and was bored doing it, and frowned with disgust, like a village cat driven by hunger to eat cucumbers in the kitchen-garden. My body ached, and I slept as I walked. At first it seemed to me that I could easily reconcile this life of toil with my cultured habits; to do so, I thought, all that is necessary is to maintain a certain external order in life. I established myself upstairs here in the best rooms, and ordered them to bring me there coffee and liquor after lunch and dinner, and when I went to bed I read every night the *Vyestnik Evropi*. But one day our priest, Father Ivan, came and drank up all my liquor at one sitting; and the *Vyestnik Evropi* went to the priest's daughters; as in the summer, especially at the hay-making, I did not succeed in getting to my bed at all, and slept in the sledge in the barn, or somewhere in the forester's lodge, what chance was there of reading? Little by little I moved downstairs, began dining in the servants' kitchen, and of my former luxury nothing is left but the servants who were in my father's service, and whom it would be painful to turn away.

" In the first years I was elected here an honourary justice of the peace. I used to have to go to the town and take part in the sessions of the congress and of the circuit court, and this was a pleasant change for me. When you live here for two or three months without a break, especially in the winter, you begin at last to pine for a black coat. And in the circuit court there were frock-coats, and uniforms, and dress-coats, too, all lawyers, men who have received a general education; I had some one to talk to. After sleeping in the sledge and dining in the kitchen, to sit in an arm-chair in clean linen, in thin boots, with a chain on one's waistcoat, is such luxury!

" I received a warm welcome in the town. I made

friends eagerly. And of all my acquaintanceships the most intimate and, to tell the truth, the most agreeable to me was my acquaintance with Luganovitch, the vice-president of the circuit court. You both know him: a most charming personality. It all happened just after a celebrated case of incendiarism; the preliminary investigation lasted two days; we were exhausted. Luganovitch looked at me and said:

" 'Look here, come round to dinner with me.'

" This was unexpected, as I knew Luganovitch very little, only officially, and I had never been to his house. I only just went to my hotel room to change and went off to dinner. And here it was my lot to meet Anna Alexyevna, Luganovitch's wife. At that time she was still very young, not more than twenty-two, and her first baby had been born just six months before. It is all a thing of the past; and now I should find it difficult to define what there was so exceptional in her, what it was in her attracted me so much; at the time, at dinner, it was all perfectly clear to me. I saw a lovely young, good, intelligent, fascinating woman, such as I had never met before; and I felt her at once some one close and already familiar, as though that face, those cordial, intelligent eyes, I had seen somewhere in my childhood, in the album which lay on my mother's chest of drawers.

" Four Jews were charged with being incendiaries, were regarded as a gang of robbers, and, to my mind, quite groundlessly. At dinner I was very ·much excited, I was uncomfortable, and I don't know

333

what I said, but Anna Alexyevna kept shaking **her** head and saying to her husband:

" ' Dmitry, how is this? '

" Luganovitch is a good-natured man, one of those simple-hearted people who firmly maintain the opinion that once a man is charged before a court he is guilty, and to express doubt of the correctness of a sentence cannot be done except in legal form on paper, and not at dinner and in private conversation.

" ' You and I did not set fire to the place,' he said softly, ' and you see we are not condemned, and not in prison.'

" And both husband and wife tried to make me eat and drink as much as possible. From some trifling details, from the way they made the coffee together, for instance, and from the way they understood each other at half a word, I could gather that they lived in harmony and comfort, and that they were glad of a visitor. After dinner they played a duet on the piano; then it got dark, and I went home. That was at the beginning of spring.

" After that I spent the whole summer at Sofino without a break, and I had no time to think of the town, either, but the memory of the graceful fair-haired woman remained in my mind all those days; I did not think of her, but it was as though her light shadow were lying on my heart.

" In the late autumn there was a theatrical performance for some charitable object in the town. I went into the governor's box (I was invited to go there in the interval); I looked, and there was Anna Alexyevna sitting beside the governor's wife; and again the same irresistible, thrilling impression of beauty and sweet, caressing eyes, and again the same feeling of nearness. We sat side by side, then went to the foyer.

" ' You've grown thinner,' she said; ' have you been ill?'

" ' Yes, I've had rheumatism in my shoulder, and in rainy weather I can't sleep.'

" ' You look dispirited. In the spring, when you came to dinner, you were younger, more confident. You were full of eagerness, and talked a great deal then; you were very interesting, and I really must confess I was a little carried away by you. For some reason you often came back to my memory during the summer, and when I was getting ready for the theatre today I thought I should see you.'

" And she laughed.

" ' But you look dispirited today,' she repeated; ' it makes you seem older.'

" The next day I lunched at the Luganovitchs'. After lunch they drove out to their summer villa, in order to make arrangements there for the winter, and I went with them. I returned with them to the town, and at midnight drank tea with them in quiet domestic surroundings, while the fire glowed, and the young mother kept going to see if her baby girl was asleep. And after that, every time I went to town I never failed to visit the Luganovitchs. They grew used to me, and I grew used to them. As a rule I went in unannounced, as though I were one of the family.

" ' Who is there?' I would hear from a faraway

room, in the drawling voice that seemed to me so lovely.

" ' It is Pavel Konstantinovitch,' answered the maid or the nurse.

" Anna Alexyevna would come out to me with an anxious face, and would ask every time:

" ' Why is it so long since you have been? Has anything happened? '

" Her eyes, the elegant refined hand she gave me, her indoor dress, the way she did her hair, her voice, her step, always produced the same impression on me of something new and extraordinary in my life, and very important. We talked together for hours, were silent, thinking each our own thoughts, or she played for hours to me on the piano. If there were no one at home I stayed and waited, talked to the nurse, played with the child, or lay on the sofa in the study and read; and when Anna Alexyevna came back I met her in the hall, took all her parcels from her, and for some reason I carried those parcels every time with as much love, with as much solemnity, as a boy.

" There is a proverb that if a peasant woman has no troubles she will buy a pig. The Luganovitchs had no troubles, so they made friends with me. If I did not come to the town I must be ill or something must have happened to me, and both of them were extremely anxious. They were worried that I, an educated man with a knowledge of languages, should, instead of devoting myself to science or literary work, live in the country, rush round like a squirrel in a rage, work hard with never a penny to

show for it.   They fancied that I was unhappy, and that I only talked, laughed, and ate to conceal my sufferings, and even at cheerful moments when I felt happy I was aware of their searching eyes fixed upon me.   They were particularly touching when I really was depressed, when I was being worried by some creditor or had not money enough to pay interest on the proper day.   The two of them, husband and wife, would whisper together at the window; then he would come to me and say with a grave face:

" ' If you really are in need of money at the moment, Pavel Konstantinovitch, my wife and I beg you not to hesitate to borrow from us.'

" And he would blush to his ears with emotion. And it would happen that, after whispering in the same way at the window, he would come up to me, with red ears, and say:

" ' My wife and I earnestly beg you to accept this present.'

" And he would give me studs, a cigar-case, or a lamp, and I would send them game, butter, and flowers from the country.   They both, by the way, had considerable means of their own.   In early days I often borrowed money, and was not very particular about it — borrowed wherever I could — but nothing in the world would have induced me to borrow from the Luganovitchs.   But why talk of it?

" I was unhappy.   At home, in the fields, in the barn, I thought of her; I tried to understand the mystery of a beautiful, intelligent young woman's marrying some one so uninteresting, almost an old man (her husband was over forty), and having chil-

dren by him; to understand the mystery of this uninteresting, good, simple-hearted man, who argued
with such wearisome good sense, at balls and evening
parties kept near the more solid people, looking listless and superfluous, with a submissive, uninterested
expression, as though he had been brought there for
sale, who yet believed in his right to be happy, to
have children by her; and I kept trying to understand why she had met him first and not me, and
why such a terrible mistake in our lives need have
happened.

" And when I went to the town I saw every time
from her eyes that she was expecting me, and she
would confess to me herself that she had had a peculiar feeling all that day and had guessed that I
should come. We talked a long time, and were
silent, yet we did not confess our love to each other,
but timidly and jealously concealed it. We were
afraid of everything that might reveal our secret to
ourselves. I loved her tenderly, deeply, but I reflected and kept asking myself what our love could
lead to if we had not the strength to fight against it.
It seemed to be incredible that my gentle, sad love
could all at once coarsely break up the even tenor of
the life of her husband, her children, and all the
household in which I was so loved and trusted.
Would it be honourable? She would go away with
me, but where? Where could I take her? It
would have been a different matter if I had had a
beautiful, interesting life — if, for instance, I had
been struggling for the emancipation of my country,
or had been a celebrated man of science, an artist

or a painter; but as it was it would mean taking her from one everyday humdrum life to another as humdrum or perhaps more so. And how long would our happiness last? What would happen to her in case I was ill, in case I died, or if we simply grew cold to one another?

" And she apparently reasoned in the same way. She thought of her husband, her children, and of her mother, who loved the husband like a son. If she abandoned herself to her feelings she would have to lie, or else to tell the truth, and in her position either would have been equally terrible and inconvenient. And she was tormented by the question whether her love would bring me happiness — would she not complicate my life, which, as it was, was hard enough and full of all sorts of trouble? She fancied she was not young enough for me, that she was not industrious nor energetic enough to begin a new life, and she often talked to her husband of the importance of my marrying a girl of intelligence and merit who would be a capable housewife and a help to me — and she would immediately add that it would be difficult to find such a girl in the whole town.

" Meanwhile the years were passing. Anna Alexyevna already had two children. When I arrived at the Luganovitchs' the servants smiled cordially, the children shouted that Uncle Pavel Konstantinovitch had come, and hung on my neck; every one was overjoyed. They did not understand what was passing in my soul, and thought that I, too, was happy. Every one looked on me as a noble

being. And grown-ups and children alike felt that a noble being was walking about their rooms, and that gave a peculiar charm to their manner towards me, as though in my presence their life, too, was purer and more beautiful. Anna Alexyevna and I used to go to the theatre together, always walking there; we used to sit side by side in the stalls, our shoulders touching. I would take the opera-glass from her hands without a word, and feel at that minute that she was near me, that she was mine, that we could not live without each other; but by some strange misunderstanding, when we came out of the theatre we always said good-bye and parted as though we were strangers. Goodness knows what people were saying about us in the town already, but there was not a word of truth in it all!

" In the latter years Anna Alexyevna took to going away for frequent visits to her mother or to her sister; she began to suffer from low spirits, she began to recognize that her life was spoilt and unsatisfied, and at times she did not care to see her husband nor her children. She was already being treated for neurasthenia.

" We were silent and still silent, and in the presence of outsiders she displayed a strange irritation in regard to me; whatever I talked about, she disagreed with me, and if I had an argument she sided with my opponent. If I dropped anything, she would say coldly:

" ' I congratulate you.'

" If I forgot to take the opera-glass when we were going to the theatre, she would say afterwards:

340

About Love

" ' I knew you would forget it.'

" Luckily or unluckily, there is nothing in our lives that does not end sooner or later. The time of parting came, as Luganovitch was appointed president in one of the western provinces. They had to sell their furniture, their horses, their summer villa. When they drove out to the villa, and afterwards looked back as they were going away, to look for the last time at the garden, at the green roof, every one was sad, and I realized that I had to say good-bye not only to the villa. It was arranged that at the end of August we should see Anna Alexyevna off to the Crimea, where the doctors were sending her, and that a little later Luganovitch and the children would set off for the western province.

" We were a great crowd to see Anna Alexyevna off. When she had said good-bye to her husband and her children and there was only a minute left before the third bell, I ran into her compartment to put a basket, which she had almost forgotten, on the rack, and I had to say good-bye. When our eyes met in the compartment our spiritual fortitude deserted us both; I took her in my arms, she pressed her face to my breast, and tears flowed from her eyes. Kissing her face, her shoulders, her hands wet with tears — oh, how unhappy we were! — I confessed my love for her, and with a burning pain in my heart I realized how unnecessary, how petty, and how deceptive all that had hindered us from loving was. I understood that when you love you must either, in your reasonings about that love, start from what is highest, from what is more important than happiness or unhappiness, sin or virtue in their accepted meaning, or you must not reason at all.

" I kissed her for the last time, pressed her hand, and parted for ever.   The train had already started. I went into the next compartment — it was empty — and until I reached the next station I sat there crying. Then I walked home to Sofino. . . ."

While Alehin was telling his story, the rain left off and the sun came out.   Burkin and Ivan Ivanovitch went out on the balcony, from which there was a beautiful view over the garden and the mill-pond, which was shining now in the sunshine like a mirror. They admired it, and at the same time they were sorry that this man with the kind, clever eyes, who had told them this story with such genuine feeling, should be rushing round and round this huge estate like a squirrel on a wheel instead of devoting himself to science or something else which would have made his life more pleasant; and they thought what a sorrowful face Anna Alexyevna must have had when he said good-bye to her in the railway-carriage and kissed her face and shoulders.   Both of them had met her in the town, and Burkin knew her and thought her beautiful.

1898